The Man in the Mirror

Thirteen Day's,

Fourteen deaths,

a few Senators,

the Godfather,

a Chief of Police,

a Defense Contractor,

a few 9 Millimeters,

some Suppressors,

a Hitman,

and some Faith.

"The farther backward you can look, the farther forward you can see."
Winston Churchill

One

"A death of one Sam Clark"

Winter would be here soon, he could tell, it was almost like smelling the rain before it rained. He could tell that the winter season was soon upon them because it was November, and because of the chill in the air, it was no chill, it was just down right cold. The locals would consider themselves fortunate not to have the first snowfall already. In years past there may be snow still on the ground from the initial winters offering, that was good for 'Conoscalo Tuttio' no snow on the ground, less to cover up by the way of foot prints, less to clean up altogether.

He had been in the cabin before. It was part of the process, when available. He did not like to go blind into buildings or homes. Having an idea of what lay ahead actually made it easier, less worrisome. In his profession, it was always best to measure as many times as possible, and then just cut once.

He liked that metaphor, not that he was a craftsman on any level. Just that, through the years he had learned and picked up a few things here and there, one, the most important in his eyes was to do it right, essentially to be prepared, which essentially meant to be ready for the un-expected.

As a prepared individual he would take his time to make sure that he was aware of every aspect. In the past, he had watched the 'targets' for weeks on end. He would check his keys and make sure that his entry would be undetected and more importantly just not noticed, by the tenant or the prying eyes of others, especially after.

The cabin was an easy mark and the target was predictable, he always wanted to get as much information as necessary, sometimes it was to be in a special way, other times it would to just be completed. As he had been told in the past, several times over, do the job as it needed to be. This target would need to be in a natural way, a way that would not cause inquiry to his death.

All the main lights had been out for an hour, the target was predictable enough to let Conoscalo know that his bedside light would be out in less than fifteen minutes.

The target was a reader and enjoyed to read before he went to sleep at night, Conoscalo had decided a few days before that would be the best time to enter the cabin. If the target did not get up during the night, then it would be just as well, a heart attack in bed would be believable just the same.

He looked at his watch. He made one final check to what he was carrying. He had his surgical gloves on and had removed his heavy gloves and his outer jacket.

He discovered his heavy jacket made a sound so he removed it. He had the usual 9 mm with suppressor, a throw away weapon on his ankle and a knife in his back pocket, the syringe with his magical ingredients were attached to his chest for easy access.

The holster for his throw away weapon, or one that he could drop without recourse, also had a knife attached to the inside of the holster.

If you had not placed the knife there, or had not manufactured the holster, you may never know a placement for a little three inch throwing knife could exist in that small area.

When he felt comfortable with the surroundings and his appearance he started to approach the cabin, he would enter through the kitchen door, that door was the easiest to him. He knew that the second step to the patio was loose and made a noise, it was difficult to hear, and to the everyday person it would be nothing, but to Conoscalo it could be life or death.

He positioned himself to avoid the step and still be at the ready. He placed the key into the lock and slowly unlocked the door and pushed it open. No sooner had his own foot hit the floor of the kitchen, he saw a flicker of light come from the bedroom his target had just turned on his bed side light. He quickly moved through the kitchen, into what would be, for normal people a dining room.

This man had changed that space into a make shift office.

A desk sat in the middle, just as a dining room table would sit a book case to one side, another small table to the other side of the desk. He quickly moved from the kitchen around the breakfast bar, and slid next to the book case.

As he had discovered during an earlier entry, this was a great place to hide, especially if someone was coming from the bedroom area. This is where he hid.

He could see the man as he walked, carrying a glass, the man walked in front of the desk and toward the breakfast bar. At the ready Conoscalo placed the syringe in his left hand, and approached the back of the man. As the man stutter stepped onto the cool tile floor of the kitchen he paused, this is where it was complete. Conoscalo had approached him in such a manner that there was no noise, none whatsoever.

The syringe was in his left hand and was slowly pushed into the neck of the target, almost center, the fluid would enter the spinal area soon if not first.

It was fast acting so the legs would start to give way before all the solution had entered the body. There were always convulsions that the body went through to try to reject it, the targets response was natural.

With his other arm and hand he guided the man gently to the floor. The glass was released as soon as the brain had the information that something was entering his body. It shattered on the floor. Once the target was on the floor, he let the individual convulse on the empty cold vinyl floor, as his prying eyes lay to watch. It was his profession and being cold at heart was just part of his responsibility.

The officials would consider that he died of a heart attack, no other signs of struggle, and no reason to understand or comprehend foul play. With the Chief of Police dead, investigations would be little, Conoscalo had reviewed the other parties within the small department of Schrader Maine, and they lacked many things.

They would not look any further. Conoscalo approached the body and moved it into place.

When he was moving the body he noticed that some kind of allergic reaction had taken place at the site of the needle entry. This he had never seen before. He had used the same material many times over and never had someone developed an allergic reaction like this.

Conoscalo checked his watch. He had been there too long. Regardless of anyone coming he never wanted to stay too long. In his mind that would be unprofessional although the person lying on the kitchen floor may have a different opinion.

He went into the individual's bathroom, with little thought to the actual size, he randomly removed the first full size one from the box.

He removed the outer wrapper and placed it in the bathroom's garbage can. He would return to that same bathroom and deposit the other wrappings from the Band-Aids adhesive side. He carefully obtained the victims thumb print on both sides of the Band-Aid and then placed it gingerly over the allergic reaction on the target's neck.

He then went in search of the files. Conoscalo spent the next ten minutes "cleaning up" as to what they wanted from the desk and surrounding areas. He already had a stack of papers, three to four files in total and four notebooks. There was no computer in the cabin, one less thing to search through, and that is a good thing since he was never good with passwords, taking a computer would certainly change things. When he felt that he had everything he went back into the kitchen to make sure that he had covered all the bases.

His job was never easy, all the research, the planning, and then the most important, the completion to get everything right as if no one was the wiser-to ensure that no one was the wiser. However, this job was easy as far as easy goes, not too many would delve deeper, it would be labeled and stated to be a simple heart attack, nothing more.

The majority of his time spent in this little cabin was searching for the files that his client had asked for. It was not his concern as to what they held.

It was part of his reputation and the sheer commitment to his job. His commitment and attention to detail was his reputation.

He was the best for a reason and sight unseen if you could find him, there would be a price to pay. Rumor had it that he was worth every penny.

Two

"An Arrival"

His arrival was not late, by his standards anyway. He wanted to arrive earlier in the day, sometimes while traveling your time evaporates quicker than one would expect on the open road. He knew that Sam was a reader and would still be up if he had called, his better judgment told him not to make that call. Nick's fear was simple, if he called Sam, to let him know he had arrived, it would become a long night of drinking and a longer weekend of recovery. Nick still enjoyed to drink and would love to relive the earlier days with his mentor. He thought that they would have plenty of time for that later, they both needed a good start early the next morning, and had already set it up to meet at seven in the morning in front of the Schrader Police Department.

Nick Sheridan was a detective. He had just retired from the Los Angeles Police Department and was looking for his Shangri La much like his mentor did ten years before.

When he had first called Sam to inform him that he had opted out for early retirement, he was hoping to get some simple patrol job and work for his mentor once again.

He was to say the least shocked when Sam called back a few days later to inform him that he was retiring, the Mayor offered and two days later, he accepted the job as Chief of Police, they had kept it close to the three of them. Sam still had to tell everyone, although for the most part everyone already knew.

He had tried to come up with another title, he always liked Detective, that was a title, he thought. The term sir would irritate him in no time, he would never get used to that. As for Chief, he knew that Sam was right and eventually 'Chief' would have to work. For the incoming Chief of Police for Schrader Maine, what else could be done?

He was typically a calm person by nature, he knew that he needed to get away from Los Angeles, and with an early retirement he got just what he needed a change of pace and, in this case, scenery.

Even though the title would no longer apply to Nick Sheridan, he was and figured that he would always be, a Detective.

He loved the job except the politics, and yes, there was plenty of that, especially in L.A. The truth was that Nick wanted out.

The early retirement was not meant for him or others like him he was one of the few that jumped on the opportunity. He had considered that maybe he would make a good private detective.

It was a thought, a fleeting one at that. In the end, the opportunity to take over from his Mentor would prove to be best.

Nick was almost forty-five years old, he was not a good-looking man by any means, although he carried himself well he was just the normal next-door type. In his youth, your mother would remind her daughters that this would be one to avoid, for she would not approve.

He had black hair, some had left him already and the other was turning grey, blue eyes, he carried a tan but would prefer to stay indoors rather than sit on a beach. He wore glasses from an early age, funny thing was he could do anything at work, get shot no problem, break a bone no problem, go through Lasik Eye surgery not going to happen, when an eyelash found its way in to his eye it would be just short of a natural calamity.

Many things were certain about Nick Sheridan, he was loyal, dedicated to his duties and had trouble letting go of the little things, even more trouble if he deemed it a big thing.

When he left his motel room, early that next morning, he was in search of two things, the exact location of the Schrader Maine Police department (Sam had told him in the center of town) and a cup of coffee.

The 'Downtown' area was about three city blocks long, strange though no parking in the front of the Police Department, and just like Sam had said, in the middle of town.

Therefore, Nick parked a block down, only available space. The parking space was directly across from a diner. Nick thought that would be a great place for a cup of coffee.

He was soon to realize that he should have skipped that part.

It was a nice day out, just like the woman behind the counter remarked. She stated that everyone was wondering when they were going to be dumped on, as they said, in question was when the first snowfall would arrive. Now as for the coffee, there could be a few things learned or should he say taught to the woman.

"Well, at least it was hot," Nick mumbled.

Nick Sheridan was a simple individual from a police family or at least the last two generations. How many people would take a job sight unseen, in a town they had never been to from their soon-to-be retired mentor who escaped the 'big' city years before.

"Could this be a mistake," Nick said in a muttered way under his breath.

He had not seen Sam in almost ten years, and it was almost seven in the morning, Sam's truck should be pulling up. Which means that maybe, no parking does not mean that much to the Chief of Police for this small town.

Maybe he could leave, send a simple note, and retire to a quaint town in the middle of nowhere. Wait, think about it you are in a quant town in the middle of nowhere.

It might just be the place to relax. More crime probably happens in an hour in LA than here in a year, "hell maybe a half hour" he said. Remember what Sam always said, "The decisions you make in life usually directly represent that life." They were words to live by if you asked the right person.

Three

"A Senator and his friends."

It was not unusual for his office to be occupied on a Saturday, if James was in the office so would be his secretary and other support staff. Someone who is the CEO and the majority stock holder for Reynolds-MacMillian Defense Contractors would fully understand that Saturday was just another day of the week, another workday in the eyes of James Bennett MacMillian.

James had seen the light on the phone, for some reason he had been staring at it, or maybe just in that direction. He declined to answer it in fact he figured that if the secretary outside his office did not catch it then it would just go to voice mail. More or less the point he knew who was calling, sometimes the people you sleep with, figuratively speaking not literally, would come to haunt you. Tom had certainly fulfilled that notion.

"Mr. MacMillian, You have a call on line two," the Secretary said.

"Who is it Samantha," James asked.

"Mr. Griffin, Sir,"

"Patch it through Samantha," exactly whom he had thought, the phone call he was dreading.

"Tom how have you been?" James Bennett MacMillian asked with great sincerity.

"Don't bullshit me, James, do you not answer your cell phone anymore," Tom asked.

"Of course I do, I left it somewhere yesterday and checked the messages this morning, all five of your messages were there, just did not have the time to call back, yet," James again with his voice ringing with true sincerity.

"Maybe our lives should be switched, you're sure sounding like the politician with an answer like that," Tom said, now with a little sarcasm ringing throughout the comment.

"I think we are way past that,"

"I do not need to remind you that as a member of the board, I would have a say in what and more importantly how things occur," Tom stated.

"Tom, you have been and will always be a very integral part of this company that should go without saying, however, we need to properly conclude everything and then we all can reap the rewards." James was adamant, he was taking the Chief Executive Officer role and as the only owner listed on paper anyway, with little precaution, he could state what he liked as far as the public record is concerned.

"Just trying to protect what we have assembled, through the years." Thomas Patrick Griffin Sr. had always protected his interests and more importantly the interests of his family.

"It seems as if our relationship is coming to an end," James said in a premonition type of way.

"James, our relationship is not ending, the world is changing and you either change with the world and its ways or be left somewhere behind,"

He continued, "We have a checkered past, we have each helped one another during our down times, that part will never end, I will always be there for you. And I would fully expect you to be there for me, or my family when needed."

Thomas Patrick Griffin Sr. was an honorable soul, he like all other good souls had skeletons in his closet and his lifelong friend and the Godfather, to his second son and only living child, held all of those keys. In addition, ironically his friend James Bennett MacMillian, the holder of those keys, had skeletons himself. Tom Griffin or as he was referred to these days as just 'Senior' did not hold all of James's keys for they were littered around like candy from a busted piñata. As good friends do, Senior had helped his friend in alleviating some of his past discrepancies in ways not used by the common masses.

Thomas Patrick Griffin was born in Boston Massachusetts in 1938.

He was from a middle-income family, whose Father had aspirations of the other side and the power that came with it.

His Father had done many things in the past to support his young family, he had most definitely profited from the Prohibition years, not so much in the Boston area, for he was one that believed you should not prosper in your own backyard. In addition, in the 1920's and 1930's you could prosper just about anywhere, if you had the courage to do so. His Father had the courage and made quite a name for himself in towns like Philadelphia, and Hartford and even in New York City. Moreover, at the age of thirty-two when his first son was born he was well on his way with legitimate enterprises of the day. He was not a visionary, he just saw many things in a different light and because of his views and thinking he would buy a downtrodden canvas company.

With his new company and his income coming from legal enterprises, he set off to Washington D.C. to drum up business for his new company. With hard work and good old American values, he bribed some and encouraged others by means of old contacts from his rum-running days. By the time he returned to Boston he had received several Army contracts, very lucrative contracts for the day.

Tommy, as the entire neighborhood called him in his younger days, was a personable child. He knew everyone and something that would help him in the future was the fact that he never forgot a name.

His Father, on the other hand, would not remember your name ten seconds after you had introduced yourself, for this earned Tommy the right of passage to follow around with his Father.

They proved to be a great team and his Father's ideas along with World War 2 and the many canvas products he made for the U.S. Government moved the family to a higher income and social setting.

By the time, Tommy had graduated High School his father encouraged Harvard enough that it was the next destination. Moreover, after earning a Bachelor's of Science in Political Science, and then going on to earn a Master's degree in Political Studies, young Tommy Griffin became a worker on the campaign of another Boston native and fellow Harvard graduate, Senator John Kennedy. The sad realization of life is that you maybe do not get everything that you want, and after a successful campaign, there was no room on staff for the young Griffin, much to his surprise he was asked to work for Lyndon Johnson, the sitting Vice President.

As history would have it, he was in Dallas on that fateful day in November when the young President met his demise at Daley Plaza and he was there when his boss became President. He was loyal to the President and through his loyalty rewarded with the assignment as the Ambassador to South Korea, with that he would become one of the youngest Ambassadors ever.

That was a great time for Tommy, newly married the young couple was to begin life together in South Korea and would have a child, their first son within the year.

As went life so went the good and the bad, their first child, which he named after his father Sean Patrick Griffin died in his second day of existence. Six months later another Sean Patrick Griffin would pass away, his Father would die suddenly from a massive stroke, it would become the same day that his wife informed him that she was pregnant once more.

Throughout all of his personal life issues, he had become a climber, even with his age this young Democrat was on a political ladder and it seemed to be moving at a fast rate. In August of 1968 a second son was born, this child survived and was named Thomas Bennett Griffin Jr., his middle name was not a family name it was for the child's Godfather and the best friend of Tom Senior, James Bennett MacMillian.

In 1970 he was asked to leave his position so the Republicans could have one of their men as the ambassador, this became more of a blessing, in 1972 with the help of all his friends he ran a successful campaign for Senator from the great state of Massachusetts.

As tragedies follow great families, this family would get their fair share in the fall of 1976. With their young son at a sleepover a break-in occurred at their home in which the wife of Senator Griffin was murdered. To this day, the murder of Kathy Griffin is unsolved. It is and has always been a hotbed of conspiracy thoughts.

Four

"Meeting of a mentor."

Nick was intelligent, good at school and many thought that he would become the first Sheridan to go straight to college from high school. His family did everything to encourage that thought, maybe a little too much. Maybe he knew, he could just not break it to the parents that had supported him in his every endeavor, he truly loved his Father's profession and so much wanted to extend the Sheridan name with the Los Angeles Police Department. After two years of College, he secretly applied to the Police Academy, he told his parents the same day that he dropped out of college the next day he would start the Police Academy. When he informed his parents, he concluded that this was something he had always had the desire for, and that one-day he would finish his degree, one day.

Nick had been a police officer for about four years. He had taken the Detectives test and was awaiting the results, at that time as a patrol/beat cop for the fair city of Compton.

It wasn't that bad compared to other parts of the city, there are actually worse places to work in patrol. He had been married for a couple of years, a relationship that started good and slowly went bad.

They had no kids, for reasons he did not know, with all the statements that he would hear on a daily basis from his fellow officers, he was glad at that time that he had none.

Nick and his partner Mike Keener were both regulars on the overtime circuit. As his Lieutenant, would say "do it whenever you could get it?" The City of Angels offered many ways for a Police Officer in good standing to earn extra money, you could always pick up bodyguard details to the stars and for special events.

Nick and Mike's performance evaluations for the L.A Police Department were always on the up and up.

Because of that, they were "allowed" to work on their regularly scheduled days off as part of the "Warrant Service Squad." The pay was good and it placed them on the fast track, you would think that it would be more like in the movies, action all the time.

This was not necessarily always the case. Maybe they had the easy ones, most of the people that they had the hard copy on, the order to pick them up, gave in rather easily. After about 8 months on the "WSS," the team had performed in such a manner that they received the opportunity to have back-up on all pick-ups. They split up and trained their new partners in order to assist each other.

Nick's new partner was Gregory Clark, Greg had actually graduated two weeks prior to Nick at the Police Academy, and they knew of each other but did not know each other, so to speak.

Nick and Greg actually worked well together almost better than Nick and Mike had.

The warrant they served on that day would end up being different, when Nick and Greg approached the door.

Nick had the warrant and a picture of the individual on the warrant. As typically, for the neighborhood, all front doors had screens, and with the recent hot weather, every door was open and all screens used.

"Los Angeles Police Department Warrant Squad, we are here to serve a warrant on a Dwight 'Double D' Dickens," Nick spoke loudly while he knocked on the door.

Through the screen, Nick could see two men at a table in the kitchen. The kitchen was located straight through the hallway. Nick could clearly see one of the men at the table was in fact, Dwight Dickens.

Nick quickly shoved the warrant in between his belt and back, he motioned for his partner to go around back.

Greg did just that and moved to the rear of the house.

Greg approached the back door, it was located in the kitchen and also had a screen door attached. The door was open with the screen door closed. Greg could see that both men were moving toward the front door, no weapons were visible.

Nick opened the front screen door and was inside the house, his instructions were loud and clear.

"I need Dwight to come forward, the other gentleman may return to the kitchen, please keep your hands visible," Nick asked.

Greg entered the kitchen and as soon as he had he felt a barrel of a gun pressing against his head, "Say a word and the gun goes off," the man said quietly.

At the same time, the man that had backed into the kitchen reached beside the refrigerator and pulled out a shotgun. In no time, he had pointed it at his partner and fired, with a sheer response Greg yelled out.

From that point, everything happened extremely fast, Nick had dodged the shot by jumping into a side bedroom. He had drawn his weapon when he entered the house originally, the jumping into the other room and then landing had jarred the weapon from his hand, and it slid under a bed. Nick raced to retrieve the weapon at the same time he was calling for his partner there was no answer.

He called again "Greg," still no answer.

He tried to remember what would be the order of process here, he could not recall exactly what was taught or how it should be handled. He was in a room, with his partner in another with at least two individuals with weapons. The fact was that the Police Academy had not prepared anyone for a situation like this, it was clearly not typical in fact it was clearly out of the ordinary. Nick called it in, he explained, he used his cell phone so that it would not be broadcasted over the radio. If his partner were in the back room, they would have access to his radio. The cell phone was the best way to communicate.

He could hear chatter from the kitchen area, he was guarding the door to the room, it was still open, his main concern is if they fired through the walls. An old house like this with plaster walls could be thin, and buckshot or bullets would easily go through. The TV was on in the other room that worked good for Nick, they could not hear him when he was on the phone, and it worked in a poor way because in return he could not clearly hear them.

All Nick could hear was mumbling through the wall, suddenly he heard the door to the kitchen open, the mumbling stopped. He heard shouting and shots fired. He headed for the door of the room, using a piece of a broken mirror to peek around the corner toward the kitchen, he saw nothing.

He tried to make sure that he was as cautious as possible, in the end it seemed that he extended his upper body and with the mirror extending from the doorway, it left a little for the imagination. Another shot fired and the shotgun blast hit Nick in several places on the left side of his body, his hand, arm and shoulder.

It was a wound, and considered by many to be nothing more than a flesh wound. His thoughts about the walls were correct; they bore little in the way of protection. He quickly tended to his wounds and again found himself on his cell phone.

Whom he was talking with changed, they had patched his line directly to the senior individual on the scene, a hostage negotiator was not available Detective Lieutenant Samual Laroy Clark was and even though his son was the hostage in the other room, no one objected for several different reasons to Sam taking charge.

Nick introduced himself, and hearing who was on the other line, made Nick a little hesitant, he was talking to the man. Highly decorated, the number one rated Detective in the area and many individuals always thought or maybe assumed that Sam Clark would be named Chief of Detectives real soon, and then maybe even Chief of Police, to say he was highly regarded would be just the icing.

"Nick, I need you to tell me everything. Start with your wounds and then describe your surroundings," Sam asked.

Nick reported on his wounds, and then described the room that he was in; he was hesitant to ask but did so anyway. "Sir, what went on in the backyard, and could you please give me the status on my partner Greg."

"Two individuals tried to leave through the back door, they opened fire and we believed are dead on the back porch," Sam was to the point, this relieved Nick. "As far as," Sam paused, "As far as Officer Clark he is still in the interior of the house, we have no other word, and we are setting up phone lines and trying to make contact."

"Tell me what you can hear Nick," Sam asked, hoping that Nick would allude to some kind of sound that could be heard through the walls. "Nothing, the TV is on and rather loud, I could hear mumbling before, that stopped when they tried to exit," Nick reported.

"Okay, hang tight, we are going to keep this line open. Where are you situated in the room?"

"Sitting with my back against the wall under the window, I'm facing the door. The door is open, I turned the single bed on its side to offer some protection," Nick's response was almost in a boot camp style, short burst with direct reflection in regard of who was on the other phone, the respect flowed.

"Good, we will get back to you, please report any noises you hear," Sam was off that phone, he handed to another individual on scene.

The situation around Nick began to deteriorate quickly, there was nothing that Sam Clark or anybody else could do. The individual that was still in the kitchen did indeed have a hostage, for some reason that individual had not tried to leave when the other two did, or at least tried. He had barricaded the back door to the kitchen, his name was not known, Dwight Dickens was one of the men that was lying motionless outside. Nick's situation was that he could not leave the room, for some reason the homeowners had decide to place bars on the window of that room, subsequently the house built next door was just two feet away. The swat team had tried to get to that area. They created a lot of noise and had no room to move and with the man in the kitchen still holding a hostage it was believed to be in the best interest not to approach the situation from that direction.

After numerous attempts to contact the lone individual, Sam decided to go with his gut. He needed to approach the situation like many others in the past.

Sam picked up the phone, and with the negotiator by his side, agreeing with every step explained the plan to Nick, "Nick we have no way of getting you out through the window, what are the chances you could see into the kitchen. Remember a baited man needs no reason, if he drops his guard."

"I have more mirror pieces, maybe I could position myself to," Nick was interrupted. The Chief of Police had grabbed the phone to mention the following. "Officer Sheridan, this is the Chief of Police, how are your wounds."

"Okay, the bleeding has stopped. I still have full movement," Nick stated.

"Good, good to hear that. Son, if you have a shot take it," the Chief of Police had a reputation, if he said do it, you had better do it.

They tried to contact the individual and he was not communicating at all, they could storm the house and if Nick did not act fast that would more than likely be the result, storming the house and not knowing positions would surely mean mistakes could be made and Greg would not fare well.

While all the conversations and waiting were in the process, Nick was busy assembling small items that he had found in the room, anything that could assist.

He was chewing some old Bubbalicious bubble gum that he had found in a drawer. He had also assembled some of the mirror pieces that he found throughout the room, he attached the gum to his extendable mirror he placed a larger piece of the mirror to it and headed toward the door. He had caught the man off guard he was not directly looking at the doorway. He was sitting on the floor, with his back against the cabinet doors.

He had Greg in a headlock with his left arm and the shotgun was in his right hand, the shotgun was mostly lying on the floor, Greg was motionless it seemed to be an eternity as he watched his partner, there was no movement. Nick wanted to take the opportunity, "Sam, I have a shot is there a green light," Nick asked in a low tone.

"Take the shot, you have a green light," Sam answered.

Nick was still watching the man. He had a few seconds to consider all of his options. He could wound the man, in the hopes that he did not have time to react prior to Nick removing the weapon and subduing the individual. He stood and tried to control his breathing, if not for a few seconds, at least until he had achieved his goal.

He literally swung around the door and fired his weapon, the shot struck the man in the shoulder, as the man started to raise the shotgun the next shot was between his eyes, the man slumped almost immediately as the shotgun dropped to the floor, he did not fire a shot this time.

Nick responded in kind and approached the individual moving the shotgun away. He was screaming "It's clear, situations clear," the swat team had entered and was inside the house before he could finish the sentence. He was removed quickly from the house and throughout he kept asking about his partner, as it ended Greg had the mother of all concussions and after a few weeks would be fine. Nicks wounds healed also and they would both be back on the force inside of a month.

Nick made detective three weeks later and Detective Lieutenant Sam Clark asked the new Detective to be his partner, it was quite an honor. When Nick started to work with Sam, he had already been on the job for nineteen years and was considered one of the city's finest detectives. Sam loved his job and everything that went with it, many times while working a case with Sam, Nick thought that Sam seemed let down when they actually caught a suspect.

For Sam the chase was the best part and in the ten years that they worked together, Sam was by far the best at assembling a case. He almost had a District Attorney's way about him as to how thorough our case files should be.

Nick had known for many years that one day Sam would walk in and call it a career. Sure enough after a vacation Sam came into the office with papers in hand, he retired two weeks later. Sam with all his due diligence to what he wanted had found the perfect oasis. He found a position as Chief of Police in a small town named Schrader located in Penobscot County Maine. Nick remembered when Sam told us in the morning Detective's meeting, we actually had to go get an atlas to look it up, some of us recognized why this would be the perfect area when we saw it on the map. Fishing galore, with many lakes all around that area, that was when we all realized that this would be an oasis for Sam.

Five

"A plan to watch."

James Bennett MacMillian had been here before, this place he enjoyed. His oasis, it hadn't been always like this, through the years it had been transformed. He would not sit long, by himself. He would be joined,
"May I join you here?" Ian Thompson asked.
"Please Ian, have a seat."

Even though he would take the offer, as they sat, neither would speak. Ian knew this drill. James MacMillian had been around the block before, through the years he had grown to not enjoy, so much, this side of the business world. Sure others did not necessarily do it like this. Maybe they had other means to clean the dirty parts, those parts that needed adjustment, or as in this case complete removal in time.
"You know, some years ago, this was all private land. Our land."
"Is that so," Ian remarked after a few seconds.
"We bought it when we expanded in the early eighties. Marcus went through a green phase, you know the environmentally correct thing, before it became the thing to do."

"Really?" Was the questioned response from Ian? That name he had not heard in some time, at least uttered by the man who had ultimately taken him from this earthly place, or had at least ordered it, James was too high on the food chain to handle "those" things.

"He would be like that, some times. Used to drive me crazy, spending all that money, for what I thought was nothing. But look at it now, pisses me off even more, the fact that he was right."

"I could understand that."

"His idea to give the land, this park that he created to the city. Again, that really pissed me off. Until the tax people explained the benefits, and write offs, still writing this little spot of land from our annuals."

"Really?" Ian questioned.

"Fucking brilliant it was. And I still get to enjoy it, just like every other swinging dick does."

"But, you're not here to listen to me groan about the past, are you?" James asked.

"No sir, don't believe that I 'am?'"

"So the business at hand, is it?" James asked, knowing all along that it was.

"Let me start by saying, we want to make sure, prior to stepping forward. That this individual and what he has been getting into, as you know, we want to make sure of many things."

"It might represent the situation best, his extortion, blackmail request changes the situation."

"I hate to wait, you know this, what if he..." James paused. He could say it out loud, he was not concerned about the surroundings. He was worried, and wanted to respond quickly.

Ian interrupted, it was something that he did not like to do. Some people with their power hates to be interrupted, James MacMillian was one of those men, "Excuse," Ian paused again. "Excuse me sir, we have looked at all the possibilities and at this time, we have concluded that the individual that was asking and taking some leniencies against you, and the past. Would be better watched. So that we may see who else he is talking with, if anyone?"

"And the team?" James asked

Ian never went into details, even with the man that paid the bills, and in this case even paid them very well.

"We decided to watch the source, and then we will decide. The other individual is not being watched so closely at his home, we have the office taken care of,"

"So both are being carefully, yet dutifully watched, in your own way of doing things?" James asked.

Ian just nodded, he wanted to add nothing else. James did not question this any further, he had already given the green light to take care of it.

He had trusted this with the man that he had used before, his cleaner. James knew with this man on the job, soon, he would no longer worry, his past would rest with those that were currently being watched.

"And what about Mr. Massena, we are keeping him in the loop?" James asked, not really caring if he was or was not in the loop. They, James and Massena had been "friends" if one were to call it that. The fact of it had been more to the point of using each other wisely in the past. A defense contractor heavy with government contracts could always use an underworld figure, or two.

"Through channels," Ian stated without further explanation or hesitation.

"Of course." James stated.

"Sir, just so you know. I understand the relationship in the past and all. I Just believe that we should keep our distance, so to speak. Something is not right about his interest." Ian wanted to say more, sometimes treading lightly is best, in the beginning.

"Of course," James repeated.

Six

"Just like Mayberry."

The front door said it simply, Police Headquarters Schrader Maine. A plain looking building with a 'no parking sign' directly in front of the building, there were windows on each side of the door other than that it was a brick building just like many others located on both sides of the street, it was located in the center of the 'downtown district'.

He opened the door and entered, immediately he thought of an old style country Police Department, something you might see on the Andy Griffith Show. As you entered the building you had a counter to your right side with various radios and dispatch equipment located behind the counter, a little waiting room right past the counter with several cubicles located on the left side of the entrance.

From the entrance, he could see three separate cubicles. No one seemed to be in the cubicles, and in fact there was no one around, the front door unlocked and nobody here. Nick almost expected that drunk from the Andy Griffith Show to come out and ask him if he wanted coffee, "what was his name" Nick said aloud.

"Whose name" exclaimed a woman in her late fifty's that came from around the corner behind the counter.

"Hello, Patty Dunbar, nice to meet ya, I'm the departmental secretary, so whose name" she said to the visitor. "If you're looking for the chief, you might want to come back, he has meetings this morning. Anything else, and I will be able to help you for the most part."

Nick did not really answer just shrugged his shoulders and mumbled that it was not important, almost in disbelief that he would have to explain that he was asking about the drunk in the Andy Griffith show.

"So, whose name" Patty said throwing her hands up in the air "can't help you if we don't have the name."

"This place reminds of somewhere and I was trying to think of the name, it's not important," Nick said

Patty's response was dry and sarcastic "You're not thinking of a place, say in Mayberry" after a pause and a chuckle from both she continued to say "Oh, don't worry about it, you wouldn't be the first to draw that conclusion."

Nick offered his hand to Patty, she was a typical sort somebody you might see in a Library, with her bifocals hanging from beaded type of chains that were holding the glasses on around her neck. If first impressions were the most important, Nick would have to conclude that she was the one who did everything around here and probably complained about doing it. This Police station was active because of her endeavors and she stayed active because of it.

"Nick Sheridan, nice to meet you," Nick said.
Patty shook Nicks hand, and exclaimed in almost disbelief

"Holy crap you're the new chief,"
Nick responded in kind "Nice to meet you Patty, and yes I'm the new Chief" although Nick was still not comfortable with the title 'Chief'.

"Patty for now, Nick would be fine," Nick said.
"Now on to the business at hand, where is the current Chief, he said bright and early and for Sam that started two hours ago" Nick stated with a little smile.

"Patty seemed curious as well, he did say around seven to eight in the morning, if I remember correctly. Maybe he decided to go fishing this morning and is running a little late."

"Tell you what, we will give him another half hour and then we will make a call," Patty said without hesitation.

Nick seemingly agreed and asked where his new office is located, Patty directed him back past the cubicles through the coffee room to the back of the building.

Nick followed her and saw that the door was open. Nick could see that the glass on the door had "Chief of Police Schrader Maine" must be a reminder if he ever lost his way.

Seven

"Too many deaths."

He walked in and found, not a soul around,
"Where's my staff and who has my messages,"
the Junior Senator from the state of
Massachusetts did not seem disturbed and since
it was a Saturday, he understood. Thomas
Bennett Griffin Jr. understood, unlike the previous
Griffin that had held the same Senate seat, a few
years prior. He had walked in with two staffers
and a few more showed their face when he
entered the office. The Chief of Staff came from a
nearby cubicle and passed the messages, along
with him was the biographer, the ghostwriter who
was to write about the not so young anymore, yet
still carried the looks of a younger man.

When Tom saw the writer, he knew that the
next couple of hours would be wasted, in his
eyes wasted. He had not been in favor of this
biography idea. It more or less had been pushed
to highlight his life and get his profile to the next
level. In many eyes it was long overdue.

As the ever-gracious person that he was, he went and shook the writer's hand, for all the young Senator knew the writer did not want to be there either.

"Senator, good to see you again, was informed last night that you were available for a few hours," Bill Clement said.

"Bill, glad to see you also, let's go into the office,"

"Could you give us two hours" he asked his Secretary as they both walked into his office.

"Senator, I appreciate your time, I know you do not want to be here, maybe two more sessions and it will all be in the past," Bill said.

"Two more sessions, what do we need to cover for this one?"

"With all the research I just need to get your personal thoughts on some issues, from your personal life. I have enough from the political side."

"You would like to talk about my mother's death and about college," the Junior Senator knew this was going to come up, it always does.

"Sir, every time you give an interview there are always questions about your Mother's death. When we previously spoke, and with discussions from your staff, by the way they are very protective of you, as I am sure you know.

I would love the opportunity to input some of your personal thoughts on the matter, something for the book for content purposes," the writer wanted to know this, something that could be new and original, something someone has not written or more importantly that the Senator had never said.

He tried to stay objective to the cause, the cause was simple, to get the best foot forward about this young simple mind.

Something that might feed the hungry Democrats of the world, which upon their horizons were bright individuals that maybe in the future could take the White House.

Bill Clement was not a Democrat and until recently had found little time in accepting what their big picture was, until recently, when for reasons he could not fathom that his mind was opened to the righteous side of politics that had escaped him in the previous 32 years of his existence. Not for the glory of God, religion had never been and he swore would never be his thing, unlike many for the temptation of lust and a strong desire to be lusted for, would bring his political thinking and with that the mindset that came with it, to a new light.

A new light named Jessica, and within a few months the one time, unknown writer became published, and seemingly plucked from the many interested, for the ghost writing experience and payday of a lifetime.

Recruited to ensure that an overwhelming lifelong republican could change and with this thought, as plucked from obscurity, ensuing interviews would open eyes of many others, or so the supporters of Tom Griffin thought.

"May we start with your Mother's death," Bill asked.

"Certainly, like I've said many times over. I was only eight when it happened, I was invited to a sleepover and was very excited to go, did nothing but talk about it all week,"

"Where was the sleepover at, whose home," the writer asked.

"The Gillespie's home, Aaron Gillespie was a friend from school, same class and all. I just remember being extremely excited. I was only eight so a lot of other things did not matter for someone that young,"

"Do you think that your memories are brought out because of the death or for other reasons," the writer again inquired.

"I think that has something to do with it, repeating it and the facts being repeated on TV so much, it is a prominent case. A Senator's wife dying, during an apparent break-in and with no one ever charged in the crime. I do remember not giving my mother a hug or kiss, I just grabbed my stuff and ran toward the door, I'm not sure if I said goodbye," Tom Jr. said.

"She had planned to spend the night at a friend's house,"

"Yes, as I found out many years later, she had made plans to stay with the family's good friends the MacMillian's at their home," the Senator continued with "She was not even supposed to be at home, that night."

"What made the plans change," the writer asked.

"Again as I found out many years down the road, she dropped me off in the early afternoon, my mother went home and took a nap. When she woke up it was close to six in the evening and she just did not want to make the trip out to the MacMillian's," it was difficult for the Senator to recall such painful memories, especially around the anniversary of her death.

"Who knew that she called someone," the writer asked in a monotone way, he knew the answers it was always good to hear it again just in case it brought forth other questions.

"She called the MacMillian's to tell them that she would not be arriving, they had even offered to come pick my mother up if she wanted,"

"Your mother decided to stay,"

"Yes, and for all the memories that I have about this, the Saturday morning memories seem to be the strongest," the Senator, remembered clearly getting up early on that Saturday morning to watch cartoons like most other children of the day. In addition, about an hour later, the cartoons stopped and the news broke in to show the live reports of then Senator Thomas Griffin Sr. wife was dead because of a break-in.

"Your maid found the body of your mother," the writer asked trying to be as gentle as possible.

"Well, not really, she came in and found broken glass in the kitchen and the den was in disarray.

She called the police, she also thought that my mother was gone, and did not even check the rest of the home," the Senator stopped, he paused and was merely reflecting on what he had already said,

"Senator, you okay," the writer asked.

"Yes, I'm fine, the police found the body of my mother,"

"To this day your father was considered by many, especially the conspiracy nuts, to be involved, perfect crime and all that," the writer wanted to change the subject, he personally thought that it was absurd to think that his Father was involved. Seeing he was in Korea at an Asian growth conference at the time, still many conspiracy believers thought it was too easy to be true.

"Yes, a couple of years ago they had that Docudrama that my Mother's murder was the perfect crime, and that my father did it. In the end we saw what that was all about," the Senator had a wry smile on his face, and the writer did not see the smile, for Tom Jr. knew what really happened to the director that made the 'Perfect Murder' documentary.

"Correct, as it was proven several years later he had paid obscure people to lie about what really happen," the writer concluded.

"Yes he did, the damage was still done for the most part, although I think we held our end up very nicely," the Senator was sure to say that.

"Why didn't your family sue, you could have made it easier in the long run," the writer asked.

"We just thought that the truth would come out, that director was extremely popular, if we would have sued. We just believed that suing and getting nothing, maybe a little detraction in the papers was not worth it overall," the Senator thought what a headache it had become right before he ran for the Senate the first time.

"I would like to move on to the college years, your roommate Robert Robinson was shot and killed during your junior year at Harvard," the writer asked.

"Yes, that was a very dark time, just a terrible time," The Senator paused.

"So many things happen for no reason at all, Robbie was a decent guy. He went to Harvard to better himself. He still hadn't decided about law school but was leaning in that direction," the Senator was hesitant and fumbled through his words.

"Many things seemed odd from the police reports," the writer asked.

"Well, with all due honesty you would have to ask the Police or detectives assigned to the case. I don't believe that they had anything to go on, not much anyway,"

"You were brought in for questioning at one time, right?"

"Yes, I was, suppose it is the same for any roommate, you know,"

"If you were to go back and read all the press reports about this, it seemed that you might have been a person of interest, as they say these days," the writer tried to be as gentle as possible to his question.

"Some would still say that to this day, always comes out like that, especially around election time,"

"And what would you say about this," again the writer tried to ask his questions as if he was reading them from something, to which he had no ownership of.

"What would I think, well I'm a Boston boy, born and raised. A lot of baggage comes with that, so many things were said. His Father got away with, the killing of my mother and now it's the sons turn, things like that. Very hurtful things,"

"And the truth would be," the writer asked, again already knowing the answer.

"Ah the truth, something most people are not interested in, something that most if not all people find completely boring. The truth of the matter was that I had a very good alibi, if it should be called that. I was in the car, with witnesses saying this, about an unknown gun man who walked away, so on."

"And your roommate,"

"Well the final Police report said, what it said. You have all that information, take of it what you will.

We were on the way to a party, in the warehouse district, was not familiar with the surroundings and so on."

"Did you get any kind of apology?"

"From the media, please, I did get one from the Chief of Police, on behalf of the city, blah, blah, blah. That was more than likely done, because of my father's position as a U.S. Senator."

"Nothing more,"

"Nothing,"

"And no one was ever charged with the crime, or anything,"

"Still a cold case, to this day, sometimes when the phone rings, when I'm feeling a little sad or gloomy in remembrance, I would want that call to be the call. The call that tells me, they have the person that did that."

"With your mother's case also,"

"Yes, with that too, law of averages could tell you that it would be the more difficult case to solve, because of when it happened and where.

She was alone in the house, or so we believe, as far as Robbie, someone had to see that, someone had to see it."

"Do you think about it often?"

"Sure, especially about my mother. Would think of her more, if kids were in the picture,"

"Do you want to have children?"

"Bill are you asking me out," the Senator had always been a kidder, it was his way of alleviating a situation when he became a little tongue tied or was trying to not ask the direct question, such as in this case. "Bill, I never really contemplated the children issue. I suppose that I just assumed it would happen, you know the old song, first comes love, then marriage and so on. Well I thought I had the love, then the marriage, as you know it was short lived,"

"In our previous interviews, you always said that you guys had a good marriage and just grew apart, children were never discussed," the writer did not know this answer.

He had tried to broach this subject many times before, he had never gotten this far. It seemed to him that whenever he touched a nerve or was getting down to the juicy stuff as he liked to say in his own journal, he would be interrupted by some staffer that would barge in, like the Senator had some button under the desk in order to call for help.

"I'm sure that it was, like I said I thought we had a good marriage, so maybe the subject was broached several times. It was a busy time in both of our lives, getting married right out of college, trying to make our mark inside our own world of business,"

"She was in marketing. You were running the family business so to speak,"

"Yeah the family business, let's not make that sound so nefarious, I believe I have a reputation to uphold."

"And then the divorce,"

"Yes, then the divorce. It was a trying time for us, her parents had died that same year, Cancer for her Dad and what I think was simple loneliness and the loss of her husband for her mom."

The Senator became silent, he was deep in thought or so it looked. "Bill, I know, for the book to sell and do well, we need the information about my Mother's death and that of Robbie's. This is obvious, so for you, we made a little package it contains everything that I can remember and has some other press clippings and assorted information. Review it and then in a couple of weeks we can schedule another meeting."

The time with the writer had ended and the Senator was back to his usual correspondence and other mundane senatorial work. His life was full and he would have to get used to all the correspondents and their future political statements as to his future. He liked his present situation, the future presented too many prying eyes.

Eight

"Maybe he's not on the boat."

The office was not big by any standards. The door was at the center of the wall. When you walked in the desk was directly in front. It was an old style wood desk. Nick thought that Sam picked this desk out and more than likely would be taking it with him or would try to sell it. He remembered that he always hated the metal type and swore that when he had his own it would be wood, big and overall very nice. The office chair behind the desk was nothing fancy, facing the desk were two armchairs. On the left side of the desk was a lateral file cabinet with three drawers and a closet. There was nothing on the right side of the desk. Behind the desk was a three-shelf bookcase that seemed to be longer than the desk itself.

The one thing that he noticed was missing was a computer.

Nick stood in the doorway and surveyed the room,

"Well are you going in, everything okay?" Patty asked

"Were there any boxes delivered?" Nick asked Patty unassumingly.

"Yes" Patty answered, "We placed everything in the closet."

"The Chief, Sam, said that you were always a fan of good coffee" Patty said with a simple chuckle.

"Hope that you brought your own," Nick's response was easy, after drinking the coffee that was still leaving a bad after taste in his mouth, "Well after the coffee from across the street, your right."

"We make better coffee over here, and it may be in your best interest not to have the daily special either, just to let you know" Patty said with a smile that left something for a later discussion.

"Chief, sorry Nick, Sam left you some reading to do on the far edge of the desk, we also put together a little explanation of things, I'm sure that he will go over all of it with you when he arrives, if you want to get a jump, there is it."

Nick looked to the left, he saw what seemed to be a pile of miscellaneous reports and a couple of notebooks, and he recognized the notebooks from Sam's time in LA. Sam had always written down all his thoughts about a case. He would then methodically go through his chicken scratch to write the more important virtues that would end up in the regular report.

Sam was a Detective of old, he understood computers and the value they had with Law Enforcement.

He just wanted to stay in an old school way of thinking, if you were to type something into a computer and you did not use it, it was gone forever.

He would use his notebooks for all his thought, they might be dumb and would never make it into the final report. He would however, have everything to remember or recall later.

"Patty, are the personal records in that pile also," Nick asked.

"Yes, put them there myself earlier," Patty answered.

"Looks like I will get started with that until the Chief makes his appearance."

Patty left the office, and Nick went behind the desk to get started. Sam informed Nick of several things, many they would get into later. He knew that the employee base was limited. It was comprised of mostly decent people that could handle the job as a Patrol Officer in a small town. Sam had trained them, not in a forceful way more to the fact of learning from your mistakes.

He had held drills, from which they all could learn how things would be properly run from a big city standpoint.

Sam had kept it simple, and he truly felt that what he had instituted here, he would profit from, so to speak, in the near future.

He pulled the personnel records from the pile and started to read, from the way it looked, Sam had laid out everything for him to get started in case he was late or maybe decided to start his retirement a day early.

With the taste of bad coffee still lingering, first things first, let us unpack the coffee pot and start brewing something that will taste like coffee.

With the Coffee brewing, Nick started to unpack a few other mementos and then went to search for Patty.

Patty was on the radio when Nick entered the room,
"Ernie, what's your 20."

Ernie's response was almost immediate
"Patty, I'm out on old Knoxville the north side, coming back in now," "Ernie, stop by the Chief's place and tell him that Nick Sheridan is here and he's late" Patty said while looking in Nick's direction.
"Okay Patty, he might still be fishing, I'll give him the message," Ernie said with no other inquiries.

Nick informed Patty that he had made coffee, and that it should be ready in a few minutes. He had unpacked his coffee maker and used a special blend for this morning, if they were coffee connoisseur's they would fully understand what good coffee was all about, and his special blend would be put to good use. In addition, if they had no idea what good coffee was, and would rather prefer to have to stuff scooped up across the street, then he would hold the door open for them.

Nine

"It's a crime scene, till someone of authority say's otherwise, you always treat it as a crime scene."

There is no easy crime scene.
Crime scenes that have children involved are horrific. On many dimensions, regardless of the situation they are always difficult.
Maybe the worst is when it involves someone that you know or have known. In addition, maybe when it is not a crime scene, just a deceased friend and you happen to be the first to see it.

Patty received the call, not by regular means, cell phone to cell phone. Ernie Fischer was a diligent sort, somewhat slow, but a hard worker. Ernie knew that his days of being a cop, might be limited.

With all considerations made, Sam saved his job many times over. If the mayor had his way, either someone else would be hired, with prior experience or the position just removed altogether. Ernie was not a bad Patrol Officer, he was, in the eyes of the Mayor expendable for the better good.

It was a harsh discovery for Ernie, many things in life you will never forget, and at 42 years old, this was the worst for Ernie Fischer. When Ernie first arrived, he checked the dock area to make sure that "The Chief" was not still out on the lake,
"Boats still there," Ernie said as if someone was next to him.

As many times that he had gone fishing with the Chief, Ernie knew the drill. Go early, finish early then drink beer. You always had time to put stuff up later. There was nothing in the boat. It did not look like the
Chief had been out fishing at all this morning, and he really did not expect him to be off drinking beer somewhere.

Sam loved his beer, just not in the morning. No poles were in the boat, nothing. Ernie walked back up the stairs to the house, he knocked "Chief you in there?" Ernie said, knocking louder even banging. Without hesitation Ernie reached for the key, even the Chief of Police would keep a spare above the door. Ernie used it to unlock the front door. While still calling for the Chief he traversed the front living room and had barely turned that corner when he saw it.

Ernie's life would change forever, Ernie went into a mode he had never used before. He hurriedly approached the body and checked it for a pulse, there was no pulse the body seemed cold.

He immediately backed away all the way through the house to the front porch. He then reached for his cell phone and made the call.

Patty was in 'The Chief's' office, when the phone rang, she removed it from the holster that carried it looked at who was calling and mouthed to Nick in a low voice that Ernie was calling. For all things considered, Ernie was calm.

"Is the new Chief there?" Ernie said,

"Yes, I'm in the office with him, were just going over the simple" said Patty. Before she finished her sentence, Ernie cut her off "Patty" he said "The Chiefs dead" complete silence followed. Patty's response was simple and sincere "Ernie, that's not funny and totally, well not funny,"

"Patty, he's dead, no pulse, in his kitchen, dining room area must have happened this morning" Ernie said.

Nick looked up from his reading he saw a look from Patty, a tear already down her cheek. She moved a little and fell into the chair with a slump, as she did she passed the phone over to Nick. Nick could hear a voice on the other end, "Patty, Patty you still there, you need to tell the new guy" about that time Nick said "This is Nick Sheridan, the new guy, what is it Ernie."

The response was slow "Sir" Ernie said, "The Chief, Sam he's dead" with the way that Patty was crying in front of him, Nick knew something was not right.

"Ernie, describe the scene to me," Nick asked.

"Well, I checked the dock to see if he went out" Ernie went on to describe everything that had transpired in the last 3 minutes or so, "That's when I backed out of the Crime Scene and called Patty, you."

Sam had taken what he was given when he first started as the Chief and molded them into a team. He had people that had good hearts and a simple understanding for what is right, more importantly they knew the difference. As Sam used to say, "Repetitive actions make repetitive responses." You say it enough you drill it into their minds and one day when the pressure is on, they will come through.

"Ernie, hold on. Why did you say Crime Scene?"
Nick asked.

"Chief always said that it's a crime scene, till someone of authority say's otherwise, you always treat it as a crime scene," Ernie stated in such a manner that it sounded as if he was reading it from the manual.

Sam Clark had a manual on all things relevant to a Police officer, it was not a book type manual, it was one of those, these are my rules just follow them.

"Ernie, stay with me here, what did it look like to you," Nick said with a little hesitation in his voice, sometimes it best not to ask.

"Well, he was just kind of on the kitchen floor, on his back. There was some broken glass on the floor."

"Any blood, sign of a struggle, anything" Nick asked, stopping him in mid-sentence, Nick continued with

"Ernie, we are on our way. Secure the scene, no one in." Nick flipped the phone shut and handed it back to Patty, he reached into the duffle bag that he had brought with him and pulled out his 9 mm with belt holster and placed it on his right side, he put his jacket on and went to the door. While he did that, he turned to Patty and said,

"This is going to be difficult for all of us. We are going to need our rock to keep it altogether for us."

"Patty" he squatted down in front of her, and gently moved his hand to lift her chin up to look him in the eye.

"Patty, we need for you to make the calls, the coroner, the Mayor," Nick wondered. "Do we have some kind of Crime Scene Kit? Is there a vehicle I can use, wait, I'm going to need someone to take me." Nick did not know how to get to Sam's cabin.

Patty removed herself from the chair wiped her eyes and "there will be plenty of time for all that wimpy crying stuff later, looks like we all have work to do."

She picked up the radio on Nicks desk and called for Zach "Zach, what's your 20."

Zach, never questioned, he just did. The call was not a panicky call just a call.

Nick was outside with Patty when Zach arrived, introductions were made. Before Nick got into the passenger side he turned to Patty,

"Better make those calls,"

"And Patty, no other info is available"

"Thank you."

The vehicle left and Patty returned to make the calls.

Zach seemed uninterested. "Going out to the Chief's place" "He's a good guy, taught me a lot," Zach said. "The way we heard the stories he taught you a lot too" Nick was silent, "Zach, pull off to the side of the road." Once the car stopped, Nick Continued "Looks like the Chief has had a heart attack" "Ernie went there earlier to get him and found him dead in his kitchen."

Zach just stared at him, maybe some shock or utter disbelief. "Are you sure, you said Ernie found him." Zach Said, "You see Ernie never did well with the checking for a pulse, we kind of joked, anybody but Ernie to help us medically." "Zach let me drive, just give me the directions." "You all right" Nick asked.

Zach response was much of the same, "Yea all right" he continued with "never knew the Chief had heart problems."

Nick was reluctant to say anything, although his thoughts were the same.

Before the vehicle came to a complete stop, Ernie was at the door waiting to pull the handle. When Zach stopped the car, Nick turned to Zach and asked,

"Zach, I need you to grab the Crime Scene kit from the trunk and a notebook."

"The Crime Scene kit" Zach replied, rather hesitantly toward his new boss. "But you said natural causes,"

"What was one of the most important rules that you have been taught?" There was a pause between them. Nick could see a blank look, not a dumb look just a blank stare. "Remember it's a crime scene till someone says it isn't."

The response from Zach was a plain and simple "sorry."

"Don't be sorry, if you have a question ask it, there are no wrong, bad or stupid questions" Nick, finished his sentence and stepped out of the vehicle and turned to shake Ernie's hand "Ernie, good to meet you,"

"You too, sir" Ernie continued with, "Sir, no one in or, well out."

"Okay, thanks Ernie, Zach is getting a crime scene kit. May I get some gloves?"

Nick had been to many crime scenes, he had seen friends, and fellow police officers dead at scenes before. He had even seen the one you never hoped to see, even this would be different. Nick made his way through the front room to the dining/kitchen area.

As soon as he turned the corner, there was Sam. Nick paused, whatever rate of speed he had used to get through the house, his anxiety, that same momentum would bring his body to a quick stop.

In fact so sudden that Ernie ran into the back of him. Nick turned around a little and back again, to focus on his mentor in front of him, he motioned for Ernie to stay where he was. He approached the body, knelt down, Nick slowly checked for a pulse, on the off chance that maybe Ernie was wrong and somehow Sam was just sleeping on the floor, in his kitchen. As it would turn out, no such luck.

Nick stepped away from the body lying before him. While standing in the middle of the kitchen he looked around. It was always a good detective etiquette, look, listen, and then decide. He started to remove his gloves, turned to Ernie and Zach and said.

"Looks as if Sam had a,"

A paused ensued,

"Boys he died of some kind of natural causes, an autopsy will let us know what exactly."

"Ernie, when the coroner arrives" Nick was interrupted by Ernie

"Sir, excuse me we don't really have a coroner. We use Doc Gooden, our local town Doctor. Not the Doc Gooden, baseball player" Ernie finished with.

"Okay, when the non-baseball Doc shows up, let him do whatever he does to remove the body, where or who would perform the autopsy."

Ernie and Zach both looked at each other and without hesitation almost answered together, "There's a coroner in the city." Zach stopped speaking and Ernie completed the tandem thought with Zach nodding appreciatively behind him "We have used the service before, cost though, Patty has all the info I'm sure."

Ernie finished with a rather odd statement, "Zach's dad is not going to like it though he doesn't."

This time the interruption was by Nick "What do you mean Zach's dad's not going to like it."

Zach chimed in over the top of what Nick was saying, "Yea he won't like the cost overrun,"

"Who the hell is Zach's dad?" the words were not completely out of Nick's mouth when once again both Ernie and Zach interrupted by saying, "He's the Mayor."

There was a long pause from all. Nick said in a low voice almost not at all,

"The Mayor, great," he continued with "Make the call to Patty, Zach," "and Zach, tell her that it is natural causes of some sort, probably a heart attack."

Until the coroner arrived, the three of them sat outside and just lingered, there was not much said. There would be plenty of time for that later. "Zach, Ernie, I'm going to need you guys to fill me in on a lot of stuff, in fact I will look to both of you to accomplish what this department needs," Nick said.

He wondered whether this turnover would be more difficult, with all that had happened. Nick had so many questions. He just did not know where to start.

The notifications were the worst. Nick had made many in his years at the LAPD. You never knew what to expect and sometimes would have to be there much longer than you wanted. The fact that he would be responsible to notify Sam's family did not dawn on him until the coroner had actually asked.

Doctor Mike Gooden was a very knowledgeable small town doctor, he was in his early sixties, he had been pursuing retirement, his love of the area and the people and his desire not to leave with no one to take his place had been the one deal buster toward that retirement.

He had Coroner credentials simply because someone needed to be, he however had a disdain for autopsies, he actually always confessed that his bedside manner would be wasted during an autopsy and that was why he did not like and had always pushed the Coroner part to the bigger city of Bangor. In addition, of course Doc. Gooden introduced himself as the non-baseball Doc. Gooden. Nick had not been in town a full day and this was getting old already, after the third time it just did not need repeating.

The sad fact was that now as the new Chief of Police it actually fell upon him, Nick Sheridan to make all necessary notifications.

The body once removed, traveled about sixty miles for an actual Coroner to perform an autopsy, and never knew that they were that expensive. After the discussion with Ernie and Zach, he had called Patty to check about the price while waiting for a real coroner.

The phone conversation was brief Nick was handed a cell phone from the Doc, and with a quick although hesitant "Nick Sheridan may I help you."

The Mayor seemed as if his day would be different because of the new person.

The only thing that Nick got from the conversation was, I will be there in five minutes and you have only been here for half a day or so and you have already depleted your budget for the next month, and with the reminder that he was no longer in, the "City of Angels" the conversation was over.

Instead of waiting for "his honor" to arrive Nick went back into the cabin to look around the kitchen. Something did not look right. What that something was, well he could not put his finger on it, it just did not look right.

As nick was squatting in the kitchen, the Mayor was standing over his shoulder. He announced himself, Nick turned and stood up, he offered out his hand to no avail. The Mayor, his given name was Zachary Taylor not for the 12th president but for a local individual who fought for the Union in the Civil War. This at one time had been an important name in the area, in fact so important that they used to have a festival or parade day to honor the Late Zachary Taylor, Union Soldier. It seemed to be an honor for all that were named Zachary Taylor to ride or walk in the afternoon parade. Those days had gone, seemed that Nick was blessed with two of that name in his surroundings,

Nick introduced himself, "Nick Sheridan, your new Chief of Police."

This time the Mayor shook the hand that extended to him, "Mayor Taylor."

The Mayor's attack was quick and to the point, "Look I know that you're new, and this is probably the worst way to start in this new job," after a short pause he continued with "this isn't L.A. we do things differently up here."

"Are you talking about the autopsy?" Nick asked. The Mayors response was swift "yes, I am referring to the request for an autopsy. You do not seem to understand what all the cost associated are."

Nick was quick to interrupt, "This will not be the best first impression, when we spoke on the phone a few weeks ago you said my duties are 24/7." Nick continued with "Unless I have cleared with you a day off to leave the area etc."

"If that is the case did you still consider Sam on duty, still on a 24/7 duty status this morning," Nick asked.

The Mayor response was simple, "Yes I regarded Sam as the Chief of Police until you guy's had turned over all responsibilities."

Some of the reading that Nick had done prior to arrival was in fact the by-laws of the city and the responsibilities of the city towards its full time employees.

"If that is correct Mr. Mayor, then Sam was officially on duty and as per your city's guidelines, and I believe it read something like 'If a person is on duty and dies under certain circumstances it can be deemed necessary to perform an autopsy for insurance purposes'."

The Mayor leaned in to Nick, "you read that from current rules."

"Yes, sir I did and I do not mean to throw that out to you, I will back off the autopsy if he had prior heart problems. I do not remember any heart problems in his family." Nick wanted to say more, he left the rest for another time.

The Mayor while pushing his hand forward said "Hello, Zachary Taylor here I'm the Mayor of Schrader Maine and it is a pleasure to welcome you, our new Chief of Police."

Nick responded by saying, "Wish it was under better circumstances, if you will excuse me, I have to call Gregory Clark and let him know about his Dad."

Nick made the call and after the initial shock Greg seemed to be in the best spirits overall.

They talked for about 20 minutes and both were curious about the heart attack.

Before the conversation had finished Nick asked for and received permission for the autopsy if it came to that.

Greg still had to decide about the personal effects and all that, there would be time for that later. Funeral arrangements needed to be made and of course other family members needed to be contacted Nick said that he would call when he had more information.

Besides the congratulatory phone call that Nick received a couple of weeks ago, he had not talked with or seen Greg in about 5 years.

Greg's relationship with Sam seemed strained when he left. As far as Nick could recall Greg had never visited Sam and Sam never returned to L.A. for a visit.

Sam was a tough nut to crack. He either liked you or put up with you and would tell you the same. His son was the polar opposite. Greg always had a good demeanor, Nick never heard a bad word come from Greg's mouth, he was always the cup is half-full type.

Nick had waited to make the call so he could have some privacy, he really did not know what to expect from Greg or the emotion that he might feel during the conversation. He was back in his new and seemingly empty office when he called out for Patty.

"Patty" Nick yelled out in a come here type of way. Soon Nick heard the clambering of shoes so much so that when she was in front of Nick's desk he leaned out of his seat as if to look over and see what type of shoes she had.

"Patty what are you wearing? Sounds like a storm on a metal roof"

"Clogs" she replied "Wasn't really expecting a lot today"

"Nor was I, can we take some time to go over the basics here" Nick wanted his tone to be, well for it to be a little caring yet strong.

The rest of the afternoon, was Patty and Nick discussing and going over all the pertinent information as to running this station and his everyday duties.

Of course, this is an area without a criminal element, so the need to have a patrol on 24/7 is unnecessary. Recently the State patrol has picked up patrol on the interstate and the main route-entering town. Patty also said that we would get Earl back from convalescence leave in the next two weeks. That would bring our total compliment of Police department workers to six, Nick Sheridan (Chief of Police), Patty Dunbar Secretary/Dispatcher, Caroline Dunbar Dispatcher, Earl Rodgers Patrolman, Ernie Fischer Patrolman and Zachary Taylor Junior, Patrolman. In the two hours that they talked, Nick had written many questions, he was sure that most would be included in Sam's notes.

He had been right about one thing, Patty was the glue, she held everything together and would probably be the calm voice when things got bad, Nick wondered if they had ever had a day as bad as today.

Patty was a long-term employee. She had been working at the Police Department of Schrader Maine for over thirty years, she was into her fifties and once she started, had decided that she did not want to go anywhere else.

She was born in a nearby town, and left after high school.

Like many others she chased, caught and married her one true love, they had a child together and three years later were divorced. She looked for work, and found it in Schrader, she never left it, and over the years, her responsibilities had increased. Patty at one time in her life was a good-looking woman, over the years, she had let herself go, and she had no worry of what others thought. She was, extremely good at her job.

Nick had gone back to the motel late. It was after ten in the evening, and after a restless and uncomfortable night's sleep, he was up early. Most of the previous evening he had not been disturbed, they all had other things to do within the normal scope of the job, Nick did a lot of reading.

He was back at the office by seven in the morning, he was the first one and would be the only one to arrive after all it was Sunday.

About an hour after he had entered the office Caroline Dunbar called, she was the weekend or as some might say the stand by dispatcher in case?

She called by the urging of her mother, just to see if anything was needed from the new Chief.

Just like her mother, she left small town life for the lights of the big city. She may have lasted a little longer, and around the age of thirty she returned, she had no children, judging by the numbers kept within the personnel records she and Patti lived at the same residence.

The town of Schrader was not a large town, Maybe there was five thousand people in the entire area. In the summer, with all the cabins and camping available that would balloon to twenty five thousand if not more. Back in the year two thousand, they had decided to discontinue the Police Department for Schrader Maine. The reason for this was financial, the city council voted on the measure and the police department would have been no more, then came 9/11.

When 9/11 happened and after all the new laws were enacted, it was determined from the state to keep the Police Department, ninety percent of all the finances for the Department was now paid at the state level. Through some quirky law, the Mayor received the ability to control the Department, and because of the size of the town and the resources, the City Council had decided to allow the sheriff's office to patrol the interstate. This removed money from the department. It also relieved the department of many daily jobs.

Ten

"Daydreaming was over, supplies would be needed."

Not that he had listened to the advice given just a few months before. He had never enjoyed vacations. Or at least the part of going somewhere else just to relax. A vacation to him, was spending time alone, amongst no one. He did that best at his home.

The method of contact had, through the years changed from one style to another, at one time he even had a pager. When he received the initial call it was to say the least strange, never had he spoken to the "new" guy. It may have been the boss, yet hearing directly from him was odd on so many levels.

The fact that it had been, like it was, with hits in three cities to essentially be spread over a six day period, with specifics was unusual. He had been busy like this previously, many years ago in a different day and age. Today he had to be careful for many things. Every street corner seemed to have a camera, not including everyone with a smart phone, who also had video capabilities in many cases.

In the society of today, the common man and woman, teenager to child would just as soon flip out a smart phone if they were to witness something, and then start to video or take picture prior to calling any authority. This was good for Conoscalo, kind of? At least there would be a delay for the authorities showing up, if ever in a situation like that, of course the pictures, the video are different stories all together. At least he blended in.

He had not been this busy in some time. The cabin job was easy, just out of his normal area if he really had a normal area.

With part one down, part two was next, soon he would ask that one question that had always escaped a place and time to ask it.
And so he went on.

Conoscalo always hid in plain sight, if someone had known him, he could be easily spotted. This is where he would be caught, drinking a cup of plain, black coffee. Sitting in a café, or as this one so proudly called itself, 'bistro'.
Previously in his career he would have thought that this was the boring part, the mundane dismal part of his job.

Times changed and the mundane part became the necessary part. Through the years he realized his preparations needed to be better than ever. He also started thinking more and more about what could be.

We all day dream, having certain fantasies that will materialize, yet still garner our attention as top the complacency of our own life and how it could be different. For a highly educated hit man, the opportunities were endless.

His life could change. He could go work at a fast food restaurant, which would be easy. The application would leave many wondering. An almost fifty year old male, looking to be a short order cook. Education some, at least for the purposes of this application, life experiences many. He could see it all now, the pimpled youth, hanging on his every word as he explained how to succeed in his former career. They would all giggle at his story telling skills.

Maybe, most would raise their hands in unison and state how much bull shit this was, as he explained the best way to slit someone's throat, to induce the least amount of pain, as if knowing that were even possible. Not even getting into the discussion of the mental side, not necessarily with the preparation, but with the deed itself.

Sure some would say that they would want to hear another story, others would just turn away, having heard enough of the old man's stories.

Yes, this could happen, he could easily walk away and never be heard from again. He could just leave it all.

He knew this was not in the cards, not as they presently were dealt. He would have to wait but his time could come. When that chance arose, he would be ready.

As for the mark here, it had been different. He had already seen him once, walking into the building itself. Conoscalo, had entered this residence previously. It had been a solid two weeks ago, when the young lady that lived in the apartment had gone shoe shopping or something to that affect. She was like those kids on TV, laundry, gym, tanning salon, nails, waxing, sleeping, eating and then some doses of partying through it all, come to think of it, she did not do her laundry, she had that sent out.

He had done the dry run, unless they fell out of the routine, he would hit them in the bedroom. He knew every step of the apartment and even had taken the time to sharpen the knife, and then place it back into its overpriced mahogany holder.

He should get friendship points for that alone, no one wants a dull knife at their neck.

Conoscalo needed no more information as to where this mark was going. At one time, maybe years before it was a well-kept secret, it no longer was. It seemed that everyone knew what happened on Saturday nights, or as it was in this case "afternoon delight" not that he knew the entire history, so much for the night time today. As usual he would not be one to beat around the bush, for lack of a better term, he would go straight at it, as usual.

The same crowd knew what happened as well on Monday, Wednesday and for that fact every other Friday evening. Even as his mark left the same building only one hour later, Conoscalo stayed, he wanted to find out how busy this building was with its non-security and the absence of a door man.

He would leave soon, daydreaming was over, and supplies would be needed.

Eleven

"Olivia, what have you gotten yourself into?"

MAY 2012

It was once said, that it was like treading water with cement shoes. She had been told this by the actual Doctor that had referred her patient. Her patient of the last six years. In that time he had divulged much, without saying anything that he regretted. Still once a week they met. It was the best kept secret unknown to all. As she had nearly promised some years before that they would break through, that between them, with her guidance he would figure out the cloudiness of that mirror that he wanted to look into.

On that spring like day in May, as the summer approached, as his campaign headed into a full time and constant affair.

To do this, to be there on that date and the others that followed he would go against the wishes of his campaign manager and his Chief of Staff, they had wanted him to reschedule the meetings with the therapist until after the November election.

In total only four individuals knew of the meetings to begin with. With his therapist making her own scheduling, the privacy was assured.

His campaign manager and chief of staff of course had known since the inception of the meetings, beside Tom Jr. no one else knew of them. As all campaign managers do, there was still a worry, last thing that either one of them wanted, was a leak at the most delicate of times.

He had been on that proverbial couch for some time, leaving in one place, trying to jog that memory that was unclear to him. It had all began some six years ago. His panic attacks had been diagnosed as sheer stress.
He was in the middle of a dirty political campaign, the death of his Mother and its unsolved state, another unsolved murder of his best friend. The stress itself was enough, then the dreams began.

Almost floating he would recall, not moving like you had both feet on the ground, that he just floated. He could see the mirror, not that it encompassed the entire room, to someone as young as he was at the time, still seeing it with that viewpoint, as an eight year old, made it larger.

He could see his mother's body, the shiny substance that surrounded her was unknown. Then in one corner he saw the movement, turning quickly he would look directly into that mirror.

That's where the dream changed, in time he would not just see his own reflection, as time went by, he would see himself at different ages.

While in college, after college, sometimes as an eight year old, a man in his mid-thirties and even sometimes into his forties, and even as a present day graying man.

This had continued for the past six years, they would not always speak of the dreams, there had been times when it hadn't been brought to the discussion for months.

As this process began Olivia Morehead had been warned, against even her own better judgment she would take on Tom Griffin Jr. as a client. She would be reminded of her late father, whenever she stepped out of the normal, to explore or what not to explore, his statement would be the same "Olivia, what have you gotten yourself into."

Sometime later on a spring day a couple of years down the road, he would make his first breakthrough, within weeks he would figure out just who was in that mirror, within weeks he would see through it entirely.

Twelve

"Oh gosh, my name is Kristi Jensen."

It had been a habit of the good old days. Picking the proper time when it was the quietest around, not that nobody would be there. In Los Angeles people were always around, certain times of the day there were less and in those times, the quietest of moments you would get the busy work done.

Nick, now had a shelf of busy work to get done. The original plan non-withstanding. They, Nick and Sam had said the process of turnover would take a month to get Nick fully up to speed. That time had evaporated, Sam was no longer around to be asked the small things that usually are left out of personal reports.

Just as Patty had stated the previous evening, "see you Monday," in which with that statement Nick took a few minutes to recall it was Saturday, "what about Sunday" he would state as he removed himself from his uncomfortable chair and followed the clog hopping secretary who was nearly out the door by the time he caught up.

"Patty, I realize you cannot work seven days a week, yet who works tomorrow?" Nick stated as his eyes rolled, as if to remember some point of what the Sunday schedule really was.

The look on her face was more of a shock, then a caring glance, not that this day, this Saturday had not had enough caring glances already.

"You don't know, you were never told. Weird, guess there will be a lot of that coming. Nick, we are closed on Sunday."

It was weird, for him, it took time to comprehend.

"Closed, how can that be? What if something happens?"

Patty was quick to respond. "Summertime is different, of course. When not in tourist season, we have someone on call. This week it is Ernie. Sam," Patty stopped herself, it had been a long day. "The Chief, may he rest in peace, he would usually take care of anything on Sundays, after he was done fishing. Nick, you're the Chief now, we can change it to what you want, how you want. Everyone just might need that day away tomorrow. Phones are already routed to the duty phone, Ernie has it."

They said their goodbyes again, this time with the conclusion that "See you Monday," from both parties. Nick would pick Sundays for the mundane, for that busy work. That would be his time.

James Bennett MacMillian had a different reason to be in on a Sunday, he wanted an update to some information that had been shared by his "cleaner" he wanted this information to be face to face.

"Ian, you're going to have to go slowly and explain this. Weren't we watching him?"

Ian wanted to go slowly with many things, he did not want to be here, not on any day, called to the mat like this, yet slow he could not go with this information.

"James, we were watching him, mainly at the office, not the cabin. As we heard, through our people, he died of a heart attack. The coroner is performing an autopsy that will be started later today, with the initial preliminary report coming out Monday or Tuesday. Of course the final report will be in a couple of weeks. He's dead, it was not nefarious in any way according to the new Chief of Police that is pretty much following the standard drill with city employees."

"New Chief of Police?" James questioned.

"The report that we have now, says that a former friend of one Sam Clark, someone that he worked with previously was hired in and it was kept quiet for some reason, no one really knew about it." Ian stated in a matter of fact type of way.

"Is this going to be a problem, the new guy?" James wondered.

"No, they are following procedure. Simple as that. Our problem up there is no longer."

"Ian, did you take care of something without..."

"No sir, following the game plan as we originally discussed, nothing further." He had interrupted his boss, which he did not like to do, he considered it rude, and even he had standards, for the most part.

"And our other one?" James asked.

"Just as we discussed, fully blanketed, we want to know what he says and to who he says it, fully covered."

For James MacMillian it was odd timing, although it was good for him, one less thing to take care of.

Nick had arrived early, started coffee and was essentially on his third pot when the phone rang. His understanding from the brief conversation of the previous day that all calls were forwarded, shouldn't that go to the on call guy, Ernie, Nick wondered.

Nick answered it by the tenth ring, "Persistent buggers," he mumbled. "Schrader Police department, Nick Sheridan, may I help you."

"Wow, thought I would get the answering machine and just leave a message. Can you get this message to whomever is now in charge? Let me start by saying how sorry I am by the loss of your Chief, I met Sam a couple of times, thought he was a kick in the pants, in a good way."

"We thank you for your kind words, and you are?" Nick asked.

"Oh gosh, my name is Kristi Jensen."

"We thank you Kristi Jensen, I will make sure that message gets to the proper individuals." Nick wasn't sure what else could be said, maybe Ernie was getting plenty of these type of calls.

"Oh, sorry, my official capacity is as your Counties Coroner. I wanted to inform the department that I would be performing the autopsy on Sam Clark later today and would be sending the results as they come in, and I wanted to know who to send them to, so I was going to leave a message asking for you guys to get back to me."

"You're the Coroner? Okay, my name is Nick Sheridan and I'm the new Chief of Police, I thank you for the ..."

"Damn that was quick?" Kristi Jensen stated this, as Nick was speaking more of an excited utterance.

"Yes, quick, yet still it was in the works, just so happened as it did." Nick now paused.

"I did not mean any, sorry. Let's just do this, If any problems arise, I will contact you, otherwise I will mail the initial report out sometime tomorrow and then the final once the toxicology reports are back, is that okay?"

"That would be fine, if you want to e-mail it that would be great as well. You should have all our information, and thank you for getting this process started so quickly so that we can close the obvious."

It was not a quick phone call, it would be the only received in the office on that Sunday, at least Nick would be able to tell everyone that it was complete or at least the process started, so that they could start to move on.

Thirteen

"What were once vices, are now habits?"

He had taken Sunday off. Conoscalo had used, through the years, many different storage places, spaces and compartments. In the old days, or in his case the not so recent past he would use lockers at bus station or have apartments in other cities to conceal items from time to time. Apartments in his line of work could get messy, nosy neighbors were just the beginning, and he never liked using bus stations. The lockers in most bus stations were not that secure, and usually a criminal element hung out at the stations. The influx of cigar smoking in the late eighties and early nineties created a relative cheap alternative for storage.

These shops with private humidors were no longer for the rich, everyone could afford them and you didn't have to belong to a private club or group just to have one.

He punched in the code for the outside door. This code had been given to all individuals that rented from the cigar company, or in this case it was nothing more than a bar, with a special ordinance to enjoy your smoke, inside.

No two codes were alike and once inside the room he would have to use his key to open his private humidor. Some things he did not like to keep too close.

It was just as he left it. He had placed a little gadget on the top of the box, just like he had asked for. Something with a motion sensor, added to a cell phone.

It looked like a regular cell phone, this cell phone would immediately send a message to his very own cell phone with a simple movement.

If it were ever to be picked up, by someone other than Conoscalo, it would call another cell phone to report the incident that it had been moved. Therefore making this place, somewhere he could never go to again. If the cell phone was never moved, then no worry as to what anyone may have found, inside those four cigar boxes that were stacked below it.

He moved the cell phone look alike, and counted to five in his head.
His cell phone would ring before he could finish the count to five. Originally there had been drawbacks. Cell towers went down, as did the power in central Boston. A few tweaks later and it would be nearly foolproof.

The nearly part being that it had worked every time that it should have, the nearly was not knowing when the next time would be and since they could build something like this, then as they would say, someone always could build something better.

Something that would certainly change the little devise that they had so perfected.

He pushed the red button on his own cell phone. Setting them both down, he started to remove the top box, then the one below it. The third box down contained what he had come for. Once the items that he needed were removed, he would place the boxes back into the same position from which they just came. Then he would punch the proper seven digit number into the gadget and place it back on top of the boxes itself.

With those items properly secured in his nap sack and his humidor properly locked up, he would go into work mode. The remainder of that Monday would be spent evading, from that point around noon, until it was time, he would constantly move, covering his tracks carefully along the way.

Some three hours prior to the time that he had been given, for the deed to occur, then he would go into his other mode. Now he needed to prepare himself.

He calmed down. He could feel his heart rate slow.

His smile faded, however the anxiety was still there.

When he began to focus anew he started to mentally go over what the needs of this job are, what might have to be done to complete or fulfill those needs. Did he have everything? Yes he had everything just in case, he thought. "What were once vices, are now habits?" he told himself, he had wished that were an original quote, it actually came from an album title for a Doobie Brothers record from 1974. He thought the title was appropriate maybe his vices were always his habits. Years ago, he thought that he had no vices, a remnant to the mentality of youth or arrogance. You would have to be arrogant to work under the conditions that he sometimes faced. No, not his vices nor his habits, this job was his destiny. We all have one. Why couldn't his profession be his destiny?

This time he did not go into the 'Bistro' for a coffee. This time he would walk every block in a slow pace, like he was just out enjoying the scenery on a chilly fall evening.

While doing this he would walk by the building itself several times, this he was not worried about. He had watched just about everything on that block, the comings and goings of everything that he could see was normal, nothing to cause alarms. This newer, somewhat upscale part of the city of Hillsborough was bustling just enough, so that his continued walking would not draw attention from the masses. A trained eye looking for something, on the other hand, maybe that would be a different story.

Just as he had been told, his target was on time this evening.

Through the years as his law firm established itself, as he was established as a lawyer who would go that extra mile for his client, regardless of what may have been legal or not so much.

Through those years he had accumulated many toys, you name it he had one, sometimes two. There was one toy, that he admired the most, this toy, assumed by his rather large ego was well hidden.

Not as well as he had thought, or assumed. His young woman was into her thirties and was a prior employee of the law firm that carried his name, Morris, Finley and Turner.

It was the one vice that had become his habit. It started as a somewhat small office romance. She was involved for her own reasons, him for his. It developed into a somewhat passionate, if you were to ask her, or an extremely passionate relationship if you were to ask him. It went to the next level when she pushed to get a little money.

She wanted to buy some nice things. It escalated further when he bought the building for investment purposes and moved her into the top floor.

He had paid too much for the building and he was paying too much for her. In turn he insisted that other nights would be involved, grudgingly she agreed in a committal non-committal type of way.

There interludes would increase even further over time, Monday night had always been theirs, he needed it especially after a long weekend with the kids and wife.

Conoscalo knew the young woman's name but didn't care to repeat it. She was in the wrong place at the wrong time. When he was done however, it would have to look like she had been the reason for the attack. He was sure there would be someone to accuse, some fingerprint left in her apartment from the other nights of the week. He suspected that she had other male callers. Robert Morris was just a meal ticket and up to this point a good one.

The intended victim, Robert Morris, casually strolled into the apartment building. He carried a briefcase and walked as if he owned the place, which in this case, he actually did. Conoscalo would wait about twenty minutes before following. There were people that depended on him and paid well, for him to be competent and quick. When his time was right, he would walk toward the building. He too walked in as if he owned the place.

As he knew, no cameras, he still would wear a ball cap pulled down low.

He walked up the stairs encountering no one in the building.

He walked to the door. He slid out his locksmith tool, four pulls of the trigger and the assembly inside the lock had opened. His fluid movement had been perfected throughout the years. He removed his 9 mm and placed in between his back and his belt. Conoscalo always had a knife and a throw away piece on his ankle, the knife he placed in his back pocket. He put on his gloves and checked his watch.

The door opened quietly, He knew that he had not been misled with the text that simple stated: "Sex first, then food."

He slowly stepped into the apartment avoiding the pile of clothes that seemed littered by the door. He went toward what he deduced from the sounds to be the bedroom. He knew this is where they would be.

It wasn't something he wanted to see, a man with his back to the door his pants around his ankles going at it doggie style with his blonde girlfriend in front of him on the bed.

He figured the man to be Robert Morris, Conoscalo was keenly perceptive like that.

He stepped back into the hall, around the corner from the door. Should he go now, he had to gain some calm. He went through it quickly in his mind her jealous boyfriend comes in, maybe he has a key maybe the door was unlocked. He hears and he knows.

He gets a knife from the kitchen for he knows what he has to do. He would walk into the bedroom, come up from behind and slit the man's throat. It would need to have a personal look, as if the killer was outraged, the easiest way to accomplish that would be a physical attack. That would accomplish his goal. It was to be in a natural way for the demise of Robert Morris if you could consider it natural at the hands of a jealous boyfriend, maybe a possible lover? He would hit her to subdue her and then strangle her, he had seen a robe, and he would use the belt on the robe to perform the task.

The thought had not even finished from his head as he went into the kitchen to get a knife, he knew which one to grab, the one he had sharpened on an earlier visit.

It wasn't his neck, although his job would be easier with one clean cut vice having to place much effort into the situation.

He was now ready, and with that thought he peeked around the corner, and entered the room. It was quick, he went behind the target with his right hand and grabbed Robert Morris's forehead. With one fluid movement and with a precision of a professional his left hand moved in front of the lawyer's throat, to begin the bloodletting of a major artery. The knife dropped to the floor as if it were still cutting the air in the room.

He moved quickly and grabbed her by the hair in the midst of her motion forward. This time her sugar daddy didn't pull her back by her hips. With the assistance of her own movements and the addition of another 215 pounds of weight, her head, and her face became one with the nightstand that stood on the left side of the bed.

In fact, the timing for all purposes would be almost perfect, for her face hit the nightstand at almost the same instant that Robert Morris's limp body hit the floor. Her body lay nude partly on the nightstand and partly on the bed. He removed the robe's belt and strangled the young woman. Her only moves were with his assistance.

He knew any forensics that he left behind could, in time catch up to him. He knew that it could happen one day. He would as always, check the other rooms, just to be sure.

He checked his watch as he left the apartment. As he walked from the apartment, in time, he would remove the hat and then his outer jacket.

The hat would go into a nearby trash can, the jacket would go into the nap sack that he had carried with him.

Another different color light weight jacket would come from the nap sack, this jacket he would wear, zipping his nap sack up and then placing the jacket on, this had all been accomplished as he walked, not skipping a beat in the process.

Fourteen

"Sir we have a situation."

"Go on?"

"We have an unknown individual entering the apartment?"

"Entering how, invited, did someone open the door?"

"No Sir, some type of tool..."

"A Break in?"

"Something like that."

"Is this individual still in the apartment?"

"Yes, has been in the apartment for almost, two minutes and 33 seconds."

"Shit, God damnit..." Ian Thompson paused. Originally, or at least in the beginning he had been a quick thinker.

Through time, things had changed. These days it had taken longer for his reaction, even though it shouldn't have.

"Sir?" Charles Norman had worked for Ian Thompson on many difficult yet always unique 'cases'. He was always the first one called when Ian was assembling a team. He had been the first one called for this, when Ian needed surveillance or any type of computer work, Charles Norman was the first call.

"When he leaves, put your best two guys on him. Low key, don't spook him. I want to know everything about this individual, try and get a picture and have that team report back every hour to you. You can report to me when necessary."

"Yes Sir!"

"And wait a solid ten minutes and have someone check out the apartment. See what has transpired." Ian feared the worst, his one charge. Not necessarily to protect Robert Morris, his charge had been to just make sure he makes the meeting on Wednesday.

"Yes Sir." Charles had always been a good 'yes' man. He always knew the proper time, when not to push things.

"Charles, on second thought, I will be there in five or less. I will enter the apartment. You stand by. I will call when I've arrived." Ian ended the phone call before he could hear the obligatory "Yes Sir," from Charles.

Charles Norman would quickly make another call. Charles was with the first team, in the van which monitored everything. The second team would be tasked to follow the individual,

"We have video on the individual exiting the apartment. Should be exiting the building at this time, do you have the mark."

"We have the mark, ball cap, and a light weight jacket, blue in color."

"That's the mark."

"And the instructions?"

"Level A surveillance, report back to me every hour at the top of the hour, understand."

"Understood? Mark has now removed the ball cap and outer jacket. The ball cap was disposed in a trash receptacle at the corner of Abbott and Sixth Street."

"Understood? Our team will remove the trash, when the availability for us arises."

"Level A, understood, out."

Charles now had the best surveillance team on it, at least the best of what was available. It was in the concept of their business to have every scenario explained prior to the original surveillance. Since they had been on a complete cover of Robert Morris, it was not difficult for the explanation to extend back to the original Level A surveillance. That would mean within the next twenty four hours, more than likely a lot sooner, they would be fully covering the individual that had just left Pamela McKnight's apartment.

Ian Thompson made incredible time, Charles was not sure where he was when he first called. Yet still, incredible time it was.

"How long was the individual in the apartment?" Ian asked of Charles.

"In total, just under six minutes." Charles responded quickly as his boss took long and quick steps toward the building.

Charles handed his boss the lock smith tool. "Stand by, out here. I will call in a few minutes." Ian didn't stop or shorten his stride as he spoke. As Charles stopped his stride, as Ian's voice trailed off, by this time Ian was nearly ten feet ahead of his slower employee.

Ian needed no tool or key for that fact to enter the apartment of Pamela McKnight, the door had been left open, just cracked enough to peer in. When he saw that the door was not closed, he did not bother to knock, slowly pushing it to one side, turning and closing the door behind him. Even though he would close it when he left, better that he closed it now, just in case. He would not speak as he entered the front room, he had felt it wouldn't be necessary. Those feelings would come true as he rounded the corner.

"Jesus H. Christ." Ian muttered aloud, for no real reason.

His first feelings once he thought of the situation that laid in front of him was to check for a pulse, maybe Robert Morris was stronger than he thought. Two steps into the bedroom, and his thoughts changed. Now his thoughts centered on the next individual, or individuals that would enter this room. They would not be looking for a pulse, they however would be looking for and at everything. Ian would have to take care of that, no one would see this, except his trusted crew. Looks like they were on a vacation of sorts, if anyone would inquire, Ian knew all too well that someone would always inquire.

Immediately he stepped out, retracing his tracks, trying to not mess up any more. He looked down to follow his feet. Ian paused, he did not move or take another step. This was his time to reflect. He was then quick to get on the radio.

"Charles, go ahead and make contact with the other team and find out who this guy is. I want him, alive."

"Yes Sir."

"And Charles, I mean alive, not close to death, well enough alive."

Again Ian would not hear the next 'Yes Sir', this conversation would be ended quickly as well.

Fifteen

"She had multiple stab wounds, he died of a heart attack."

Nick decided that Tuesday would be a good day to go out to Sam's cabin and clean out his personal items. He was in the office by six thirty in the morning prior to Patty or any Patrol Officers. Patty arrived a little later and was surprised but not actually surprised that the "New Chief" as he had been referred to behind his back, was in his office reading away. When Nick first heard Patty in the outer office, he called for her. His demeanor was quick that morning, Nick had asked Patty and wanted to be sure if it was all right to bellow her name, he originally suggested an intercom. She suggested that maybe he could e-mail her to come into the office. Her response was actually good witty enough to get a dry smile from the chief.

"Yea, Yea and in a few seconds if I did not come running you would yell if I had received that e-mail yet," Patty said in a sarcastic manner above all.

"Guilty, yes I probably would and then I would yell and curse the fact that our e-mail is so slow," Nick said.

They had discussed the autopsy and that the report would be coming in on Monday, at least the preliminary report.

Not that he wanted to read it, not that he really wanted that report at all, it would still be nice to conclude and move on, so to speak. As it would end up, late that day he would receive an e-mail stating that there was a delay and that she would be calling or contacting them on Tuesday, that she was sorry for the delay. Nick had concluded that the autopsy was bumped for other more pressing reasons, it was understood on the police side of it, they always seemed to wait for the coroner.

For the most part when they met they would discuss the office and how things used to be with Sam, and as usual Nick would end most conversations asking what she thought, Patty liked that. It gave her the respect she deserved without making a big fuss and that was most important to Patty.

Patty was her usual self that morning, a little bubbly and more to the point than the first few days. It seemed that they were getting closer as the Chief and his Secretary should so that the Department does not suffer at its time of need.

Nick had looked over the how's and ways of the department, he wanted to take his time with any changes, he certainly did not want to upset them any further during what would be a time of mourning.

Overall, as he explained to Patty that it was, his goal to stay similar to the way Sam had done things. Patty was about to leave his office when Nick suggested the following.

"Patty, put out the word to not call me the new Chief, just Chief will do I don't like it. I will have to get used to it."

Although the conversation was over, he found himself following her not less than 20 seconds after she had left.

"Patty" he called out

"I forgot, could you please tell me about the Charlton case."

Patty turned and looked perplexed,

"The Charlton case, Chief,"

Nick exchanged a shrug of his shoulder type of look to Patty.

His answer was "Hell Patty I don't know, Sam mentions it in his notes that I should review it, his gut feeling?"

Patty went directly to look for the old case. She was unable to find all the correct files in fact the only file that she found was a one page write up that said little to nothing...of the case.

"Chief looks like we might have a problem here" she said in a low tone to Nick who happened to be right behind her looking over her shoulder as if he would find the file first.

They both took a step back from the file cabinet. Nick started to name off several places, "could it be signed out. Do we even have a sign out system, small office and all?"

Patty's remarks were of a generic sort, "never needed it, before maybe it is a good time to start."

After a little tapping of the clogs and wondering aloud, Patty's only conclusion was to think, "It might be at the Chiefs house."

"Patty, call for Zach or Ernie to run out and, no have one of them swing by and get me we can go out there and clear his house of all the personal items," He was going to do that anyway, no better time than the present.

Nick figured he could clear the house of personal items and find this missing file.

As Nick walked back to his office he could hear Patty on the radio telling Ernie to come into the station and pick up the Chief, she then instructed Zach to get some boxes from the local supermarket and some newspaper for packing. It looked to be that she was certainly the glue that held it altogether.

After Nick explained to Ernie that they had the arduous task of getting Sam's personal stuff together, and during the drive out to the Cabin Nick inquired about the Charlton case.

He had remembered that Ernie was a member and since Schrader or the surrounding area did not get much crime a Murder, as Sam had described it in his notes would surely make everyone available and at the scene. He had thought that Ernie's knowledge would be decent. Nick would be pleasantly surprised at the level of knowledge.

When Nick mentioned the Charlton's case, Ernie's first response was "Sam's pet project is that going to be your pet project too."
Nick response was one of confused indifference, "Sam's pet project what do you mean, Sam's pet project."
Ernie went on to explain, "That Sam was not obsessed with the case he just happened to mention it a lot lately."

"What would be your definition of a lot," Nick asked.

"We would be out on the boat fishing and Sam would just bring it up. He would always ask if we missed something," Ernie reported.

"Just out of the blue, no provocation," Nick said.

"Pretty much"

"Okay Ernie what I would like from you is if you could give me an overview of what happened," Nick asked, he hoped that it would be accurate and not lengthy.

Ernie started in about the case, "the Charlton's," he could not remember their first names "had a summer cabin on the other side of the lake."

"They usually came up for 6 weeks late in the season, it was questioned why they would be at the cabin this late, in the September time frame, they were both professionals he worked at a bio firm and she was a registered nurse at a local hospital."

They lived outside of Boston," Ernie looked over at Nick to maybe receive some kind of appreciation. Ernie went on about the Charlton case, "he could not recall the town just that it was outside Boston."

Ernie went through everything that he could recall about the case, and by the time that they arrived at Sam's cabin Nick felt comfortable with what he knew about the Charlton's and their missing file. He was also pleasantly surprised as to the answer he had just received.

Zach was waiting when they arrived, he had a couple of boxes hopefully they could do this quick for it was something Nick had not looked forward to. With his most recent conversation with Sam's son Greg, it seemed that they had not been that close and as far as Greg was concerned there was nothing that he wanted except Sam's retirement gift from the Los Angeles Police Department.

Ernie's last statement on the Charlton's began with I did not tell you how they died, Ernie continued with "She had multiple stab wounds and he died of a Heart Attack."

Nick stopped dead in his tracks and exclaimed "How, he stabbed her and then died of a heart attack over the grief."

Ernie looked at Zach and once again, they both replied, "Sounds like Sam."

"I have not found one file let alone anything to do with the Charlton's case." Looking at Zach and Ernie, Nick asked again more aloud to no one let alone to the individuals standing in front of him.

"We have one file missing where else could it be."

It was already 3 pm after all the trash or what was deemed trash had been removed, Nick had Sam's personal stuff in the back of Ernie's squad car.

"Zach give Ernie a ride home, I will take Ernie's car back to the station house, Ernie you can pick up the squad car in the morning. Or if you would prefer I will call you when I get into town" said the new Chief. "Chief if it's all the same I'll help out with whatever's left," Nick did not have time to say anything before Zach chimed in with the same response "If you're still looking I'll help,"

Nicks response was clear "Looking for a file, but where." Nick had gone through the complete house, if a stranger would have walked in and watched it would have looked like the three stooges.

Nick would walk over to an area and search it, with nothing discovered he would go to another, Ernie or Zach would follow him to the original spot and search the same area, it was total overkill, and the result was still no file.

Nick called Patty just to make sure that she had not found the file somewhere, he was hoping that she would discover that it was, misfiled or something. It was wishful thinking but a solid no, Patty had torn the place apart, (her words,) and to no avail.

Nick was not surprised to hear that it was not there, after hearing those encouraging words he gave Patty some things to finish with tomorrow.

"We need to get the locks changed," Nick said. "Patty is it normal procedure to send copies somewhere, because of the location was it totally our jurisdiction," Nick asked.

"No, not on a normal basis, maybe Sam sent it somewhere. I would have no idea where." Patty's response was dry, even Nick thought it might be a long shot.

Nick asked, "Try to call someone,"

"Who," Patty asked.

"I do not know who," was a dry reply in return.

Nick thought that if you did not try what would you know. He grew concerned that an official file was missing, it was better that it was a non-active case. After all, it was a twelve plus-year-old murder-suicide. The only person who still talked of it was Sam, what was the big deal with this case and more importantly where is the file.

Nick did not really care about the file or its contents, he was curious as to why Sam would refer to it so often in his notes. What Nick really cared about was the black eye that it might give his new regime.

He did not want the headache of all the explanations, and then again, maybe he should have a chat with old Zachary Taylor the senior.

Nick could use his vast knowledge of bullshit, just talk with the 'Mayor', and smooth it over and after all in a small city as if this missing file was not a big thing.

Nick gathered up Zach and Ernie, they had loaded up Sam's boat with his fishing stuff, they had decided to the leave the boat in the Boathouse and would return in the morning and take the boat to Ernie's for now. That would allow the Mayor or better yet the City Council to sell or rent out the City property, Sam's old place.

Nick called the Mayor and sadly, interrupted his evening meal, when Nick started to explain that they were just leaving Sam's and that the cabin and all attached properties would be available at the end of the week.

Nick was rather surprised that the mayor already knew of the search for the file, and was pleased when the Mayor stated, "Does not mean much to me, it's a closed case so not to worry if you want to talk about it we can."

In one hand Nick was relieved on another he had a problem and it was time to take care, the sooner the better.

"Ernie, have Zach pull over and then pull in behind him," looked like this would have to be the first change. Nick never raised his voice, which was a surprise, only said shit once, and never used the 'F' bomb, which was more of a surprise.

He talked to both of his Patrol Officers with respect, he told them, "That what happens in our official Police community stays there," and at the end of the conversation, it was obvious that they both understood.

"Nobody, nobody gets information on any official Departmental task or job, regardless of whom they are or what position he or she holds, the statement from now on is 'ask the Chief.'"

The worst part was that Nick would have to repeat everything to a Police Officer that he had never seen, the convalescing Earl Rodgers and then to Patty and her daughter Caroline. First Nick would have to approach the Mayor, maybe it was a little oversight something between a father and son, and then again, maybe he, the Mayor, liked being involved in all aspects of his city. Nick had not stepped completely out of the vehicle when his cell phone went off,

"Hello, this is Nick."

"Yes, the new Chief of Police, this is Kristi Jensen, the coroner?"

"Yes Mrs. Jensen, have that report do you?" Nick asked, not sure why else she would call.

"Actually I have some questions for you?" She asked.

For me, Nick thought? "Okay, go ahead."

"Would there be any reason, why there was some type of injection site in the back of Mr. Clark's neck?"

"Not sure, how do you mean?'

"Well there was some type of injection site, with a band aid over it, just struck me as strange?"

"What was injected, do you, would you know?" Nick asked.

"Not sure, sent it off, toxicology will take some time, as I'm sure you know?"

"Well, I will have to do some checking from his doctor, you know, glad that you caught that. When the report comes in, then we can assess it all, if that is alright. Give me a couple of days, let me talk with some people and we can go from there, okay?" Nick was perplexed as to where he could start to ask the question, and to whom. Kristi was okay with the wait, after all she was waiting on her own report. It just struck her as curious.

Sixteen

"She is in your office, waiting for you?"

His reasonable assessment was that something was missing or he had missed something, for Nick had read the contents twice. Everything, Sam was always the one to keep the facts correct, in some kind of order. He had always done this on a case, for official reasons and for Sam's own reasons. When Nick originally arrived, there was material that he would need to read, for Sam, not knowing at the time left this material as a precursor. Sam's death interrupted this process, and left it incomplete in too many ways. Nick wanted to conclude, he had only one direction to conclude. Knowing as Sam arranged things in the past, Nick could assume that something was missing, the two notebooks that he read on the first morning mentioned several items. One was the Charlton case.

Nick was deep in thought, a thought he could not shake from the forefront of his mind as if something was there he just could not reach it.

This was somewhat of a new feeling for him maybe he had these feelings before, he was able in the past to bounce these ideas to another person, sometimes his partner, sometimes Sam. The provocative question was where, if Sam had this other information, and they removed everything from his home, where could it be? They had searched the office, his truck, and his home. In fact, they cleared his home out. Besides the furniture nothing was left in the home.

The drive to Sam's allowed Nick to think, to talk aloud and not have interruptions. It would sound strange to anyone else, so he thought, talking aloud made Nick go over everything, and yes even sometimes he corrected himself, the rationale to this was that no one else knew, again so he thought, aloud.

In an hour of searching, essentially opening and closing drawers, he had found nothing, he did not move any furniture, in fact for the last half of that hour he had not moved from the chair at the desk. When he started to look there was nothing that he would consider out of place. If Sam had something, it was gone, he never had it or someone removed it.

His focus shifted, Nick always lived in the city, city noises were a part of his life, sometimes so much that he could not think straight. Here at the cabin, there was no noise, city or otherwise. His thoughts and his presence had migrated to the bedroom. He had been in the cabin for a while and had never really noticed the floors, all hardwood, much of what you would expect in a cabin.

In fact, the only area that did not have the hardwood showing was in the living room, for a carpet covered a majority of the room.

Nick went back out to the living room, he went to the one corner of the carpet, the corner that was clear of furniture he bent down and lifted the carpet.

The carpet would not move, somehow it was secured to the floor. From frustration he sat back down, he had removed every wall hanging, picture, painting and mirror from the walls he still found nothing. He would later remark to what an idiot he had been, he would remark this to himself, for when he kicked his feet up into the chair that sat next to the desk, on the corner of the carpet he moved the chair enough to make a scuff mark on the floor.

It was not the only scuff mark that became visible.

It did look like the chair was repeatedly removed or slide on the wood floor, in a direction away from the carpet. When Nick moved the chair completely off the carpet, he bent down and again tried to lift the carpet, this time with ease.

Moreover, as he moved the coffee table, this assumption would prove correct, it was easy to see that loose floorboards became visible. He dropped the carpet and knelt down.

When Nick pulled the loose board up from the floor, and before removing anything from beneath the floorboards he exhaled.
He had no idea why Sam would have a secret hiding place or what could be in it, he just hoped that it would answer some provocative questions that he had. He pulled out the two notebooks and a file that was about 2 inches thick. Why here, this place was not easily accessible by any means, why would Sam go to the trouble of putting some files and notebooks here when he had a file cabinet with a lock just eight feet away. He never remembered Sam as being paranoid, and this would clearly rate as some kind of paranoia.

Nick checked under the floorboards to ensure everything was out, he placed the floorboard back into place, without conscious thought he placed the carpet, coffee table and the chair in their original spots. Nick thought that there might be other hiding places, he still could not comprehend why his friend would hide these papers in the manner that he did.

Nick had decided that he was not going to look further, he might damage some of the cabin if he did.

He locked the cabin and headed for the car with the materials he had just found under his arm, he placed them in the passenger side and started the car.

His thoughts traveled just as the car did on the way back to the station house, his mentor was not the paranoid type at least he had never previously been a paranoid type.

"Chief." Nick glanced at the radio in the car. "Chief Sheridan?"

Nick picked up the radio, "This is...Chief Sheridan, go."

"Chief, there is a Kristi Jensen, County Coroner waiting for you." Patty stated.

"Go ahead and let her know I will call her back in a couple of hours or so, if that is okay?"

"Chief, she is in your office, waiting for you."

"Be there in ten."

Seventeen

"The Godfather."

Appearing on page three of the post, or for that fact any page of any newspaper, anywhere, was part of the past. If you were to inquire with those that thought they knew, they would tell you that they did know who the godfather was. That he, this current godfather was being watched like all the past godfathers as they were known.

This information would be the standard statement, if you were to crawl under the skin of some Department of Justice type it would be more unfiltered. The real fact was they had no idea, and for the most part, as long as they kept things quiet, no rampant death, no public in fighting, they really did not care. Of course this goes without saying, if someone breaks the law, then their just rewards is just that, what they ultimately deserve.

The current godfather was unknown, totally unknown. There was that inner circle, the most trusted of the most loyal, those handpicked men and women that knew who he really was. That number that knew had never exceeded ten in total. Today, besides the godfather, only a few individuals knows the true identity of the leader of the syndication or crime families.

"Stand by, 2 minutes." The system had extensive research behind it, the principle was simple. To communicate with the other family heads, yet stay behind the scenes. The electronic side of it was a controlled system that was fully cyphered to include any possibilities of being hacked. The world's top hackers had been employed, some blackmailed, others by choice to maintain a system that was beyond believe as to how it worked, and secured like no other.

The personal side was the other families.

They had agreed, maybe not some particularly, maybe their fathers or uncles, predecessors none the less. They had agreed to go legitimate, or at least have that side to them. They all still dabbled in the old ways, drugs, prostitution, gambling, and that money was good. The legitimate side of it brought them the casinos back, and other interests. It was one thing to own the casinos, it was entirely another to own the land, the shops, the parking, and other interests that lay around them, the less watched interests around them.

And so the godfather before him had gone underground, one day he was gone. He had not died, more importantly he had taken the spotlight from those that watched and turned it back onto them.

It was like the blind leading the blind. As this godfather was ready to pass the torch on, he did not pick someone from the family, who would know who he picked, this person was never to be seen or witnessed in a position as the godfather, nothing remotely close.

"Gentlemen." The voice said.

"Godfather" came the replies, from the other ten that now hooked into the system.

As the man spoke, certain graphs would come up on the screens that the ten watched. Each man was alone, in a room fully designed and built by the godfather's men. Each room was located in a facility of choosing by the other men, this was the agreement. All electronic services were conducted by the godfather's people.

As the general business would go, business would be discussed first, then new ideas, then general questions. If any problems were present between different families this was the time to "adjudicate" those issues. All told, this meeting would take just two hours. They would be monthly, unless circumstances interrupted this.

Eighteen

"It looked peculiar."

Nick was back to the office in a flash or something like that. He wanted to immediately delve into the notebooks, and the file that he found under the floor boards. Why would he keep anything under the floor boards?
"Why there?"
He now mumbled to himself.
"Why?"
He could never remember a point to some type of secrecy for Sam, more facts were kept in his head than anywhere else. Have two safes in the office, one for general use, another with only two knowing that combination.
"How long have they been there?" This brought another question to mind, if they had been placed there recently, from who was he hiding them?
"Chief she is in your office and says that she can talk to only you about it, sounds fishy in a way, if you ask me." Patti stated this as they walked in the general direction of his office, at the door, prior to entering Nick responded, as if he did not hear anything.

"Patti, what I need from you right now. Is everything from this Charlton case, this missing file, pictures, who developed them, are they digital, maybe someone has a copy, just find out."

"Hello, you must be Coroner Kristi Jensen, sorry for the wait and all."

Nick would, in most cases compliment himself on his "detective sense" figuring out the intricacies of an individual, a suspect, a certain condition or situation was essentially what he had done for the last twenty years or so. He did not picture this individual as a thirty something straight out of school type. By the voice and complacency that she had on the phone, he thought mid to late fifties, seasoned, rode hard or at least moderately and then put up wet, this was not the case.

"Good to meet you Chief, although it was pointed out by your staff that you might be a little, put off by that title?"

"Well let's just end that, call me Nick, leave it at that, okay."

"And please call me Kristi, we do not need the formalities in your or my office, as far as I'm concerned."

"So what brings you up here, I thought you were just going to e-mail me with any information and the preliminary report?"

At this time, his thoughts lay elsewhere, the file and notebooks were still fresh in his mind, he wanted information, the coroner, regardless of how cute she might be, surely was not going to provide him with the knowledge he so wanted.

"This could not be done over the phone or through an e-mail. The injection site that I spoke of, well I rushed it, and discovered that it was a mix of Ketamine and potassium chloride." She handed a file across the desk. Nick had meandered to his side of the desk, she remained in the chair across the desk.

"Ketamine, isn't that for..." Nick stopped himself and flipped open the gray colored file, what he was reading, or as to where his eyes went was all over the page that was open in front of him.

"Mainly for larger life stock, horses primarily?" Kristi responded. Standing up she moved closer to the desk and then pointed to a portion of the paper.

"What is that?" Nick asked.

"The amount..."

"Sorry, I get that this is something extremely, I just can't fathom, why, and is that a lot?" Nick was back to asking why.

"Yes, it is considered a lot, as far as a lot is concerned. Why, I'm not sure, have no earthly idea, guess that is why I'm here?"

"Okay, start from the beginning. And why is there a finger print report here, where did you get that?"

Nick was looking at the pages underneath the first page, it was a typical finger print report, not with all five prints from each hand, that most coroners would take to ensure they have the right individual, more for insurance purposes and one of those things that became mandatory because it was always done and therefore expected more than for any other reason. This was of each thumb, both the left and the right of Sam Clark, side by side.

"So like I said, the injection site. It looked peculiar..." She would go into extreme detail, by the time she was done, Nick thought he could detail a coroner's report and this was not even the preliminary.

She started with the injection site, directly in the back of his neck, centered, something that both Kristi and Nick would agree would be to say the least difficult to do by yourself. Especially after many times of trying to do it themselves. Finally figuring that it could be done, yet would be of a high difficulty.

"Typically, if a needle goes in and some type of solution is disbursed, when you draw that needle out and you are sloppy with it, some of that solution will discharge at the site of the injection.

So I tested that dried portion of the solution. There is no way to calculate the exact dose or total amount of what may have been injected into the body at that point yet, it is a ketamine-potassium-chloride solution."

"Enough to kill?" Nick asked?

"If the ketamine didn't do it, the potassium chloride would have, and in some type of combination who is to say for sure, the amount would..."

"Could this mask or contribute to a heart attack to an individual that had no real history of heart problems?"

"Without a doubt, the final toxicology report will answer some questions. His heart, showed no signs of disease or defect, just so you know."

"And what about the finger or thumb prints that were listed?"

Kristi looked around the smallish office, "Can I erase this?" Kristi asked this while pointing to a small white erase board that was attached to the wall, at one side of the desk.

"Sure."

She would erase the board of the two things listed at the top and draw a band aid or what looked like one in the middle of the board, oversized, yet still a band aid looking thing.

"How would you put that on your body?"

Nick looked around, glancing back and forth, wanting to ask, what part of the body, back of the neck?

He would raise both thumbs as if he was giving someone the thumbs up with both thumbs up. He would place his thumbs over the band aid, semi in midair.

"Exactly." Kristi responded

"Just like each thumb print on the band aid."

"Who did the prints?" Nick asked.

"CSI lab for the state, have a friend there, he sent some one over right away. Not a smudge, he said it was a perfect pull?"

"No smudges, perfect pull?" Nick responded, her look at the statement of a perfect pull, gave a face of understand yet not fully understanding. Nick would explain, "A perfect pull means that the print you just dusted for was found in a perfect state. If that person was in the system or you had their prints, they would be easily matched, without any worry, a perfect pull was an easy six point match."

"When I pulled the band aid off his neck, I placed it correctly, it was not upside down, it was if you placed it, just as my poor picture would represent."

Nick sighed.

"His prints placed perfectly on a band aid, no smudges, over an injection site that is on the back of his neck, somewhere you would have some type of extreme difficulty to place it, let alone smudge free. An injection site that contained Ketamine and chloride potassium. With two note books and a large thick file, that I just found under the floor boards of his living room."

"Under the floor boards?" Kristi remarked.

"Yes, under the floorboards."

"What's in them, what do they say?" Kristi was interested now, the other items, she could possibly suggest as explainable? Possibly.

"Just found them, have yet to go through them. Was planning to do that, and then you brought me all of this." Nick's hands now waved over his desk, as if he was Vanna White showing a letter on the board of fortune.

Nineteen

"The Charlton's."

David and Julie Charlton had a terrible ending to what would seem a lovely life. David Yancey Charlton was born on July 23, 1953 to Michael and Bernadette Charlton. His father was a mechanical engineer and his mother was a homemaker, due to complications at delivery David Yancey Charlton was an only child. He grew up an average child, he loved the home he lived in, and later in life made it his own. He went to college and became a Bio-Chemistry Engineer, he married his college sweetheart and accepted the first job he was offered. In hindsight, he married for all the wrong reasons and divorced after ten years of not so wedded bliss.

That was a rough year for David Charlton, not only did he have to deal with a divorce he also had to deal with the death of both parents. His father while driving home from dinner swerved and ran his vehicle straight into a tree, seems that his highly educated father and homemaker mother were not into wearing a seatbelt and they both died upon impact.

Julie Glass was born on September 10, 1957 to Gregory and Juliet Glass. Julie grew up much in the same way, nice neighborhood outside of Boston, actually not too far from David Charlton's home.

They had no contact between them. There was a 4-year difference in age. Julie's Father was a Doctor who worked at the local hospital, her mother was a registered Nurse who worked only part time while Julie was growing up, this gave her at least one parent at the home on a regular basis. Julie's father was rarely at home, for he was dedicated to his job.

Julie graduated from high school with honors and it was always suspected that she too would become a doctor, after college graduation she twisted them all and decided to go to nursing school perhaps that was the last straw for her father, he could never understand why she would waste her intelligence as he would say, just on nursing. Maybe Julie was smarter than all of them, by the time Julie graduated from nursing school her father had drank himself into deep trouble with his liver and within three years he would be dead, sadly enough so would her mother.

It was on Julie's first night of work while tending to a small leg cut that she met Marcus Reynolds and within 6 months, they were married for what seemed all the right reasons. In addition, what she learned soon after that she loved him very much and he her, she also learned that the love he really held was for his work and was never at home. After false promises, and lonely nights, Julie divorced Marcus after 10 years of marriage.

With mutual friends in the medical field David and Julie were set up on a blind date of sorts, and to the surprise of everyone involved they were married the next year after about 14 months of dating. David always remarked that he was way out of his league, she was so pretty and he was nothing more than a researcher geek. They were extremely happy together and had tried just about every way to conceive a child, sometimes you just have to give it time. Due to both of their work schedules, their annual trip to Maine would be later in the summer that year. It would be a joyous trip and would be a great 44th birthday for Julie.

It was the usual trip, no cell phones and especially no computers. This was their time to catch up on reading, to cook, to enjoy one another, and with the possibilities of the future to continue this happy union. The 10th of September was a great day, a great birthday, it would be for anybody excluding the fact of a husband stabbing his wife repeatedly in the belly and then himself dying of a heart attack.

Twenty

"Like it never happened."

The updates had become more necessary if you asked James, asking Ian would get another comment if the truth were told. Ian hated the updates, allowing for more of them was not his choice, he did not make the decision so it was what the boss wanted or possibly needed. James wanted the updates, he wanted to stay on top of who had killed his lawyer that was for sure. He did not like to have them every twelve hours as he had demanded.

Since the initial call there had been nothing else. This person, as James had stated had returned to a non-descript, flea bag of a motel and had not left the room in what was almost 48 hours. If he was still in the room at all, James repeatedly questioned this, in fact Ian had changed his tone, "we believe, that he is still in the room," had become the statement, even Ian was not so sure.

Self-doubt had become to roost on Ian's mind, more to the point of what would occur if he was not in the room.

"So shall I ask?" James asked before Ian had closed the office door.

"Yes, we believe he is still presently in that room." Ian was more exact or was it rehearsed, by the tone of his voice.

"Who does that?" James mumbled a loud, not expecting a response, although would welcome a good one, or at this point, possibly a bad response would suffice.

"I take from this situation that he is trained, although he has lapsed, I'm coming to my own conclusion that he is a professional." Ian stated as he took a seat in front of the overtly large desk.

"Because of his actions, and how he just strolled away from Robert's?" James inquired.

He had strolled, James and Ian, on several occasions had watched what Ian's people had put together.

The man, that really never showed his face, leaving the apartments, removing and then replacing clothing, walking down the sidewalk like he owned it. The video that they had pieced together was from various sources, their own, an ATM, the convenience store parking lot cam and finally the hotel in which he stayed, or as James would consider it, the flea bag where he now was holed up.

"So what is the plan now?" James asked hoping for more than we will wait.

"We will give it another 24 hours, if no movement then we will breach, at night we will do this. Assembling the men for this action now." Ian had not really finished what he wanted to say, when his cell phone rang.

"Ian," it was the only way he would answer his own phone, unless he knew James or whatever boss of the day was on the line, then it would be a more responsive and professional "Ian Thompson."

"He's on the move."

"I'm placing the phone on speaker." Ian stated this as he held up the universal one finger over your lips, so that hopefully his boss would not speak. As the way of business, his people did not know who they were taking orders from, less things to worry about later on. As far as they were concerned, Ian was calling the shots.

"How many teams on him?" Ian asked.

"4 at present. One to stay at the motel and go through it when we feel comfortable that he will not return within a certain time frame."

"I want to know everything about everything, nothing slips by us, nothing. Call every thirty minutes for updates, unless one is necessary sooner, Ian out." Just as quick as he had flipped the phone open to take the call, it was flipped shut ending all transmissions.

"I really believed, this guy, was playing us and had left that room by some means." James had stated this, although deep down inside Ian's own thoughts was a similar response.

Ian said nothing.

"And what about Robert, and his lady friend?" Ian was happy to respond to this, "You're the boss, tell me." Ian stated this, he was not in favor of the plan that James had suggested and the one that they had followed.

"He's done this before. Of course he was not dead and showed up a couple of days later. We could always put him into a rehab."

"Yes Sir, always a possibly, a rehab for those that are having trouble catching any breaths, we open ourselves to more people knowing. Right now it is you and I, and my highly paid and completely qualified team." Both men were now silent, it would like that for a few seconds that seemed like a few minutes.

"James, let's stick with your idea, it is already in place. Everyone expects Robert Morris to walk back into the offices of Morris, Finley, and Turner.

So what if he never does, we should pull the trigger with the off shore accounts so it looks like they were pulling funds out. In a couple of weeks we call in a good reporter that owes us one and they start the story of embezzlement and other nasty stuff."

"Lay out his laundry?"

"Precisely."

"And the apartment?" James asked.

"Like it never happened, we had to remove and replace some carpet, some other minor things, nothing too bothersome."

"Her family, any somebody calling, or something like that?" James asked intentionally wanting to know, more for the protection of all things considered, rather than knowing at all.

"No, her side of it is completely out of the picture, kept woman, married man turned them off some time ago, that will not be an issue. His wife on the other hand, well." Ian had stated the obvious, Robert Morris's wife was usually the problem.

She liked the money that he had, and she spent that extremely well, she actually liked the hours that he kept, being gone a lot was good for both of them. What she did not like was the fact that he really no longer tried to keep his muse, or whatever he was calling her these days a secret. It was the secret that all parties knew of.

Twenty One

"So he gave the "lot" the rundown."

It would be strange by many accounts. Seldom, if at all would you see the lights on this late, yet they were on, more so to the fact it was all hands on deck. Even the convalescing Earl was at the station, when Nick had finished with the meeting from the coroner, after flipping out his wallet to buy dinner, he announced rather authoritarian that he needed everyone back, Caroline, Zach, Ernie and the one guy I have yet to meet.

He was pleasantly surprised to find that Kristi had semi volunteered to stay and explain the medical report, preliminary as it was, and she still wanted to explain it none the less. Nick was happy to have her if anything just to explain the band aid and those troubling prints.

While he stayed in the office and leafed through the notebooks, taking notes of his own as to the contents, the others all of them, after eating, were asked to clean out what once had been the conference room.

It had been transferred into a storage room, even with papers that covered the windows that looked into the conference room.

Sam had deemed it an unnecessary place to have for such a small station. Nick on the other hand, wanted a place to have meetings, to discuss the topic as it was, and to have a couple of white boards so that they could all confer as to what really happened to the former chief. So as directed, they had removed everything, and then set up a table in the middle of the room with white boards that had been borrowed from the high school just a few hours before. Much like the two computers that Zach had removed from the Mayor's storage, unbeknownst to the Mayor.

He had informed the lot, as he referred to them in an openly manner that he would give an update at 10 pm. That should last for an hour, and then other assignments would be handed out as needed.

The first words to assembled lot, were close to what he had uttered before about what should and should not be discussed to anyone outside of the office. He had covered this previously, except to Earl and Kristi, who sat attentively listening as if she belonged as well.

"This stays with us. You feel uncomfortable about a question, that individual that you're talking too does not like what they hear, then you send them my way, have them call me. I will set them straight. We do not discuss ongoing investigations, period."

"Sir, Chief what do we label the Chiefs death as, I mean..." Earl had asked this, to him this was new. He had heard through the grapevine amongst other places that it was a heart attack, "Is it still ongoing."

"Sam Clark's death has not been ruled anything, so technically it is still ongoing. Were we might have thought one thing, it is safe to say in my mind it is something else now. We will get into that in just a few minutes."

There was nothing asked, the blank stares bounding back him were obviously waiting for what was to come next.

So he gave the "lot" the rundown. From what had been reported about the Ketamine, the Potassium Chloride, and the band aid. Kristi readily stood and discussed what she had discovered, ending with a similar yet better drawing of a band aid, this time with thumbs or what looked like them to each side of the band aid, with the direction of the prints.

He had tried by placing an imaginary band aid on the back center of his neck, only to be caught several times, once by Kristi, twice by Patti, while trying to do this, at the same time that he was looking through the notebooks. He had told Patti that he would explain, not she sat in front of him trying to do the same movement, without any luck.

"Are you sure the band aid was not upside down, and maybe the crime lab reported it wrong?" Zach asked this, after his facial expressions changed to an "I got it" type of look.

Kristi was exact in her work, her paper work and her due diligence for the facts showed this. She immediately pulled out some photos of the band aid prior to removal from Sam's neck. It showed a little indentation on the top right corner of the band aid. That was the top, just as the prints on the report stated. Both prints of each thumb were pointed to the top of the band aid, in the direction of the head.

Nick, then went into the note books and the file.

"The file that was found under the floor boards contained Sam's insight into the Charlton case, it was some thirty pages long, and it however contained no pictures. So, Patti, we need to find out who took the pictures for this case and if there are backups, we need copies. As far as I'm concerned, that is job one for you, finding the original file or at least the pictures from the scene itself. And try to find the lead detectives of the case."

The "lot" was quiet, Patti just nodded.

"Caroline, I need to know everything there is to know about Robert Morris, he's a lawyer out of Boston I have a number for him. I do not want anyone to contact him, under any circumstances. I just want background. I also want background information on Marcus Reynolds and or Reynolds Defense contractors, not sure if they are one and the same. Start with that and we will go from there."

Caroline nodded, almost moved from her seat to start, then she slowly slide back into the chair, as if she wanted to listen more.

"For everyone else, it is work as normal. No comments, no discussions about any of this. Earl, upon your return in the next week or so, we will get you back into the grove of things. I do appreciate you coming out tonight and your work. Just as I appreciate everyone and the daily duties that you perform."

Again, no questions.

"This is command central. This is where Caroline will set up, the whiteboards will have a timeline soon."

Twenty Two

"My gut says we have crossed paths previously."

In a mahogany paneled room they spoke, "Did you check this room out, Ian is this room clear have your guys done the wand thing in here," his usual nature was to wait, to make his decisions in a practical manner. He was never one to jump the gun, "I want to know where that son of a bitch is, all the time, without any interference. I want him watched, if he shit I want to know where and how much." James was quiet again. He sat back in his seat behind his desk.

"Sir, we have swept all your offices and your apartment. We are in the process of checking out all the vehicles right now," Ian spoke with a calm about him, he had dealt with demanding individuals on a regular basis, James MacMillian was the utmost of demanding bosses. Ian had worked for Mr. MacMillian previously, never this close and as it would seem always in the background behind the scenes as it were, one thing was for sure.

Ian Thompson reputation was stellar, if there were a problem he would fix it, if something needed settled he could settle it.

Ian Thompson was of a legal mind, his reputation for this, for getting his employers, what they needed to perform their duties at whatever or whoever's cost, was unprecedented. His life was not different from many others, your normal kid growing up in Manhattan. His parents were both professional, his father was one of the largest brokers on the east coast. He may have been the original "you're the man," if someone needed it, he would get it for him or her. You had a child in trouble, he could take care of it, and there were no limitations for this. Ian's mother was probably at that time the only woman lawyer for the mob, she was attractive and that made her very good with juries.

It used to be, that she could wink at a jurist and you might as well have terminated the trial, after that it would be a foregone conclusion as to the results.

Ian was getting ready to move on to college when his life changed forever. His mother died in a drive by shooting, or in mob terms-a hit. He would never really know the reason why.

His father the fixer that he was, with all the connections he had, never made headway as to his mother's death.

In fact it would be almost twenty years before Ian would personally take care of it. His father had always drunk too much, his mother's death and his father's inability to find out why or whom, lead to a sad demise of "the man."

He died with a broken heart and a spirit that had been gone just as long, some twenty years later the same day his only son took care of the problem that he could never find. The rosy colored glasses that Ian had seen life through were suddenly flung from his face in his second year of college.

Unbeknownst to all of his remaining family and very few friends, he was asked to join an intelligence agency that for years had been actively recruiting at his college.

He would spend summers training and with special permission he was allowed to attend Law school, by the time he had completed law school he was asked to go overseas and for the next fifteen years Ian Thompson was a figment of who's ever imagination that could remember him.

It was a good life for him. After all, he seemed that a position, in which he held, was in fact the perfect position for one Ian Thompson. He spoke several languages and had the overwhelming ability to adhere and adjust to anything given him. He too had built a reputation that exceeded most.

He had no name, not even his supervisors new his real name, or for that fact cared. One day he had enough, he was tired of what he considered "the grey area," bosses above him that were not competent enough to perform the task that they told him to do and then annoyed him with statements that they would have handled it differently.

He had always thought that if they wanted to do it, because they could better then more power to them.

And then one day, that was exactly what he told them, he said it was his time to go to the next level and retired. At the height of the cold war with so much more to be made he walked away from it all. Several years later he reflected that it was the best walk he had ever taken, he dedicated himself to solving the one thing he needed to finish not for others to benefit but for his personal satisfaction.

It ended by being very easy, he used connections that he had made through the years, connections that did not want to know why, they just wanted what was in the envelope his envelopes were always full, that spoke their language. Some things can be forgotten because of the content. Others may be remembered especially for the content. This was something he would not forget anytime soon.

He had found the individual who was responsible for the hit on his mother, not the individual who pulled the trigger, Ian considered that person to be following orders and in his book not guilty for that reason alone.

He wanted the person who ordered the hit, through channels he found him, and was even given the green light by other individuals who would not be upset if that individual would go away.

Ian through several years of service knew that if you got permission it would be better in the end. He received permission and was told even when the best time was.

He entered the facility overpowered a napping 'guard' and with both guns drawn stepped into the back room, he was using silencers just in case, and even though it was ordered or in this case permission had been given, he was told to make it look like a robbery. After entering the room, he immediately shot the only person who drew his weapon the conversation was short.

"Did you order a hit on a female lawyer back in 1964," Ian asked rather calmly.

"Do you know who you're fucking with, you're a dead man," the man said in a loud way.

Ian shot the man next to the one that had just spoken. He knew his target it was the man speaking.

"I'll ask again, did you," the belligerent man cut him off

"Yea, I ordered that hit, was glad to get rid of that fucking bitch."

Ian pulled the trigger, he shot him between his eyes. Ian slowly backed up and put two more in his heart. He grabbed a bag from the other table and filled it with cash from the three tables in the room. When he left the building, he did not run or even walk fast, he strolled.

"Ian, what's the status?" James asked.

For Ian, that memory was a good one. Regardless of what others might say, it was good for Ian. Something's you wait a life for, others just happen, Ian had waited.

"The status is simple, he went to your money man." Ian did not know this for a fact, they had watched and followed. At two o'clock in the morning, they had enough information to surmise.

"He did not mislead anyone, straight to the house. Well actually pulled up next door. Strange thing about it, for a professional he did not try to cover any of his steps."

"Pulled up next door to whom?" James asked.

Ian had left that part out, "The Schmidt house, Harlan's place."

James jaw did not fall to the ground, as he may have expected it would have, after hearing that.

"I have to ask, who or why now. This is my people, my lawyer, my investor and longtime friend the both of them, although we might be in a questionable place now..." James stopped, he had other ideas running through his head.

"This person that was extorting us, or at least attempting it. And I wonder if it isn't my old friend, he knows a great deal, could he..."

"No sir, he is...." Ian wanted to choose his words correctly, this was an old friend that he was talking about, regardless of the fact that James had mentioned or hinted on several occasions about the demise of this old friend.

"He has been a kept man, since the acknowledgement of that little whore and his involvement."

"A work of genius that was, thanks again...."

"I can't take all the credit, that one kind of fell into our laps and all, and to answer your next question, she is where we placed her for future reference and all." Ian had used a remodeling and landscaping of a certain residence for a better purpose, it looked nice above. For James and Ian in their eyes it was much more impressive as to what was underground. For them it was that Christmas present that they really could not un-wrap until it was necessary.

"Sir, we will know more real soon, trust me. Then we may decide to burn it all down, to take care of all loose ends. So for the moment let's see how the next 24-48 hours goes, okay that all other decisions can present themselves."

"What do we do now, then?" James questioned.

"We allow you to determine their value, and then..."

"Then, what?"

"We use them with your permission..." There was a silence, both men hesitated to speak next. Ian, knew what should be said, he waited on the saying portion of it. James, knew what was next, he just was not sure this time.

"What do I need to do?" James asked.

"Get them out of the house for a couple of hours the sooner the better, just in case. One thing that I have discovered is that this guy, well he works fast. So that means we need to work fast as well."

"I call in the morning, I will get them out of the house around lunch time will that work?"

"That will be fine."

"Ian, do you have any idea about this guy, anything." James asked, it was always on the tip of his tongue, he just did not want to over stress his cleaner, as the previous conversation had led, he would need his full capacities running at a high level soon.

"Not anything to say for sure, keeping him alive would be my best bet to find out, although I will say this, he reminds me of some particular happening in the past, just not sure. I will say this, my gut says we have crossed paths previously."

Twenty Three

"When did he die, Mr. Reynolds that is."

Becoming something, anything is part of a learning process. Only so much information can be garnered from a book or manual. Of course, this ultimately depends on what you want or what you may be doing. Nick knew this all too well. He had good parents and a solid family life, when he went through the police academy, he had other teachers and instructors as well, many of which he would also work with in the police force through his years of service.

When Nick put on that detective's shield he possibly had the best of the best. It is one thing to be the best at something, when your peers continually call you the best that is when even the critics take notice. Sam Clark was that teacher. He hated the term for many reasons, "he was a cop," "not a teacher" would be the one most used, by Sam.

Through the years Sam instructed, Nick listened. Many might conclude that Sam had finally decided to retire once he had trained someone to take his place, essentially Sam had taught everything that he could, it was time to move on for Sam.

Nick never materialized to the instructor level of his former partner and mentor. Nick, for the most part was a loner, not the type you might worry about, Nick just wanted to be left alone. He was always the believer in work is work, personal life is just that, personal.

By no means was any type of savant, in fact, most afternoons he would have to be reminded as to what he had for breakfast. Sometimes it would be just concluded with it must have "been something." Through the years, he had adapted too many ways that were different from where he had begun, he now took notes.

Recently he had adopted a voice recorder, one that he could hook up to the lap top and by sheer science it would translate from his voice to the written word, no transcribing for him, all done automatically. This created another problem, when did he say it and where was it, these were for another day, at least no notes to transcribe.

Nick was also a listener, he liked to listen, picking up on the small things worked well. As a, now seasoned detective, he also liked his quite time to observe the scene or other like things.

Of course, with any situation, sometimes things just happen. That was the case for Thursday morning. He had left assignments for some in the department, mainly Caroline, he had no idea that she was a night owl, and when attached to something, she went all out.

She also liked Mountain Dew, that was her addiction, and even though she was close to thirty, it affected her like she was a ten year old.

Nick had not cleared the door of the station when he noticed that most of the lights were on in the place, at 8 o'clock in the morning this might not be odd for some in certain situations, it just seemed odd for this place. "Chief, glad that you're in, was going to call, I wanted to give you an update on what has been learned." She continued to nod, as if she was waiting for an answer that she already had, waiting to go forward with her on going statement.

"Sure, you have been busy, started early did you?" Nick asked, trying to be considerate of her time. He had given the directions for what he wanted to learn, he had not been specific for when to start. He implied starting fresh in the morning, didn't he?

He had not slept, he had actually done some research himself, by two in the morning he was wide awake thinking. It was surprising, at least to him it was, since he had forgone the "computer age" as no one really called it was just a way to add a title to what he was using.

He knew the power of the computer, of the social networks that are intertwined within it, he had seen this before, and one case had come to mind?

At least started some research apparently, unknowingly at that time it was in the latter stages of being finished by Caroline, which was good for Nick, less to do, more to absorb.

"Okay, what do you have," he added.

"Well, Morris, Finley and Turner is a law firm out of Boston, they have many individuals and companies as clients, their largest client is Reynolds-MacMillian Defense Contractors, remember that name it will come up later..."

Nick knew that they were a defense contracting company, a larger if not the largest one, excluding the plane makers like Boeing, and McDonnell Douglas. The law firm and the defense contractors were throughout the notes of Sam, he had referenced that he had contacted them, although it never said a specific purpose.

Caroline was still talking, "And that Robert Morris is the head lawyer for the law firm and also listed as the senior lawyer for a James Bennett MacMillian, who is presently the President, CEO and as listed on their website as the majority stock hold with some 90 percent of the stock. Obviously pretty good for what is considered a publicly held stock, just saying."

"And Sam had made contact with them, or at least Robert Morris several times."

"That is correct...or at least in some manner, according to the notes." Caroline had answered this while holding a small notebook in one hand and a can of Mountain dew in the other, Nick would swear later that she had taken a drink, while talking, and continued to talk during it, didn't she?

"So what does this have to do with the Charlton case and what is up about them, any information?" Nick asked.

"I thought the same thing, a little digging, and some legal, maybe some not so much..." Caroline now stopped and took a complete breath, was that her first? She then turned her face and gave an awkward smile, as if she was asking permission, after the fact.

She would make a good detective, Nick thought to himself, yes she would.

"We will discuss that later, no way for it to come back on the department..." Now Nick gave a weird smile of sorts.

"I always wear protection, no need to worry about that, trust me."

Nick wanted to ask, but hesitantly avoided it, the simple "okay" was enough to be said. He had heard so much new lingo about computers lately he would chalk it up to just that.

"So get this?" Caroline asked, yet moved into the next sentence. "Marcus Reynolds was MacMillian's partner, until he died anyway, his ex-wife was Mrs. Charlton..."

Nick held up his hand to force her from speaking, the international stop sign was understood by Caroline, even in her hazy too much Mountain Dew stage.

"When did he die, Mr. Reynolds that is."

"Oh, I have it right here, wait, let me get that..." Caroline would scurry off toward the newly set-up conference room. Nick was two steps behind her. Caroline fished through one stack of papers and then went to another, "I printed his obituary off, and it is here...somewhere?"

Nick himself looked around, it was just last night that he had been in the makeshift storage and now back to the usually or what should be a conference room. It had changed again, the easels notwithstanding, some were in the room others were in the hallway as he entered. They had nothing on them, the easels were blank for now, he was sure that would change. He didn't think or even conclude why a department would have them at all, as he looked over the room, there it was, taped the white board in the center of the action.

Nick tapped on Caroline's shoulder and then pointed, "See, I knew it was somewhere?" She reached over and plucked it from the board, "He died on the second of September..."

"What year?" Nick asked?

"2001..." Caroline paused. "His wife, ex-wife was killed 8 days later."

"I think it is time to find out who Sam was talking to. And since a Mr. Morris is listed so many times in the portion of notes we have, contacting him might get us to where we need to be with all of this."

Twenty Four

"Vaffunclo lo conesce tuttio."

The hair on the back of his neck began to stand up. He hoped it was just nerves causing this feeling. He looked all around. Only once before was he aware that someone had been following him. That time hadn't turned out well for the followers or himself. It was the only time that he needed help and had to call for assistance. That number had always been available to him. That he had called it only once in over twenty years was a testament to how good he was at his job.

He drove by the house several times. The house was in a higher class neighborhood but the house was ordinary. The next time through he noticed something that made him apprehensive. He varied his route through the neighborhood.

Once he even stopped his vehicle, stepped out at a 'house for sale' sign and removed a flyer. This house was located directly behind the target's home. He noticed a car that had been parked in another place earlier. He spotted the same vehicle in a third spot when he returned five hours later. This was no coincidence. This would require extra attention. Was there a connection? Had he been set up? Was his time near? This was not the first time that these thoughts had entered his mind.

He had not protected himself as he had in the past when he left the apartment building the other evening, he had been cocky. Sometimes when you feel as if it is perfect, there is always something. That other night he had that feeling, now it was followed with another, this is not what they expected, this was not how he trained.

His life had begun easy what he could remember. He had a normal childhood and a stable family. It seemed that he had loving parents who had been married before his older sister had been born. At the age of eleven he started to notice that his home was not a typical family home after all, he began to notice that his father made trips to his sister's room more than maybe was necessary. He noticed that his father loved his sister a little too much. Six months later and his family life was no more. His Mother had discovered or maybe always knew. One day it became too much and his mother, sister and he left while his father was away on business.

They moved and would continue to do so, his mother tried to make it into a game, he did not understand it at first and his sister was constantly upset. They had seemingly escaped what his father had brought on to them, until the one day that his father found them, that happened to be his mother's and his father's last day.

His mother had gone to the store and when she returned, his father approached her from behind, two bullets later, one for her and another for his father and his family would be no more. Though the Foster care system of that day had improved, they were light years behind where they should have been. Keeping a brother and sister together was difficult, and so they were separated into different foster homes and after two years of hell and abuse at the tender age of thirteen, he left for school one day and never returned.

He somehow, for no special reason found his way to Philadelphia and became homeless for a while, doing things that do not need repeating or remembering, things that kept him alive and sometime put a roof over his head for a night or two. Maybe that is why the comforts of home seemed so dear and private to him. After a couple of months on the streets of south Philadelphia, his luck changed.

Benny "Two Eyes" Montesano was a thug, a thug with a heart. He had been a minor want to be gangster of south Philadelphia, a few street wars and through some family attrition, Benny became a player, a made player.

Benny was always liked by his uncle, his uncle had concluded many times that young Benny saw with two eye's open, unlike the normal thug tunnel vision and with that, young Benny had a nickname a moniker of sorts. Moreover, when Benny's uncle took the lead role for the family Benny became pivotal.

After a couple of years of the good life Benny started to get paranoid maybe a little itchy to the everyday beat downs and muggings on the south side. Benny changed his way one night. He went through the back door of his little convenience store. Somebody was on his back steps, a boy, a boy of 13. It would change both of their lives.

Benny allowed the young man to sleep on a cot in his storeroom, out of sight out of mind. As time would go on, he would become Benny's errand boy, as Benny rose in the ranks around his uncle the boy, or as some of the old Italians called him "Ragazzo di Errand," simply put, he was the 'errand boy'.

Moreover, over time he became a favorite of the new Godfather. In fact, it was the Godfather, who bought him his first book. He also gave him access to his library in what the 'errand boy' called the big house.

He would sit and read all day, and into the night and when his uncle had meetings in the library the 'Ragazzo di Errand' would go on one, when he returned he would continue reading as if he had never left.

The Godfather discovered that the errand boy had other qualities, a photographic memory, and he allowed the boy to abuse his abilities, this earned him another nickname.

All the Italian men who never left the big house or the Godfather for that fact, found themselves paying for the boys answers, and they would start calling him 'Conoscalo Tuttio'(Know it all). Moreover, through time and other factors he would be more affectionately called 'Vaffunculo lo conosce tuttio' (Fucking Know it all).

This brought much pleasure to the Godfather and to his young Consigliere, the Godfathers counselor and Cousin in this case, they saw something else in the newly named 'Conoscalo Tuttio' they saw a future. They brought Benny into the picture, Benny could be trusted and had seen to the young boy, and by all concerns was thought of as the former 'errand boys' father or Guardian. The Godfather and his right hand man, the Consigliere, were intent of finding someone they could mold and educate to become an asset in the future.

For it was their desire to find an individual of non-Italian descent, someone that they could control, whose life would change for the positive, it did not take long for the godfather to figure that 'Conoscalo Tuttio' would be just the person.

Benny removed 'Conoscalo Tuttio' from other prying eyes and his training began, the group lead by the Godfather, Consigliere and Benny "two Eyes" Montesano. He was sixteen when he held his first weapon, he would be seventeen when he fired one at another human being.

After the proper time and thought given, the perfect opportunity arose, the Godfather found the perfect victim, one of his very own Captains, as he said and as many said before him, 'keep your friends close and your enemies closer'. With this thought and the idea of impending turf wars, between some captains of his own and another family from New York, he would need a catalyst, a catalyst that could spark retaliation prior to an attack. As the Godfather would say "always easier to start something than finishing something", as time would go, many adjectives would be added to that statement it would never change the fact that this Godfather and the one that he would mold in the future would become thinkers from outside of the box.

A death, or even better an assassination, of a high ranking Captain within his family would be just enough to inspire others to follow more so than lead. When the day approached, the Godfather asked Conoscalo if he could, if this was something that maybe he wanted to do.

The comforting note between them became the thought of taking a life, taking the life of another, could he do this for his Godfather, do this one little thing for the man that had done so much for him, so much to better his life.

"And if I do not like it, can't do it," Conoscalo asked.

"Then you tell me that and we will just go from there, but before you tell me this, make sure to take your time with your thoughts. If you can perform this duty for me and others like it in the future, your rewards will be overwhelming, you will never want for anything else ever."

The Godfather wanted to be clear in what he said, as he wanted Conoscalo to succeed, for failure would certainly mean Conoscalo's demise. In addition, if he succeeded and then asked not to do this again would mean some type of future, a very limited future.

"Conoscalo, Benny will give you all the details, follow them," the Godfather who stood in front of him, kissed him on each cheek and then sent him on his way. For this to work, others would be standing by to clean up if necessary.

On the drive over to the location only Benny spoke,

"Conoscalo, you know what to do, no one survives," in one hand a handkerchief was unfolded showing a 45 caliber automatic weapon. In the other was the box of chocolates that he had delivered every week without fail.

It was a simple shoot and run, one behind the bar, a bodyguard and the actual contracted target. The police would report later that it was one of the cleanest hits on record. The bartender standing behind the bar had no weapon, in one shot, he dropped to the floor, and he would bleed to death from the bullet that hit him square in the face. The bodyguard was located on the left side of the target. He died with his hand on the butt of the gun, still in its holster. He had been given one fact, the target did not carry a weapon and he had to die in a specific way. It was how he was instructed, once to the heart, three to the face. This man would not have an open casket at his funeral.

He dropped the weapon and left the bar as clean as he came in, by the time he reached the curb the vehicle that was to pick him up stopped, he was not completely into the vehicle when it started to move again. His heart rate never changed and when the driver asked,

"Is it done?"

The answer from Conoscalo came in a clear and precise tone, as the driver would report "not a waiver in his voice."

"Yes it is done,"

When the vehicle stopped on a desolate back county road, the Godfather was there to greet him.

"Is it done," the Godfather asked.

"It's done, Godfather," Conoscalo Tuttio said.

"This seems to be your calling, you will not want for anything ever again. If this is to be your profession, know your profession better that any other," the Godfather hugged him and then told him that they would never see each other again.

The remarks from the Godfather saddened Conoscalo. He understood why, but it still saddened him. Another vehicle waited, that vehicle and the contents would be for Conoscalo to start his future in. His life would be different from this point on, only three people knew of what he had become.

His instructions were basic. Disappear and start a new life. His identity was legal and unassuming to others they had manufactured everything for him including a bump in his age for he was now eighteen. He could do whatever he wanted, even though he had his profession thrust upon him, he would have five years to establish himself, always to remember if he was to find trouble and bring shame amongst the people that supported him he would meet the fate upon himself, for they would know where he went.

Can you teach someone to be a killer, or do you just get lucky and pick the right person. After all this Godfather's nickname used to be lucky, had the luck struck again?

Just like that, Conoscalo Tuttio slid into a waiting taxi with just one bag, unsure of where to go or what to do when he arrived, those who did not know what he really was would only call him Conoscalo.

He found himself daydreaming, recalling the good days, when the days were simple and unassuming.

He had been doing this type of work for many years now, he had grown accustomed to not knowing the full story he never needed or wanted the full story.

He was a good-looking man. It had not been his conscious thought that had driven him to the idea that he was good looking, it was something he had always been told. He had always thought that in this business being a good-looking individual went far when it was necessary. With this being said he was not your typical memorable type of good looking, it could easily walk through a room and be noticed, just not remembered. In his type of work, that would be the priceless part.

He was tall and slender, he worked out on a regular basis and even though he was tall and lanky, he had extreme strength for his size. His hair color was originally a sandy color, he had dyed it so much that he was not sure what color it might be now without all the dyes. As part of his process he was always changing the particulars to what he wore, contacts, glasses whatever was necessary to blend in even more.

He had learned many things through the years. He always had a popular brand of shoes, harder to match directly if it ever came to that. He wore jeans and a long sleeve jean shirt, like a common work man's shirt, when that style was out or a more proper dress was necessary, he would wear that.

He made many precautions with his
duties, for it would not matter for Conoscalo over
the years he had many things go his way in life,
or more to the fact of taking lives and then he
always had the ace in the hole that he was
completely off the radar, no prints and no DNA in
the system. In fact, he did not exist, or had not
for some thirty plus years.

Twenty Five

"Did he mention Mr. Morris at all?"

"Welcome back, don't worry about the easels they are on loan," Patty said with a wry smile.
"Okay, I won't worry about the easels. What are you trying to do and why are there red marks all over these papers," Nick asked?
Ernie was quick to jump in "Chief, these are calls we can't account for. I, Zach or Patty did not make these calls,"
"Or Caroline," he continued with "Sorry, did not mean to leave you out" as Ernie glanced over at Caroline.
"Earl Maybe?" Now Nick looked over at the three in a wry attempt of a smile way.
"Or earl, he has been out for a while and all." The truth was that he had been gone for some time, a broken leg that was not set correctly, another surgery, time adds up.

Nick was amazed, now that he thought of it, it did take a few days to get their shit together, surprisingly enough in the computer age. He was glad that they had the LUD's back and could possibly find out who the Chief, Sam, had called.

Nick was quick to summarize about the calls, so that would mean that Sam made all of these calls, to whom. I would suggest that some are to the Morris, Finley and Turner law offices.

"Looks as if most of these calls are a Boston area code, dealing with the Charlton case," Nick assumed that, and suggested the same.

"There are ten numbers we cannot account for," Ernie said, seemed that Ernie was taking the lead on this. That was good for Nick to see Ernie take a leadership role. He had wanted to stress to Ernie that he was the senior member of the team and a leadership role, from Ernie, might be a good 'career' move.

They concluded, with a little 'Yellow Pages' search through the Internet, that calls had been made to both Charlton's' places of work, presumably bosses of both and maybe co-workers. Of the ten numbers listed, four numbers were generally the same except the last two digits, and again Nick assumed that this would mean it was the same office just two different phones within that office.

Nick headed for a phone. He dialed the first number of the semi-unknown list and waited to hear who would be on the other side.

The receptionist answered with a cheery voice "Reynolds-MacMillian, office of the President may I help you."

"Hello, good afternoon, my name is Chief Nick Sheridan of the Schrader Maine Police Department and I would like to speak with the President, please" Nick said with a force and distinction all its own.

"Just a minute sir, I will see if he is available, please hold,"

She was good at her job, Nick could tell with the tone.

Maybe it was just a minute or two, he was in the conference room, Caroline, Ernie, Patty and now Zach had joined him one by one. With all the on-lookers it seemed much longer.

"Excuse me, Mr. Sheridan, what exactly is this pertaining?" Nick thought for a few seconds.

"What is this pertaining, this is about Marcus Reynolds, Mr. Morris, Chief Clark who had previously called, I'm sure of that, and about Mrs. Charlton. That is what this is all about...."

The next voice on the line was quick and to the point, "Stephanie, I will take it from here."

"Ian Thompson, may I help you,"

Nick wanted to think that he was the President of Reynolds-MacMillian. He had to ask just the same, while he was asking he also wrote the name on a pad of paper with a question mark.

"Are you the President of Reynolds" Nick was interrupted halfway through.

"No, I'm Mr. MacMillian's attorney, and you are?" he asked.

"As I said before, Chief of Police for Schrader Maine, Nick Sheridan, I would like to speak with Mr. MacMillian," Nick said this time with a little more force at least in his voice.

"Mr. MacMillian is a busy person, actually in a meeting. If you may, explain to me what this is all about and I will get the information to Mr. MacMillian."

"We are looking at several angles about the Charlton Murder/Suicide case, and the death of our Chief of Police. Going by his notes, the short of it is that had previously contacted this office and more specifically this number." Nick said.

Ian started speaking, he interrupted Nick in his conclusion "Well sir, then your notes should say that Mr. MacMillian had no information to assist in that case, and that they should state that I actually discussed the matter with your Chief. Sorry for the loss and all, you said he died, recently?" Ian replied in a rather blue blood way.

"Yes, recently." Nick answered somberly or at least trying to expose a narrative that it was a recent and sore loss. Any good detective would want as much information as he could garner with giving the slightest amount possible, trying to make the fish into the fisher in this case he wanted the discussion to go on as long as possible, for many reasons he was unsure of at this time.

"Like I said, sorry for your loss, he seemed like a nice enough guy and all. How did he pass, if I may ask?" Ian asked?

"Still under investigation, right now it is pointing toward a heart attack, although, as we do, nothing is ruled out. Like I said, still putting some pieces together and all,"

"I see, well our conversation was limited really. He asked about Mr. Reynolds death, since he was looking in to the death of Mrs. Charlton. I have to admit it all seemed preliminary, maybe not going into any direction." Ian stopped with that.

"Did he mention Mr. Morris at all?" Nick asked?

"Mr. Morris?"

"Yes, Mr. Morris, the lawyer for Mr. MacMillian?"

"Not sure why he would. He did not mention him to me, like I said no real connection there. Mr. Morris is Mr. MacMillan's lawyer and all, not connected. I don't get the connection or why he would ask that or about Mr. Morris."

"Well sir, Ian Thompson was it? Depending on where this goes, we might have to call you back if that is okay?"

"Sure, I understand Chief, by all means if you need too. Not sure what I could add, we really did not speak all that long."

He did write down the name of Ian Thompson with the label of Counsel to Reynolds-MacMillian, and then in parentheses he wrote 'The President'.

"Zach, go to the drug store and buy me two disposable phones, by at least an hour of phone time, through a phone card or something." Nick pulled out his wallet and removed everything that he had in the way of cash, it wouldn't total more than fifty bucks, yet it should be enough.

"That number that we called, I want to know every time it was called, what day and time and how long the call lasted. Once you get the disposable phones I want all the other numbers called, keep track of who it is etcetera. Do not say you are from this office or use your real names, say you're selling something. Whatever it is, whoever makes the call, stick to the same thing each time, give as little information as possible from our side."

Zach would return with the disposable phones, Ernie would step up to make the calls, Caroline would be next to him to write down any pertinent information.

Mr. Morris and his law firm would have to wait.

Twenty Six

"Get me to a Doctor?"

Conoscalo went into observation mode. He had been watching the men in the car he'd spotted for three hours now. He believed this kind of paid security was good when the action started, but got lazy just waiting. Their attention was limited to the house. They neglected watching their own backsides because they thought they were invisible. Those that had watched him previously had stopped. They had actually lost him, and felt it was better to watch what seemed to be the next target. They were growing edgy and uncomfortable. In this state of inactivity they knew the action may be delayed, but the need to relieve themselves couldn't be.

The first one to leave the vehicle would be the first to stop breathing. Conoscalo approached the man as he unzipped his pants after walking just far enough to be in the shadows. Conoscalo's long blade penetrated the guard's body puncturing both sides of his heart. Conoscalo quietly laid the body on the ground. He located and removed the weapon. Another nine millimeter was always a good thing to have.

The man in the car would be a different story. For this, Conoscalo simply opened the driver's door and slid in. During his surveillance he'd noted that the passenger had used his door frame for a pillow which indicated he'd been dozing.

His last words were a little slurred from sleep, "Had to take a piss did you?"

"PFFF, PFFF" were the only sounds. Both bullets entered the rib cage and passed through his heart. One bullet ended up in this throat and the other lodged in the door frame of the car. Conoscalo believed this cleared the back of the house, but he knew there would be more men out front.

Before silently entering the residence he checked his gloves and other materials, his throwaway gun was at his ankle, a knife concealed behind it, his nine millimeter with suppressor was in the special pocket in his jacket.

The 9 mm that he'd taken from the first man was in between his belt and his back. He worked the lock pick smoothly and had the back door open with three quick twists on the locking mechanism. As soon as he opened the door, he removed his primary weapon with suppressor from his jacket pocket.

From this point on, his eyes and the barrel of the weapon moved as one. He was on high alert now. If need be he would shoot first, there was no need to ask questions. He moved carefully taking short steps.

He walked from his entry point through the kitchen, into the living room and up the stairs. He had expected a layout such as this, not much changed from how he imagined it. He had reviewed similar plans, and through his source of information, he was told that no remodeling had occurred that would change any portion of where he was to be. At the top of the stairs he turned left, then took the next right. He looked one last time at his watch, three fifty two a.m.

He could see the target and his bedmate, both asleep, one on his stomach, the other on her side. As he leveled his weapon he felt a presence. He had thought about the others, those that watched, he knew others were around. He would agree as to the protocol of how it should be, not that there was a protocol. He would suspect that no one would be in the home, possibly even those he had come to kill. This one time he had speculated incorrectly, it only took one time.

"Now, don't be stupid. Slowly lower your weapon, move your finger outside the trigger well, and hand it over your left shoulder. Do it now." whispered a man with a heavy Irish accent.

Conoscalo did exactly as he was told. Once the gun was confiscated by the Irishman, Conoscalo's arm slowly lowered back to his side, without prompting.

"Now, we are going to quietly back out of this room without disturbing anyone." Conoscalo obeyed. Once they were clear of the room, with the weapon still pressed into the back of his skull, Conoscalo wordlessly walked as directed.

"Stop at the bottom of the stairs then walk straight ahead until your nose touches the wall." Again Conoscalo did precisely that. He expected to hear sounds from others arriving to assist, but he heard nothing.

"You may call me Jimmie. I'd like to kill you but I can't, you're needed alive. Just follow my instructions and you won't be hurt, for now. Call it professional courtesy." Conoscalo nodded his understanding.

Jimmie used the next few seconds to frisk Conoscalo, he removed the 9 mm from his belt and the knife from his back pocket. Once he completed the upper torso he ordered, "Bend your left leg, at the knee bring your right foot up." Conoscalo shifted his weight to support himself on the left side, then bent his right knee placing his right foot into Jimmie's hand.

When Jimmie finished, he switched his weight and did the same with the left leg, not bothering to wait for Jimmie to prompt him. Jimmie discovered his ankle throwaway, and removed it. Neither the pressure nor position of the barrel pressed to the back of Conoscalo's head ever varied.

Jimmie then ordered Conoscalo to enter the living room.

"Walk forward, another three steps. Then stop." Jimmie said.

Conoscalo followed the orders accurately, as he had with all the others.

"Now turn around carefully and slowly drop to your knees. Keep your arms at your sides. Place your right ankle over your left. Then sit on your ankles."

Again Conoscalo followed every direction.

"So here we are." Jimmie sat on the only couch in the room, directly across from where Conoscalo was uncomfortably waiting.

Conoscalo made no reply. Jimmie brought his wrist to an unobstructed level, not blocking his line of sight to Conoscalo, enabling him to see his wristwatch, while keeping an eye on the man before him. Three fifty seven was the time. Jimmie could make the call anytime. As had recently been the case, he was on Jimmie time, he was finally master of his own future. If he were able to get the needed information and earn brownie points with someone like his boss, and his bosses boss it would cement really what Jimmie Rodgers was all about.

Over time Jimmie had heard all about the reward Ian expected to claim by providing the information. If he could get the correct information that Ian so wanted,

"Don't want to talk? Nothing to say? No questions as to how you got into this position...? Any last requests, maybe?"

Conoscalo shook his head.

Suddenly Jimmie barked, "Arms out, both of them. Extend them toward me." Jimmie would play games if he couldn't get him to talk.

Conoscalo extended his arms fully, just as the man on the couch ordered. He put a smug look on his face knowing that he was in charge. The look on Jimmie's face told Conoscalo more than any words could.

"Okay, relax your arms, shake them out. Let the blood get back into your fingers."

Conoscalo did just that, he brought his arms down, shaking them as he lowered them to his sides. Once down, he swung them back and forth by his sides looking as if he were shaking out a tingling sensation.

"Okay good enough, now raise them again, same position." Jimmie felt comfortable in these surroundings. He had things under control. He no longer held his silenced nine millimeter. It was at his side on the couch, next to the one he'd removed from Conoscalo.

Conoscalo complied with the seated man's orders.

Jimmie looked at his watch again, raising his arm in the same way that he had previously. This time it was two minutes after four in the morning. Jimmie was surprised at how slowly time was passing.

As Jimmie glanced at his watch, Conoscalo's mind raced. He needed to know more, without asking. He knew of the two in the back, but how many more were out front. He wondered why they hadn't extracted him yet. They were waiting for something, but what? He'd had the assassination and escape all planned, but how to get out of this current predicament eluded him. He'd just have to stay alert and play it by ear.

"I see your mind racing, there is nowhere to go. We have both the front and rear secured." Jimmie noticed a smirk appear on the face of his silent prisoner. Jimmie reached into his pocket and pulled out a cell phone. He quickly dialed a number from memory.

"Do you?" Conoscalo asked as Jimmie held the cell phone in his left hand.   It wasn't necessary to hold it close because of the hands free device stuck in his left ear. In case a quick response was needed Jimmie placed his right hand over the weapon lying next to him, not gripping it. Just covering it with his hand.

Conoscalo's arms were still straight out in front of him.
After starting to speak he just smiled, the smirk had grown into complete contempt for the person seated in front of him.

The phone continued to ring without response. "Lower your arms to get the feeling back." Jimmie said as he noticed Conoscalo's hands start to quiver.

Conoscalo obeyed. But once his arms were lowered and swinging loosely back and forth Jimmie shifted his attention back to the cell phone glancing at it as he heard the sound of another person, one who had answered the call, finally.

"Yes," Martin stated calmly.

"Give me five then approach, individual is before me. No problems with the acquisition."

"You have him?" Martin asked.

"Isn't that what I just said you moronic fuck?" His heavy Irish accent coming clearer as his voice raised while chastising his partner, of sorts.

"Five minutes, it is." Martin said, ignoring the verbal abuse.

"Let's just get this over with. Taking control of this guy is all that matters right now." Martin paused,

"Regardless of what was said, last thing we need is for that cowboy to fuck it all up." Martin didn't care what his so-called partner had ordered.

Conoscalo had always been a toy lover. Not children's toys. No, his toys were for work, such as the holster where he kept his ankle weapon. It had been specifically designed and was one of a kind.

A blade was deep inside the leather holster, tucked behind the small twenty two caliber pistol.

It wasn't visible or detectable during a pat down, unless someone took the time for a second pat down after removing the little gun. When the .22 was removed it triggered the blade to pop up slightly. While the weapon stayed in the holster the blade would be secure underneath, unnoticeable to anyone without prior knowledge or a secondary pat down. He doubted the original design took Conoscalo's present situation into account, yet if it could be reached, all the better.

As his arms swung by his sides, his fingers felt for the handle of the blade which he pulled out inconspicuously. As his right arm swung forward he released the blade with a vicious flip of his wrist. He didn't intend to kill, he needed answers quickly.

Jimmie's reaction was too late. He was looking around, slighted unnerved by the phone call, as the blade was released from Conoscalo's hand. He dropped the phone as the two inch blade buried up to the hilt in his neck.

Jimmie's hands went to his neck. Before he had a chance to reach for his weapon, Conoscalo was up and moving around the couch. He stood behind Jimmie and pushed Jimmie's bloody right hand away from the gun. Conoscalo grabbed it first and held it up to Jimmie's temple.

"See how easily things can change?" Conoscalo sneered.

"How many out front?" Conoscalo demanded.

Jimmie did not respond. His right hand was back at his throat, trying to staunch the bleeding.

Now Conoscalo looked at his watch, the five minutes would soon be up.

Instinctively Jimmie pulled the knife out of his neck which caused the blood to flow even more. He regretted it as soon as he'd done it. Jimmie threw the knife onto the couch and resumed clenching his neck with both hands.

He never considered using it as a weapon, his existence hinged on being able to hold out until his guys got here and got him to a hospital. Conoscalo picked up the other weapon from the couch. It was the one he'd taken from the first man outside. He picked up the bloody knife, wiped it clean and replaced in his ankle holster. He figured death was a certainty for Jimmie, who wasn't talking anyway.

He swung the butt of the second weapon and knocked him out. Seemed the least he could do. At least Jimmie would be unconscious when death came. Maybe it was repayment for the so-called professional courtesy Jimmie had extended earlier.

Conoscalo stepped away from the slumped, dying man on the couch. As he walked away he stowed the other knife to its original place in his back pocket and the secondary weapon in his left jacket pocket. That pocket now contained the nine millimeter and extra clip. As he continued walking he reached back and fired two rounds into the couch aiming to hit Jimmie and put him out of his misery.

The muzzle flare was seen by two men who were approaching the house. Both men immediately drew their weapons. One man entered the house just seconds after Conoscalo had run up the stairs, barely out of sight.

Conoscalo walked back toward the bedroom, where the two people were starting to awaken. As he heard the front door open, Conoscalo leaned up against the wall outside the master bedroom. The two inside the bedroom started to move as those do that are awaken unexpectedly by a noise, or in this case, their front door opening.

Conoscalo waited, having a perfect view of the stairs, if anyone came in his direction he was ready. His silenced weapon, pointed in the direction of the stairs. As his eyes watched the stairs, he would then turn to lay watch inside the bedroom. He would walk in just as the man reached for his bedside lamp.

Conoscalo shot him twice. Each bullet entered the man's head. Without hesitating he walked further into the room and fired two more shots at the other person in the bed. One hit her in the chest near her heart and the other hit her heart dead center. She would probably die before her husband.

Conoscalo automatically ejected the clip from his weapon as he rounded the foot of the bed. He reached into his pocket and replaced the empty clip for a full one which he slid into the weapon. He cocked the automatic effortlessly, the whole time fully aware of his predicament and surroundings.

He sped up as he headed toward the window. He shot twice and the window glass exploded just in time for him to jump through head first. As he noted earlier in the day and with the plans that he had reviewed the overhang of this roof was about fifteen feet to the edge. Conoscalo was able to turn over so that he slid the remainder of the way on his backside.

As his momentum took him over the edge, his left hand grabbed the gutter.

This slowed his fall somewhat but the sound of the gutter coming loose caused the man who was trying to pick the back door lock, yet upon hearing the glass had gotten up to check out the noise. Problem was he had taken a right, when a left was necessary. As Conoscalo swung from the gutter, he was to the back of that man, the two shots would enter the back, transit the heart, and exit into the siding of the house on the back patio. Conoscalo's grip released and he fell the final four feet to the ground.

This job hadn't gone as planned but it was complete.

In his frustration, while walking toward the house Tim Martin picked up his phone to speed dial the team at the back of the house. They hadn't made the scheduled call at four a.m. Tim was starting to worry, it was almost four minutes after four.

"Those guys better not be sleeping, Ian and Jimmie will have their asses, it will be the worst day of their lives." The other man nodded. Another team made up of two men in a van was on its way. The van was being followed by Ian Thompson. It was not always the case for the boss to come along. Something had prompted him this time.

He wanted to be there, he wanted to talk to that guy. Jimmy had objected, he had been hired for a specific purpose, to kill people.

Now he had to capture and then what, for Jimmie that took the fun out of it. When more money was offered because of this guy and what Ian thought, it did change the mindset somewhat, although as Jimmy said, he was still in charge for the ground forces as Jimmy would say. They, now had some four cars and one van for this ground force. And no one was certain if he would even show up tonight, yet as it worked out, their guess was correct.

Still no answer.

Martin checked his watch, it was four o' four. They were in the front yard of the house when they both saw the muzzle flashes coming from the front living room. Martin quickly pointed toward the back of the house, signaling his current partner to go around back.

They drew their weapons simultaneously at first sight of the flashes. Martin entered through the front door within eight seconds of the flashes. His weapon in one hand, a small flashlight in the other, he quickly, yet cautiously, went toward the general area of the flashes. He didn't hear the quiet footsteps of a man as he hurriedly scrambled up the stairs. Martin found Jimmie slumped on the couch.

Then all hell broke loose, he could see that Jimmie was conscious, but barely, blood was everywhere. Martin made a phone call, quietly speaking into his hands-free device.

At the same time he heard the unmistakable sounds of a silenced weapon firing two sets of two shots and then two more shots and glass breaking, then a commotion coming from the back, first a metallic popping sound, then two more shots.

"Get the van to the front of the house, all hands, the target isn't here, I repeat, the target's not here." Martin waited for a response, "I have a medical emergency, need a vehicle to transport..." Martin would be cut off as he spoke. "We're pulling up to the front of the house," The driver said. The conversation in the vehicle had been terse and quick.

"Do it, go assist." Ian was in the town car behind the van, as one vehicle pulled up to the closest point at the front of the house, he would follow with that town car.

"Sir, we cannot risk leaving you alone."

"Do it damnit,"

Martin was using all his strength to drag Jimmie through the front door. Martin was only concerned about Jimmie. The others knew their jobs.

Between Martin and the first guy out of the van, they carried Jimmie across the lawn and hoisted him into the Lincoln Town Car.

"There's a first aid kit under the passenger seat." Ian shouted, and then summarily pulled it out and handed back to the men, who now sat on each side of a slumping Jimmy.

Ian glanced at the bloody man, this was not the person he wanted. This was his main guy, the guy that is hired to finish what others cannot, he wanted to talk with him, and he hoped they or other forces could keep him alive at least long enough to get some type of description.

"He's going to need more than just a kit of band aids." Martin exclaimed as he looked down at Jimmy's injury.

"Do we have any friendly doctors nearby?" Martin asked of everyone.

"Yes, I have a guy." Ian answered this time, no sooner had he stated this that the car was back into drive and going forward once again.

Jimmie hadn't spoken up to this point. It was difficult talking as two men had hands about your neck Suddenly Jimmie reached up and grabbed Martin by the collar, pulling him close to his lips he whispered "Get me to a doctor." Jimmie's grip relaxed and his body slumped back to the floor of the car.

It did not take long for the trip, which for obvious reasons was a good thing.

Ian would deliver Jimmy to the man with the nickname 'the cutter'. He now preferred 'Jackson'. That really was his last name. The days of 'the cutter' were over. But he could still operate when necessary. It took only minutes to arrive at a large industrial area. The warehouse that they wanted was one of the first they came to. As they drove up, the garage door opened.

"Whoa, we still need to work out some arrangements, understand?" He pointed to the body they placed on his operating table. His two fingers and thumb rubbing together told the men that Jackson was negotiating for payment first.

"How much?" asked Martin. Ian had not followed the three men into the warehouse, his orders were specific anything it takes to keep him alive.

"Let's say ten grand?" Jackson said as he wet his lips, and smoothed his greasy hair away from his eyes.

"Ten grand, I don't have ten grand on me. Just fix him. You'll get it." Martin replied edgily and a little frightened.

"Hey partner, sometimes cash up front is a must."

Unexpectedly the other man, the one that had jumped out of the van to help carry the body to the town car reached into his jacket pocket and tossed a roll of bills to Jackson.

Ian had taken it from the glove box and handed to the man as he walked from the vehicle, apparently Martin had not seen this.
"This should cover it, get to work. If he lives, you get a handsome reward."

That roll, regardless of how much it really was, he did not disband it or count it, no sooner was it flipped to him that he placed into his front pocket, which of course caused an unsightly bulge in the wrong spot. The Kooky smile that appeared on his face almost simultaneously made the fake bulge even worse. All of his skills were focused on keeping this guy alive long enough to collect the balance. After a quick examination Jackson saw that the neck wound was his only damage probably due in part to the Kevlar vest he removed. Jackson started a saline IV to replace fluids from the blood loss then went to work on stab wound.

The unconscious Jimmie was the only one here who knew of the two shots that had penetrated the living room couch and hit his vest. If he survived the neck wound Jimmie would be sore from the hits but he was alive.

Ian sat in the now bloody town car, a good cleaning was furthest from his mind. His mind now raced to cover what had happened, he should have had two people on the inside, which was obvious even after the fact which made it more so. Now he had to make a phone call he did not want to make.

Twenty Seven

"The garage door did not close?"

If you could see the steam rising from someone, not because of body temperature and the mix of the outside air. More to the fact as in a person being steamed, pissed off, or generally just over-upset with himself, this is how you would now witness a person driving a vehicle who was following a town car.

Conoscalo was generally upset with himself, more so than any other. He had caused this debacle, and he would be the one to clean it up, or at least he hoped he would have the chance to do so. Somewhere, they had eyes on him at one time, did they still.

He had raced back to his vehicle, a dead sprint to get to the vehicle and then pursue. He had not really replayed the events, he just wanted to pursue and kill them all. He knew the layout of the sub division well enough to suggest that if they went one way, essentially going to the left they would encounter traffic, more so than if they went to the right.

This was the back exit, less traffic. Conoscalo quickly went to the right exit, he would end up just a hundred or so yards behind them.

He would have to get over it. He needed to move on. As soon as he had seen the garage open, and the town car slide into it, he would wipe his oversized SUV, just in case. If time allowed, depending on the end of who was in the warehouse he might just come back and burn the vehicle to be sure. Now there were more pressing matters.

He thought that it was strange, "The garage door did not close?" He mumbled to himself. "What the ....?"

Hell did not get out of his mouth, the town car would back out of the stall, almost as fast as it had entered.

He quickly ducked behind a garbage area, as soon as the town car had left he would survey the surroundings, especially looking for cameras. Still the door had not closed, could he?

He approached the door, weapon drawn. He did not want to go into a blind area guns a blazing.

When he heard the voice he thought it might be the only option, he saw the man come from a door off to the left side of the garage door. This guy he did not recognize, he did recognize the smallish 380 with silencer that he held, that was clear as day, even though he had just glanced at it.

The man walked out to the top stair, yelled something back into the inner building, and returned to the inner portion of the warehouse.

That was when Conoscalo took action, he ran toward a tall cabinet that was on the right side of the garage area, it wasn't much cover, yet it was the only cover available at the time. No sooner had he opened the door of the cabinet, in order to provide more cover, the same man returned.

This time he walked down both steps, mumbling something to himself along the way. He walked to the left side of the door, and hit a large unmistakable red button. Lights flashed inside the garage, the garage door was now closing. As quickly as he had walked to the door, he walked back to the interior door and slammed it behind him.

Conoscalo would conclude it was a regular type of warehouse, this garage area had two doors, the garage door from which he had just entered and that interior door that the man holding the little 380 with suppressor had just exited into.

Just past that door, was an access ladder that looked to go to the roof, only one way to find out?

Twenty Eight

"Yeah, sloppy seconds if I want, but leave nothing
breathing."

Martin looked back at his watch. It was
already past eight in the morning. He'd been
told by the 'Doc', it would still be a little longer
before they could take Jimmie away. Under his
breath Martin had nicknamed the guy 'Hackman'
after his favorite video game but changed the 'p'
to an 'h' for hatchet and obvious reasons. He
had been given the 'discharge' instructions and
decided to look around for Stinson, who had
been with him since he helped carry Jimmie out
of the house.

Martin found Stinson who reported, "I've
checked this place high and low, and it's as big
as a warehouse, just cut into a lot of rooms. I
swear I heard something earlier."

"What did you hear?"

"Thought that I heard a door close," the
bodyguard said.

"When?" asked Martin.

"Earlier, when you were playing nurse, uh assistant to the whack job, up front." Stinson now pointed in the direction where he'd left Jackson working on Jimmie.

"Sure you checked everything?"

"Think so, but I was coming back to ask Jackson if anyone else is supposed to be in this place."

"Don't ask. Just keep looking, remember what we talked about earlier." Martin wanted to remind him without saying it aloud of their exit plans.

"Gotcha, only three people are leaving this place, no one else." Stinson said this with a follow along thumbs up, and then with the motion of slicing his own throat. He didn't realize just how accurate that might become.

"Hey, Martin. Get back here." Both Martin and the Stinson looked around at the sound of the tinny voice of Jackson. It never dawned on them that he would have an intercom in this big old building.

"Keep searching. If you find anyone, kill them. I'll go see what 'Hackman' wants." Martin turned back toward the front of the oversized space.

"What's up 'Doc'?" Martin asked in jest.

"Your friend. I've done all I can for him. Bleeding has stopped completely. He has good blood flow. His pulse is strong in several places which means it's just a matter of time. When he wakes up, he'll need to rest as much as possible."

"That's it?" Martin asked.

"Like I said, nothing more to do until he wakes up. He's going to be fine in time. He'll be back to doing whatever it is he does if he takes the proper time to heal. I can baby sit him if you like, but time is money, if you get my drift." Jackson, held out his hand, he was ready for that final payment.

Martin was more than happy to give it to him.

As Jackson turned back to admire his handy work Martin raised the silenced barrel of his weapon. The sound of the shot was followed by two distinctive sounds. The first sound was of a body hitting the floor.

The second was the gasp from someone witnessing Jackson's fate. Her gasp had been clear and resounding. Martin turned to see an open closet off to one side of the room. By instinct he did not fire. Maybe he should have but when he saw the cute strawberry blonde trying to retreat back into the closet to flee, he could not. She had gotten there by entering through another room's closet. That other room connected the operating room with a work area, lab, and all around drug making space. She just happened to be at the wrong place at the wrong time.

Martin quickly reached in and grabbed her by the hair, dragging her out of the closet. She looked to be of average size, but as Martin sent her flying across the room it seemed that either she was smaller than she looked or Martin was much stronger than anyone would expect for his frame of just under six foot.

She tried to run as he began to beat her. Screaming, she fled from one room to another down the hall. She kept trying to get away, but he easily caught her and beat her some more.

The beating ended when she ran into a bedroom. Martin threw her onto the bed and started ripping off what few clothes remained.

"What the hell is going on?" Stinson had drawn his weapon with the first sounds, understanding that the deed had been done, he continued to search as suggested until he heard the sounds of a beat down. Then he saw the beaten woman lying on the bed and Martin unzipping his pants. "Get the fuck out, keep an eye on Jimmie. I'm going to take care of something here...now leave." He did. Martin finished fifteen minutes later, leaving her where she laid.

"Everything good now?" Stinson asked as Martin returned.

"Go ahead, it's your turn to finish that off, then finish it. Understand?" Martin smiled as he remembered the last few minutes.

"Yeah, sloppy seconds if I want, but leave nothing breathing, right?"

"Yeah. Now I'm going to get Jimmie and take him back to a safe house. Let him recuperate if he can." Martin motioned toward Jimmie, who was conscious but not coherent. "Stinson, you're on foot to return, got it. Call in when you have arrived at the alpha."

"And you guys, hoof-in it?" That would not be the case, Martin had arranged for a vehicle to be standing by.

Stinson had already moved Jimmie into a wheel chair he stumbled across earlier in the warehouse. Without further ado, he thought about the prospects of the other room, it had been a long night, and a little longer since he had really been able to get what he wanted. No sooner had Martin removed Jimmie from the operating "room" he had shot down the hall. Before they left, Martin had one more call to make.

"Ian, Jimmie got through it okay, it seems. Doctor is done, another witness is also finished."

"Vehicle is where we discussed, keys are under the driver's side mat. Can Jimmie take the travel, or will you wait longer?" Ian asked.

"The Doctor's last words were that he was okay to leave, but keep him calm. He said there was nothing left for him to do." Martin said sarcastically.

"Okay, and Stinson?" Ian asked.

"Going to stay behind and clean up. He will make sure that all loose ends are tucked in. He knows where to meet us."

"Okay, I'll be in touch." Ian was relieved that Jimmie was alive.

His earlier conversations with James left Ian feeling that he was disappointed, Ian understood how quickly things had gone wrong because he was there, but James was not so easily soothed.

A face-to-face confrontation was always tense and Ian couldn't be everywhere at once.

The one person that Ian wanted alive for questioning had gotten away, he also wanted him for other things. At the same time James just wanted him dead, of course after that one question was asked and properly answered, who hired you.

To James MacMillian it was one thing for his past to be kept secret if he gave the kill order but it was totally unacceptable if it was done without his consent and beyond his control. Both his lawyer and his number one money man were dead, and he didn't know why someone else would also want them dead.

Twenty Nine

"Maybe you didn't start it, but I watched you finish it?"

This wasn't typical for Conoscalo. Usually he did not place himself in such a precarious position. Opening himself up to danger was not his custom. He did not even try the interior door, he had walked right past it. Later he would discover that he had shelter if things were right, nice to know in hind sight he would guess. He needed to keep people talking and that meant breathing. He needed to know who was giving the orders, and more importantly a lead or a location.

So he was putting himself in this position by choice. He climbed up to the roof looking for access. One good thing about these old converted warehouse lofts, they had large air ducting.

They also had an access ladder down to a lower level, yet still above many of the rooms in the warehouse This warehouse also had a cat walk at about fifteen feet above ground, some of the panels on the sides of the cat walk were solid, for reasons that Conoscalo did not know, or cared to know, this provided him with the most cover.

He needed to remind himself, these cat walks that he was to walk on, were old, creaky, and sometimes if not more than normal, poorly maintained.

It was a slow step by step procedure. He had taken the ear piece with him, he liked to use it in places unknown, and it would enhance his hearing. The 9 mm would be gripped firmly in his hand, it would not be holstered for some time.

After the slow movement to one level then to another. He would stop his movement behind a large grate, garnering protection from three sides was the best that he could do. He would relocate when the coast was clear, he could, in the beginning see two people in what looked like an operating room, the other man, the one that had come out and closed the garage door was acting more of a rover, he was just looking everywhere.

As he meandered down, taking his time, he had been there some 3 hours already and traveled maybe a hundred feet both vertical and horizontal. Now, he had a clear view, just as one door had slammed. He had witnessed the wheel chair with an individual sitting down. Could that be that Jimmie character?

"No way, could it."

"Tough bastard..." He mumbled.

This gave him a view, almost in its entirety of what seemed to be a make shift operating room. There was bloody gauze strewn about the room which meant someone had just been treated here. It must have been Jimmie.

Two bullets and a knife surely could have caused this disarray. Then he saw a body underneath the metal table. Conoscalo deduced the man had been killed recently judging by the uncoagulated pool of blood. He strained to look to his right and was able to see another room because the walls connecting the rooms didn't reach the ceiling.

Conoscalo moved on to survey the next room. As he inched silently along the cat walk, exposing himself again, if anyone were to look up it could become difficult. In the other room he saw what he would call an old lab. Piles of papers and boxes were stacked on a long workbench. It must have been turned into a storage room. He kept crawling another fifteen feet beyond the storage room. Even for Conoscalo, this was sickening. The body of what seemed to be a young woman, laying partially covered on a bed and she was not alone. At first glance he thought she was under a red sheet, but then he realized it was a bloody white sheet.

He didn't want to watch while she was being violated, but the need for self-preservation prevented him from helping her. His help may only consist of putting her out of her misery but right now he couldn't take the risk.

From his position he wouldn't be able to remove himself from what cover he had, to somehow jump out, and kill the rapist while staying invisible. He had to wait which made it worse. Even though he had been a party to many contemptible acts, he would never rape anyone. That was beneath his ethics, and yes even he had ethics.

He didn't wait much longer. The man who had been violating the young woman left the room and headed toward a bathroom, this space was not visible from his view point. It was one of the few covered rooms in the building itself.

Conoscalo used the time well, as soon as the man left he engaged his cat-like prowess and slid down a load bearing post onto a table, then to the floor.

He stumbled slightly and fell to one side, luckily enough he would land on his side on some boxes in the lab, which luckily happened to be filled with packing peanuts and small glass items.

Upon impact he knew that he broke some of the glass but nothing of his own, as he bounced from the boxes he planted his feet firmly on the floor, weapon drawn, facing the door. No longer having his overhead view, he couldn't be sure where the man was or if he had heard the commotion.

Conoscalo opened the door to the hallway. The operating room with the body was to his left, the bedroom was in the adjacent room to his right. He had watched as the man reappeared from the bathroom. Although they entered the hallway simultaneously Conoscalo had the advantage. His weapon was already drawn, the man's gun was still in the bedroom on the night table.

Two shots and he slumped against the wall of the bathroom. These were not Conoscalo's usual double tap shots to the head or chest. He remembered in time that he needed information about the others. Until he knew what the man knew, killing him was not part of the plan. The first shot entered his left shoulder, the second entered high in the chest cavity. The final shot would eventually collapse his lungs without proper treatment, although even if he cooperated he probably wouldn't live long enough to die that way.

He walked up to the man, leaned down with the weapon pointing directly at his forehead.

"Whom do you work for?" Conoscalo asked.

The man did not answer. He showed no emotion whatsoever, he didn't even look like he felt any pain. Although Conoscalo admired his bravery he pointed the weapon at the man's right knee.

"I'm going to let you in on a little secret. Answer my questions, or you will be in more pain than the young lady you left back there."

The man said nothing, still glaring at Conoscalo.

Conoscalo shrugged and pulled the trigger even though he realized that the shot might be heard if there were anyone still in the building.

The man finally showed the pain response that Conoscalo had expected, he screamed while reaching for his leg with his good arm.

"Ian Thompson is my boss." The man hissed between clenched teeth. He didn't need any more persuasion.

"Is there anyone else in this building besides the young woman?"

"No."

"There were two or three others in here. Where are they now? I saw the dead one, where are the other two and what are their names?" Conoscalo demanded, wondering just how much the man actually knew.

"He's not dead but he's in bad shape. Not sure where they went. I have a number to call for instructions on where to meet them. Their names are Martin and Rodgers." The man hesitated. "Please don't kill me?" he begged.

"Which one was injured?"

"Rodgers was."

"What's the number?" Conoscalo asked.

"It's in my wallet," the man answered immediately.

Conoscalo reached behind the man and easily removed his wallet. He found a couple hundred dollars inside and a single piece of paper with a phone number, above which was the name Ian.

The number was labeled simply Ian. Conoscalo would never have something like this on him, either it would be memorized or if the number was necessary it would not have a name attached.

Conoscalo paused, "Jimmie is the one with the heavy accent?" He wanted to make sure.

"Yes. Don't kill me, I have a family." The man groaned. He hoped there was a chance to find a chink in the armor of the man that held his life in his hands.

"I'm sure the young lady also has a family." Conoscalo pointed to the bedroom where this man had just committed rape.

"I didn't start that, Tim Martin started that!" The man was shouting as loud as he could. As his lungs were filling with blood the sound of his wheezing worsened.

"Maybe you didn't start it, but I watched you finish it." Conoscalo rose to his feet and addressed the man, "this is for the girl." The next sounds exploded from the 9 mm and two holes appeared in the rapist's forehead as his wheezing stopped.

As much as he wanted to, he did not enter the bedroom yet. Not trusting everything he'd been told, he searched through the warehouse first then he checked the bedroom.

Conoscalo leaned down over the bed. "At least your pain is over" he whispered lightly. Conoscalo assumed she was dead.

He felt for a pulse in the young woman's neck anyway. He pulled back her matted bloodied hair. Gently he checked again, leaned in to look directly into her open blue eyes. He heard a faint wheeze. She was breathing! This young woman was still alive!

"Now what should I do." Conoscalo wondered aloud. He had watched for a while but he had no idea how long she had endured this cruelty. Conoscalo checked his watch, it was just past twelve noon.

He ran to the 'operating room'. It was equipped almost as good as a hospital. He filled a bag with bandages, needles, saline drips, a suture kit, and sterile dressings.

When the bag was full, he hurried back to the storeroom for clean linens, more bandages and blankets. He quickly returned to her side to gently lift her so that he could toss the bloody sheets aside and carefully wrap her in the clean linens and cover her with a blanket. He placed her near the exit and ran to retrieve his vehicle. As he ran, he pushed speed dial 'one' on his cell phone.

He waited and then punched in the code. The person that answered only wanted the pertinent information. Conoscalo would inform this first person, he would then be transferred.

"I need a doctor, not for me. Not sure what I should do but I need a doctor. Will explain everything, in..." Conoscalo was interrupted.

"Where are you?" The Godfather asked.

"Southside, warehouse district."

"Standby..." The phone went silent, it would be nearly three minutes before another voice returned to the line. This gave Conoscalo time to lift the woman and place her into his oversized SUV, putting the bag of equipment next to her. He was driving away from the warehouse when he heard a different voice. He knew that his own protection, and therefore for those that he worked "with", should be his number one priority, but he couldn't just leave this woman in the warehouse to die. The conscience that he had always wondered of, if he even had one, was now Omni-present, maybe after all the years, all the killings, deep down inside he had a conscience.

The new voice gave him directions and then started asking pertinent questions about the patient's vitals.

Thirty

"Yes, they were former clients, both David and Julie."

Nick did not sleep well, or at all, might be the better way to pronounce it. They had continued to work on the calls, to where for how long and with some other information attached. They had not called, well they called, and they could not reach anyone at the law offices of Morris, Finley and Turner. Surprising for a Thursday afternoon, even if it was after 6 pm. Nick had been surprised by the work load, or the non-existent work load. If it wasn't for this boondoggle, they would have nothing going on. Although it had been pointed out that Zach had written two speeding tickets, on this shift.

He had suggested that maybe on Friday he would start writing tickets for parking and the like downtown. As this idea left his mouth, Patty started shaking her head in the no, and hell no positions. Nick glanced at Zach, then over to Patty and then back down to his papers.

"Only if you start with your Father and his parking area behind town hall." Nick eschewed as if he wasn't really paying attention. He then glanced back up toward Patty, who was now shaking her head even more ferociously.

Just as Zach was to agree and be happy with his next endeavor, Nick chimed in again.

"Tell you what Zach, let us finish what we have at hand and then I will evaluate how things are done."

Zach would soon leave the station, the bummed look on his face was still ever-present.

"Time to call Mr. Morris, or at least try to." Nick said reluctantly. He had ensured, through the yellow pages and the web that it was numbers attached to the firm. Now he just needed an answer.

"Morris, Finley and Turner, how may I direct your call?"

"Mr. Morris's office please."

"Yes sir, let me see if his secretary is in." The young lady was curt and quick on the phone, Nick did not even have the chance to thank her. The wait was not that long, all things considered, their musical choice while on hold was all together another point.

"Miss. Halvorson, how may I help you?"

"Yes, I'm trying to get a hold of Mr. Morris?"

"And you are, and what does this pertain?"

"Excuse me, should have stated that in the beginning. My name is Nick Sheridan. I'm the Chief of Police for Schrader Maine. And this is in reference to previous phone calls by the former Chief about a cold case."

"Mr. Morris is out of the office, he will be back next week. I will relay the message to him and he will return your call when he is back into the office."

"There is no way to discuss the matter with him?" Nick asked, lawyers were always out of the office, sometimes as a police official you just had to change the way you asked.

"No sir, he is on a..." She paused, "a vacation."

"Are you sure about that, this is official business?"

"I realize the importance of your call, what case and do you have a reference number?"

"I have no reference number, it is Charlton Murders and this also pertains to a former client of this firm, Mr. Marcus Reynolds."

"Stand by, let me see if Mr. Finley is available." Nick tried to utter a word of thanks, again, he would not have that opportunity, the music was back on and it seemed louder than usual, certainly louder than last time he thought.

This time the wait was a good five minutes.

"This is Jameson Finley, Miss. Halvorson said that you were inquiring about some former clients and since Mr. Morris is out of the office, she figured it was best that I answer what I could?"

"Thank you for your time, Sir...." Nick paused. "I'm not really sure where to start?"

"From the beginning has always worked best for me." Jameson Finley responded in a cool, clear and un-obstructed way. Typical lawyer, at least the good kind, in Nick's eyes.

Nick did just that, from the beginning, or at least from Sam's death and his arrival. He was sure at any point this lawyer would cut him off, he did not.

"Sorry to hear about your friend, the Chief. This has been a long time, many years ago since their deaths. Are you going to reopen the case or is this really in the preliminary stages?"

"We are putting it all together, there are some files missing. Which is why, compounded with some other information that I cannot speak of the specific per say, since this is an open investigation on some parts of the total."

"Some of the files are missing?" This intrigued the lawyer. Usually cops do not like to submit to something that they may have lost, this guy did it without much concern by the way of his voice.

"That is why we believe there was a cover up or action at Mr. Clarks home. That is why it is so important to discuss the previous phone calls with Mr. Morris."

"Mr. Morris, well he is on vacation so to speak?"

"His secretary or assistant said he was out of the office...Vacation." Nick was used to or even expected the run around from lawyers, two different stories, not so much.

"Well, let's just say Robert has pulled this trick before, too often if you ask me."

"Of course this, his just up and going somewhere, leaving the phone behind and so on does provide for more work from all of us in the office." The lawyer stopped there, he had more than likely said too much already.

Nick was taken aback, as he thought to himself, the silence on the phone continued. One lawyer had just slammed his partner and sounded mad about the whole just up and leaving thing.

"Where did you say you were from?" the lawyer asked.

"Schrader Maine, Schrader Police Department, where the Charlton Murder Suicide, if you want to call it that, happened," Nick tried to give him the roundabout without stating the whole case.

"According to what we have, they were clients?" Nick asked tentatively, after he had told that some stuff was missing, just not what specifically.

"Yes, they were former clients, both David and Julie." Jameson Finley had not said those names together under this pretense actually became relieved. Over the last eighteen hours or so he had talked too much about his partner and friend, with many other clients, seemed that this time it was not the best to just up and leave. This would bring a welcome change. He then continued almost under his breath, "I never wanted to consider it a murder/suicide either." Nick was quick to pick up that part of the statement, "Are you, do I understand you correctly that you believe it was not a murder/suicide?"

"Well, you have to understand that I, I knew both of them rather well, I just never got behind the fact that David Charlton could do that, then again you never know," the lawyer seemed contrite, if that action for a lawyer was possible.

"Sir, Mr. Finley I believe we have enough to reopen this case, especially as to how it ties to Mr. Clark and his death." Nick hated calling his former mentor and friend Mr. Clark, it seemed so distant.

"So, I guess that I'm asking for any information that you may have as to the Charlton's. And would ask if you or those clients had any connection with Reynolds-MacMillian Defense contractors, besides being married to Marcus Reynolds."

Nick again paused…

"I have to admit, this was a while ago, sometimes some things sit with you better than others, Marcus's death and then that of Julie and David, it was a rather bad time. "The odd thing about it, Marcus died a week before Julie did. She opted with David to not go to the funeral. She was very upset, I do remember that."

"Why would you consider that odd," Nick asked.

"I was his lawyer, we weren't best friends although we did talk a lot and I never remember any mention of heart problems and at the age of 43 he dropped dead of a heart attack, maybe I never got over that one."

"Oh, as his lawyer, is there any chance I could get copies of the wills and the divorce settlement?" Nick figured it could not hurt to ask, after all you never know.

There was a pause, this answer was not immediate. Nick figured that the lawyer was devising some strategic wording that he could not, just besides saying no outright.

"Sure I don't see a problem with that. I will also send you Marcus' will. It has his ex-wife in there and it may help, I'll ask Robert's secretary to fax that part over," the lawyer stated.

Nick was curious as to why he would need his late partners help "Why would his secretary need to fax it over, you said that you were the lawyer."

"Yes I was, Robert was chief counsel for Reynolds-MacMillian and all of Marcus's personal wills and decrees were placed into that file, at one location and all."

"So who is Ian Thompson," Nick asked.

"I'm not familiar with that name, who is Ian Thompson," the lawyer asked because simply put he did not know.

"According to the office of the President of Reynolds-MacMillian he is the lawyer for James MacMillian," Nick retorted wryly.

"I believe that you have received some erroneous information, no offense Mr. Sheridan," the lawyer stated this fact truly. As it would seem he was the one with the incorrect information or at least the last time he talked.

"I tried to call the president of Reynolds-MacMillian, Mr. MacMillian this morning, and Ian Thompson stated those sentiments to me, about being the counsel to the president of the corporation," Nick almost blurted that out.

"This morning, that was quick, I've not spoken with Mr. MacMillian. So I would have to look into that," the lawyer had spoken in a low tone, for it was clearly visible by his reaction that he did not know of this and at the same time was taken aback by the comment altogether.

"I appreciate everything you've done to assist us Mr. Finley, we will look forward to receiving those faxes," Nick said. Nick gave the proper fax number and then his personal phone number in case there was anything else.

"Mr. Sheridan, could you keep me informed of any information, I would appreciate that. Like I said we were not best friends I do have a fond recollection of them all"

"Yes Sir, I will keep you informed, you have a good day sir."

When Nick placed, the phone's receiver down he took a minute to lay out in his mind all the information he had just received.

Caroline had been tentatively waiting for any information, much to Nicks surprise Kristi Jensen had walked back through the door, holding yet another file.

"Let me paraphrase, Mr. Finley is sending the wills of Marcus Reynolds, Julie Charlton, formerly Julie Reynolds, and David Charlton. He is also going to send the divorce decree of the Reynolds. He said there is some pertinent information in it" Nick was not finished with his statement.

"Of Reynolds-MacMillian" Kristi blurted out.

"Let me finish, yes of Reynolds-MacMillian. Of course we already knew about the death timeline..." Nick looked in the direction of Kristi "Seems that Marcus Reynolds died a week before Julie Charlton was supposedly killed by her current husband, the lawyer. Mr. Finley said that surprised him.

He never thought that David could do something like that. It did not surprise him as much as his friend, Marcus Reynolds dying of a heart attack at the ripe old age of forty-three. He thought that it was very suspicious, for it was never mentioned that his client and more than likely, by the way it sounds, a good client. Could drop dead because of heart problems,"

"That sounds a little familiar," Caroline threw out that statement a little hesitantly, it was more on course than she thought, for everyone else was thinking the same, or just about..

"Does remind me of a few things, the faxes will be sent shortly, he said to call back if they do not come through." Nick was done, he needed time to think.

Thirty One

"Hell, I don't know her name?"

Conoscalo had waited for updates from doctors too many times to remember. Most of his memories weren't pleasant. Now he was again waiting in this hospital-like place, hoping that this young woman could survive. He was afraid to fall asleep knowing that memories of his mother in a place like this were likely to plague his dreams. But he did let his mind wander a bit.

He had tried to do "good" one other time. Not that he was a bad person. After all, we all have jobs to do. Some of those jobs might prove more respectable or just on a higher ground, I guess it would depend on your values, ethics and morals on many of those levels or stages. Conoscalo had his, he had been provided a good life, with perks, this time he had cashed those in to get this young girl the help she needed, he could not let another one go to waste, just because.

He had not pulled up to the front of this clinic, he was directed, and again followed those orders to the tee. The back of the facility was in an alley, not that unusual.

They, two individuals that came out, did not have a gurney, or something that you would see in a hospital, they carried her in on a sheet.

Actually the door was not wide enough to support a wheelchair let alone anything wider.

They were expecting him, he had pulled up and not completely placed the vehicle in park and that back door was open. He did not have to give the details again, the woman that he had been speaking to on the phone met him in the hallway.

Conoscalo finally nodded off, he was in a room by himself, two other chairs sat across from the smallish loveseat that he occupied.
He had removed the 9 mm with the suppressor still attached and had placed that weapon under a magazine. This was on his left side which was the furthest from the door. He needed to sleep and this was a prime opportunity to do so, staying vigilant and not letting another occurrence happen, like the one that occurred just some 6 hours ago would be paramount. He was still trying to go over what he had actually fucked up, although he was ever aware that he had done something to cause this, being lazy was what it was coming down to, this he did not like.

Conoscalo suddenly came awake, oriented himself and looked around. His hand was still holding the weapon that was still under the magazine next to his leg. Just as a common person would have to get orientated, and sometimes even remember where he was, Conoscalo would do this as well, possibly quicker than that normal individual.

This time as he waited in the make-shift hospital it was for other reasons. He had no idea how things would turn out even though he had read a lot about the treatment for trauma. But this recovery was now in the hands of this unlicensed doctor and maybe God. He truly believed that her fate also depended a lot on her ability to want to live, but he didn't know her well.

"Hell, I don't know her name."

Or what her inner strengths are. He had no way of knowing that this young woman had the heart of a lion, and the will to do almost anything if given the opportunity. He believed that she should have a second chance, even if this was his chance to change his past. In that past he would have left her, certainly he would have ensured her quick death to remove her from the pain. Reminiscent this was, just as was done to him when Uncle Montesano found him at death's door, or at least the beginning of it.

Conoscalo believed he had done well in his profession, now he wondered if she could succeed as well with a second chance, if she were lucky enough to survive.

The door had opened without Conoscalo being aware, "Sir," The doctor approached cautiously, knowing the kind of people who came to him for help. He warily touched the man's shoulder. Conoscalo grabbed his hand. He didn't hurt him, but the doctor gasped at his speed.

"Yes?" Conoscalo calmly replied as he released his grip. His other hand did not twitch, move or even with the movement of his body displace the magazine that covered the weapon. The doctor slowly and carefully moved the released hand back down to his side. He knew quick movements might cause an unwanted reaction.

The doctor delivered his news with a shaky smile, "Your friend is going to be okay. She will need time to recover."

"Can I go in and....." Conoscalo was not sure what or how to say it. This girl, don't know her name and all, yet I want to what?

"Well, she might not be awake anytime soon with all the drugs that are in her system. We are in the process of cleaning it out, we will see what other things we need to do in time? You are welcome to go into the room." The doctor carefully backed away from Conoscalo and returned to his patient's room to find her still asleep.

Conoscalo sat there relieved and started thinking about what had brought him here. He would shift into the other room, he would take the magazine with him, for the same purpose as before, he certainly was not going to read a three year old sports illustrated. By the time, he had situated himself in the other room, watching the strawberry blond breathing, casually glancing up at the monitors that occasionally beeped he would reflect once again.

Conoscalo was not the type to dwell. He knew what would have to be done. He must finish off the guy with the accent because he could identify him, and then he was going after his partner who beat and raped her just for the pleasure that cruelty brought him. They may be in the same business, but Conoscalo couldn't stomach his peer's moral code. Right then and there he promised himself and her inner being to kill that monster.

Thirty Two

"No balls, too many shadows that spook him."

Ian did not like the prospects of being summoned, although if the boss calls, you go and take your medicine, so to speak. He would expect that James was over the edge, angry as hell, in general just completely pissed off that nothing had gone their way. Ian would agree, he would actually shake his head up and down, if this was said. It would not be, James had moved on, he needed closure on it all.

"Ian, let's get down to business." James said this prior to Ian even taking a chair before the big desk.

"Okay."

"Somebody does not like me, this is clear. Why else kill the guy that tried or was going to blackmail me, my lawyer, and my chief investor. Robert and Harlan were old friends and we were really tight at one time in our past.

I might have known were their secrets lie, yet they knew little about mine, except for what we might have done together." James was not really done speaking, yet he motioned to Ian, shrugged his shoulders as if he was looking to Ian to jump in with something he had not thought of.

Ian had nothing as to whom.

"And what about that Police Chief, this new one?"

"It was curious. The former chief is dead, labeling it as unknown, although leading to a heart attack. This is an active investigation. Just as it should be in most eyes?"

"You're going to have to help me with this Ian?" James suggested this.

"It just seemed like he was fishing for information that maybe he did not fully have, yet wanted some type ....." Ian paused.

"Some type of what?" James asked as he poured a drink for himself, he motioned over to Ian. Ian waved the drink idea off, at least for himself.

"Justification."

"Oh, so now he is going to take over from the other guy and get some money from me. Find out everything about this new chief, and if it looks slightly bad, put him on the list." James stopped.

"And who else is on that list?" Ian asked.

"Only loose end that I have remaining, senior."

"And how would we get through a retired Senators security?" Ian wanted to ask, he had ideas of his own.

"Seems with budget cuts and other reasons, if a retired Senator wants security they have to justify it, and we all know how cheap my friend is. It also seems that it was propositioned to him to pay some of the cost, he balked and therefore his security is limited. 1 guy, eight hours a day and no more, Monday through Friday."

"Perfect." Ian answered with a wry smile on his face.

"Make it tonight, one less thing to worry about, and if he is behind all of this, then we will kill two birds at the same time." James was reluctant to conclude anything.

"Do you think that he even could?" Ian asked.

"No balls, too many shadows that spook him. Which is better, he is alive when they find the body that is in the front yard, or is there too many holes. So we finish him and then ruin the reputation of the great Senator?" James now had that smile on his face, more to the point, they both did.

Thirty Three

"I learned from the best, you know?

Tom Griffin was the new breed of Senator, a very active Senator. He was extremely active in his home town of Boston, as many of his brethren were not as active and rather enjoyed staying away from their perspective home states. Tom actually would rather stay in his home state and especially in the city where he grew up and ultimately went to college, found love and heartache several times over for the later. The town that brought back so many painful memories also provided Tom with an air of calm. He, after all, was the son of a former Senator, former Ambassador a man that was truly loved by all. He used to make the comment to many of those teary eyed younger ladies that followed so closely, that every morning that he awoke, he was three steps behind where he finished the night before, so he had to do better, get further the next day.

This was something he still thought, for the young Senator who now held the same seat that his father had once occupied, these shoes would never be easy to fill.

Tom was a good-looking kid, always had been, some would say that those good looks got him to where he is.

He was tall, slim and lanky, the women that worked on his campaign and now in his Senate office swooned every time he passed, regardless of their status.

He was an honest man and his loyalty was far reaching, he had separated himself from his father and his father's business early in life, he had done this for several reasons. He gave loyalty as much as he received. He would become someone that you would not want to cross, intentionally or otherwise. Moreover, when the Committee Chair called out for the Senators vote, unlike many times in the past and with some hesitation he briefly spoke. He believed speaking during a vote was wrong. It should be a simple Yea or Nay, this time he made the exception. "Senator, Senator Griffin, the floor is yours," The Committee chair said.

"Thank you Chair, as others have repeated themselves in the words of others, I will not. I used to think that this was cut and dry, and no more. I have changed my original stance and it should come as no shock, my vote is a resounding 'YES', our government should regulate and control how the business of 'WAR' is handled.

It has been a free to roam society for too long, there should and hopefully will be more control on the Defense Contractors and how they do business."

The Senator said it. His vote was not the deciding factor. He would let another Senator have that power, that Senator had changed his vote also, for many of the same reasons, and a few different ones as well.

With the votes counted it became a victory for the Democratic Party, at least initially, this was a wake-up call for other bills.

This Bill would regulate how all Defense Contractors did business, according to the Bill. It would regulate how funds became available. Moreover, would not necessarily guarantee that the lowest bidder would get the contract, in fact, the language of the Bill stated that an impartial group of experts would decide who received the Contract. It would come with its downfall, the system in which it was, for all intense purposes the Government would get bigger by some degree. There would be another committee set-up especially for the ultra-secret.

The original writer of the bill was the Committee Chairman, a Democrat, and thought it would be best for the Department of Defense and for all Americans. His original idea was the desire for all Americans to have a tighter rein on the money wasted, as he stated it, on misleading contracts and the companies behind them.

Originally, this bill was to force the republicans to give a little, when they did not the Chairman expanded the bill to grip a little tighter on some fundamental 'money' items.

The Chairman was an honorable type, however, he became disillusioned when a small company in his district, could not get any defense contracts. Not even a small bite as he once said, after a holiday break he came back with the bill in almost its present state.

As typical for the Senate Committees of the day, there were fifteen members, eight Democrats because they were the majority and seven Republicans. If this were, merely a 'party line' vote as some suggested it would have been an easy vote to decide, since the outcome was a 'YES' vote then it would go to the House and then to committee to iron out the entire bill, then back to the Senate for a vote, along 'party lines' again a 'YES' vote would result. There is no way to determine the outcome, it was up for much speculation.

Since this was a preliminary vote, meaning another would happen in three to four weeks, as for future votes and their processes this would require much speculation for the beltway boys and other pundits.

This vote even a preliminary as in this case, would be different from the beginning. Along the party line, and with the military interest the vote should have been ten votes NO, and five votes YES, the bill would have been defeated it should have been defeated.

The Democrats had three individuals on the committee that had always been staunch Military backers and Defense Contractor loyalist, their votes would have been a NO and nothing would change that, not if they expected to retain their Government jobs in the next voting season. A republican victory would be at hand and this bill would never, at least for the time being would not be included for a vote.

As the vote turned out, three Republicans and one Democrat changed their mind, seemingly at the last minute, the Democrat who changed his vote, essentially swung his vote to the Party lines, no big deal. The three Republicans were an entirely different story, Senator Karla Miller, from Washington State had no real reason to change her vote.

Another, Senator Ben Whitefield from Utah, received little attention when the President searched the Junior Senator out to convince him in which direction the vote should go, his change of mind was a surprise, not as much of a surprise as the Senator from New Jersey.

Senator Tyler Hansford received many reasons to vote along party lines and at the last minute without word to his aids or assistants, changed his vote to 'YES', therefore swinging the vote to eight 'YES' and seven 'NO', therefore carrying the bill, there would be another vote in three weeks.

The Chairman of the Senate (Select on Intelligence) Appropriations Committee was incredibly taken aback from this and when he did not react to his name, the Assistant Chair needed to tap his arm to collect his attention. Moreover, when they left the chamber, he was so overwhelmed, in his time to present this positive matter, as he had stated previously, to the press he merely ducked out through the back chamber and cautiously retreated to his offices.

The Senior Senator from Oregon never expected this to pass, regardless of the preliminary vote status. It should never have made it this far. He should have never gotten into the trouble that caused all this, he thought, as he closed the large doors to his offices.

The other Committee members filed out of the Senate room to little fanfare, some aids had waited outside the room and joined them as they walked away. The results, a 'YES' to what some had tagged the Contractors Terrorism Bill, A-4179, even though this was a preliminary vote it would still make the six o'clock news.

The surprise would be that the vote was a 'YES', for the President had thought, and if he were a betting man, would have bet on 'NO'.

It became the news of the day, Fox news Channel discussed it for over two hours that very same evening, of the four Senators that had changed their vote. Three of them began answering the hard questions. Moreover, the one Democrat, Senator Tom Griffin Jr. became an instant success in his Party, many gave him credit after all how could they give credit to the other Party.

This call he expected, he did not want to take and wished that he could avoid it all together, this he could not.

"Dad, figured you would call. How's things going?" Tom Jr. asked this just like a politician would without waiver.

"Cut the crap, Dammit." The tone was usual for the retired former Senator and Ambassador, ever since he left the office he wanted nothing more than to get back in, he liked the power, those waiting at his every breath and the younger ladies.

"Look, it is just preliminary. Those three that voted in that manner, they will change the vote back, you know this. I'm friends with them, somewhat, they are just taking the Washington two step into a different direction, and you know that game better than anyone?"

"That may be true, yet still it is a shocker, just making waves and taking all the credit from the party."

"I learned from the best, you know?"

"That will get you somewhere kid, as you have obviously learnt."

"Well look at me now, good genes and all."

"Just thought I give you some shit, I'm surprised I have yet to receive a call from James." Senior was actually wondering why James had not called, his cohort in crime or whatever else they were up to had called earlier, he needed to come over, or send somebody over with some papers that needed to be signed by the board members, other than that he had not heard even a whisper from his old friend.

"Well good luck with that call and all, stay healthy, I have a full schedule to get too."

"Yeah you too kid."

Their conversation would end as it had started. There was some love-loss between the two, the father and son that had done so much and seen their fair share as well. I wasn't a hate relationship, it was just more complicated than others.

His schedule was full, or at least as full as he would let it get. The vote in the morning took pretty much all morning, then he had some time slotted with the biographer, and then he had to slink of and see his shrink, hopefully this could be the last appointment for a while anyway, hopefully.

Thirty Four

"My Name is Faith."

The doctor had made it clear to Conoscalo that she couldn't stay here. The doctor did not have the facilities for a prolonged stay, even though the young woman did not necessarily need further medical attention, she would require round-the-clock care until she became more ambulatory, then she would still require some assistance with ordinary tasks. What were his choices? He had never brought anyone to his home before. Would the girl be prepared? When she was awake enough to be aware of her surroundings would she freak out? But Conoscalo saw no other way, he would get her somewhere.

The doctor, with the nurse or at least some one in that capacity that followed the doctor around like a nurse or better yet a puppy, had given no time frame, just that they had to leave. No sooner had they left, when the doctor quickly returned and handed a large vanilla envelope to Conoscalo,
"I believe this is for you?"

"Why would you believe that?" Conoscalo shot back at the doctor.

"The person that delivered it said it was for the man that brought the girl in..."

He quickly added, "Who else could it be?"

Conoscalo would not open it now, he knew what it was, the next assignment for him, now what to do with the young lady that lay next to him.

The doctor gave Conoscalo discharge instructions and enough painkillers and antibiotics to last for quite a while. He wasn't sorry to see them go. Conoscalo was well aware of her injuries but listened carefully to what she would need.

Conoscalo again called the number. The first person to answer was not the same as last time. Conoscalo only said one thing, "I need a place that will watch over her and take care of her medical needs."

"Stand by."

He would be told of a long term care facility, although she would not require the "long" portion, she certainly needed the care side.

As they left, Conoscalo recalled carrying her limp body from the warehouse to his SUV and then into this 'hospital'. During the ride he had watched her eyes. They stayed open. He couldn't remember if she even blinked while he was near. Her eyes watched his every move. They seemed to look right through him. He began to feel an emotion he thought of as love when he looked into those eyes. But the consequences of her trauma could mean months of recovery and then probably therapy. Was he prepared for that?

He knew this move might not be in his best interest or maybe even hers, but he decided to do it anyway. He would take her to the location they had given him, she would not be booked into that room under her name, or would they even use his.

As she began to stir. "It's you," she sighed. "You saved me," the young voice said, as she focused her eyes.

"She speaks. The doctor said you would sleep for a while longer. You need rest to get well," was all Conoscalo could think to say.

"Where are we?" she asked tiredly.

"Someplace safe. Sleep now, we'll have time to talk later."

"You don't even know my name, do you?"

"No I do not, what's your name?"

"My name is Faith."

"Nice to meet you……" Her eyes closed before he could say her name, "Faith, what an appropriate name."

Thirty Five

"What the hell is a baby clause?"

Kristi was Nick's new hero. Not only had she brought the toxicology report back, a rushed one at that, normally those things take weeks. All she would say was that you may be surprised what a sixty dollar bottle of scotch can do for those lonely lab workers.

She also had a surprise. Some might wonder, Nick certainly did, that Sam was extremely paranoid. Or was he a brilliant fox of the past, Nick would hope for the later of the two, he was extremely happy that Sam had sent a copy of the entire Charlton case, the complete file, with pictures to another sheriff's office. This had not been by normal circumstances, Sam originally started the dialogue with that sheriff's office, because that sheriff had thought that some of his investigators were bored, with a real lack of work.

So Sam sent two cold cases to the sheriff, one was the Charlton's case, the sheriff upon receipt proclaimed that this case was solved, regardless if you liked the ending or not.

That the husband killed the wife, not pretty, and understandably difficult to swallow, yet still solved. That file in its entirety, was placed in the bottom drawer of the investigator that had been assigned to it, for review. It had never been returned, obviously.

How would a coroner, like Kristi Jensen, discover the file? Pure luck. Kristi wanted to go back to Schrader, to work with "the team" and especially if possible with Nick. Her investigative juices were flowing, it was different more so than her normal work. It was that rekindling that she had looked, hoped and even desired for, for some time.

So in order to have permission from the bosses to take "time off" and help out, she had to clear her desk of all cases, were possible. One was an autopsy for a possible victim in a home invasion out of Portland Maine, that investigator was the same, as the one that held that file in the bottom of his drawer.

Kristi Jensen's office was in Portland, not too far from that sheriff's office, she decided on this day to just go over, to get out of the office and take care of this one last thing. It was not unusual to discuss an autopsy report, sometimes they would go to her, sometimes, as in today she would go to them.

"Kristi, thanks for coming over, glad we could reschedule this. Getting it next week would have been fine." Investigator Kenny Franklyn was a seasoned pro, he had been in this position for some eight years and would be soon moving to an administrative role within the department. This might be his last investigation.

"No problem glad we could get together, thanks for making time."

"What's the rush, we always like to see you, and you know this, getting a report early is really never the case."

"Just clearing my plate, so that I can go and work on an investigation at the Schrader Police Department."

"Heard about their chief, heart attack out of the blue. Terrible thing, although in this line of work it happens frequently." They both would agree to that, and that was for some reason when the light went on, and the room grew brighter.

Franklyn would hold up his index finger, as if he asked her to wait a minute, reached down and opened that drawer that had not been open in some time, or at least as long as he could remember. Fumbling toward the bottom, he would pull out an almost two inch thick file, written on the top was the Charlton name with the case number listed next to it. It had a thick rubber band wrapped around the middle of the overly thick file.

"If you're going up there, save us some postage and return this to the new chief, would you." Kristi was elated. They would take the next fifteen minutes to go through the autopsy report, which usually would take an hour. She was gone with thanks in twenty minutes.

She did not go back to her apartment, she had a go-bag with her all the time, it had proved useful many times over the course of the last couple of years, she would just have to buy toothpaste in Schrader.

She would hand the toxicology report over to Nick immediately. He would immediately sit back down at the desk and flip through it. She would join him, standing on his left. In her right hand she would hold the two inch thick Charlton file, with the name toward Nick. She wanted to see if he would notice it, how could you not.

"What the hell is that?" Nick asked.

She explained it all, who had sent it, where it was. Now they were both elated. The file contained everything that was pertinent, the autopsy report for both David and Julie Charlton. The complete picture file as taken by the investigator, every note of the case.

"Who was the investigator, why didn't we get a hold of him?" Kristi asked, wondering more out loud than anything else.

"He died a year or so before Sam was hired on, I looked into that first. Just never said anything about it."

Nick now had the complete case file for the Charlton's, he had already the received the wills for both Julie and David Charlton and surprisingly enough the will for Marcus Reynolds and the divorce decree for the former Julie Reynolds and Marcus Reynolds, his hands were full.

He started to read.

Kristi was involved as well. She would scour the autopsy reports for the Charlton's.

She had already time lined the deaths according to the original coroner. The Charlton's died just minutes apart from each other. The toxicology report from the Sam Clark death, brought together more somber thoughts, Nick concluded it should no longer be called a heart attack.

Nick asked Patty to assemble everyone, he wanted to be on the same page. No sooner had all parties entered the conference room, Nick erased the white board, he wrote the names of Julie and David Charlton, Marcus Reynolds and James MacMillian. He stepped away from the board to get a clear view of all the names. He said nothing. When the faxed wills and the divorce Decree came in it was one after the other, Marcus Reynolds will and the divorce decree came in from the Office of Robert Morris, the others came from Jameson Finley.

As soon as they came into the office, he split the work up, Caroline took the divorce decree, Kristi started to read David Charlton's will and review all coroner type materials or anything medically related. Nick thought that was best, let the medical person look at the medical stuff.

Nick started in with the lengthy Last Will and Testament of Marcus Reynolds, he would wait on the will of Julie Charlton. Nick read all eighteen pages or so of the will it was pretty basic, for a man whose wealth was nearing a billion dollars it was a simple will.

As he wrote he spoke "Some key words of this will, we need to call Mr. Finley back to make sure, 'baby clause', 'ex-wife', 'within expectation'." "What does within expectation mean," Kristi asked.

"What the hell is a baby clause," Caroline said.

"Well, as far as I can tell, from what I read. Marcus Reynolds still loved his ex-wife, he tried to give her his money in the case of his premature death, and she refused it. So with her permission he placed a 'baby clause' in his will, which read as follows. If his ex-wife (Julie Charlton) has a child or is 'within expectation' of one his wealth, entire wealth' will go to the child, she would become the guardian until the child's twenty first birthday." Nick concluded, as he was speaking he drew the lines that connected each of these statements to Julie Charlton.

"And if she was not 'within expectations' or already had a child then what," Kristi asked.

"Curiously enough, if she did not it would all go to his business partner, James MacMillian," Nick once again drew a line, connecting James MacMillian to Julie and David Charlton.

"Is it that easy, you're saying that James MacMillian, currently one of the wealthiest men in America killed his business partner, his partner's ex-wife and her then current husband," Caroline did not ask this she merely stated it a loud.

"Well, I do not believe he did it by his own hand, we will discuss that later, what was in the divorce decree," Nick asked Caroline, she was still stuck on the previous statement and it took her a few minutes to focus on what should have been a quick answer.

"Uh, nothing really, just that Marcus Reynolds would pay Julie Charlton ten thousand dollars a month for life and would pay all college fees for any future children if she had any."

"Kristi, what about David Charlton's will," Nick asked.

"Just the usual, everything would go to his wife, and if they both met death at the same time, his lawyer, Jameson Finley would dissolve all assets and create a scholarship fund in their name, for her alma mater."

"No mention of children, or what if," Nick asked.

"No mention, would you like me to read Julie's will and see if there are any differences," Kristi was quick to ask, she did not like thinking about the what ifs attached to all the deaths that had already been mentioned.

"Sure, might say something different," Nick had come to the realization of what they concluded, there were a few facts missing, but the writing was clearly on the wall and easily read.

"We established already that Marcus Reynolds died about 7 or 8 days prior to his ex-wife and her new husband," Nick asked.

"So, Mr. MacMillian, the partner of Marcus Reynolds, killed his partner in order to take his half of the company."

"Or so he thought," Kristi was not reading Julie Charlton's will anymore. She was fully focused on Nick who was standing in front of her.

"Or so he thought, until he discovered or was told about a baby clause, and then he was given really bad news, that Julie Charlton was pregnant," Nick again paused.

"And in order to reap the reward, he arranged for Julie and David Charlton to die in a way that would not cause suspicion to anyone."

"Until a small time Chief of Police started calling the right people or in this case the wrong people to ask questions," Caroline interjected, she was not the only one in the room that saw the conclusion or at least thought it aloud.

"And that Chief, Sam, received some kind of information from Robert Morris," Nick removed himself from the room and went to the white boards that still lined the inner office, as he did this both Kristi and Caroline followed him closely with their eyes, they never left the room. Nick turned. His finger was pointed to a call that had been circled, a twenty minute call to Robert Morris's office.

"Right here, his last call was to Robert Morris's office and for almost twenty minutes, and it looks like what was said now lies with Sam Clark that is until Mr. Morris returns from his impromptu vacation?" Nick had reentered the meeting room. All of the other calls had been placed, some to Julie Charlton's old work, some to David's work, the other calls listed were to Robert Morris's office or to the office of the President and CEO of Reynolds-MacMillian.

"The time frame of those calls do not really work with the timeline of Mr. Thompson, that they were short calls. Although, he could have been on hold for a majority of that time?" That was the question to Nick, his gut told him that this MacMillian Character and his lawyer had something to do with it, he was not sure to what extent.

In the corner of the white board, he wrote the following:

>Marcus Reynolds, heart attack.
>Julie Charlton stabbed to death,
>David Charlton, heart attack.
>Sam Clark, heart attack
>Robert Morris (Vacation)?????

Nick immediately went to the song from that kids show, "One of these things do not look the other?"

Thirty Six

"Too bad Michael was so inexperienced with the technology?"

The two men arrived and parked the van on the street out of sight from the main house. This was Michael McKinley's first job of this kind. His usual function was for the clean-up side. Like this morning at the Schmidt mess. He was the body man. He removed bodies that could be linked back to his boss, who as far as he knew was Ian Thompson, and really nothing more. This morning's task was simple, scout the place, identify any others on the premises, and then subdue the target. His partner would do the actual wet work.

"Do you have a vehicle with you?" A voice asked through the intercom.

"Yes, I parked it on the street. I didn't know for sure..." He didn't finish his statement before he heard a buzz coming from the gate mechanism as it started to open. As he stepped through the small opening he noted that the gates were already closing.

The front door was opened by a lone man who stood and waited for Michael to walk up the long driveway.

"Mr. Griffin, it is a real honor to meet you sir." McKinley sounded respectful hiding any hint that he was there to help kill the retired Senator.

"What did you say your name was?" Tom asked.

"Michael McKinley, I work for Mr. Thompson. Didn't he did tell you in advance that I would be coming?"

"It was mentioned that someone was coming over. I was expecting Ian." Tom Griffin Senior was prepared for the worst, sending Ian could only mean one thing – he'd outlived his usefulness. This he was ready for. Sending this kid over hopefully meant there really were some things that needed signing.

"Mr. Thompson had other things to do I guess. May I come in?"

"Certainly, let's get to it. Are the papers ready?" asked Tom as he stepped back slightly allowing Michael to enter the foyer.

"Thank you Senator, give me a minute here."

He set the satchel down on the table nearest the door and pulled three or four manila folders from it and laid them to the right of the bag. He reached back in and pulled two more files from the satchel and set them to the left. Then he turned quickly with something in his hand. It was too late for Tom to respond. He was shocked to see the stun gun aimed directly at him.

McKinley depressed the button on the device. The electric arc between the two contacts looked powerful, powerful enough to make anyone totally submissive to the controller. Too bad Michael was so inexperienced with the technology.

Thirty Seven

"Let's get all loose ends finished by Monday,
including that new Chief of Police."

James wanted the meeting as early as
possible, having a get together at 8 am on a
Saturday was not that unusual, what was
discussed might have been.
"So, do we have an update on last evening?"
James asked.
"As we discussed, so that nothing comes back to
us. He has been removed, and according to our
people there was another individual that had to
be taken care of. The home was left as we
discussed, and presently they are in a certain
place, waiting my next call." Ian did not want to
give details, this time he had lied. He had no idea
of where they were. In-fact a search was currently
on-going. Iin a roundabout way, James not having
specific information on this was best.
"What's next?" James asked, already knowing the
answer.
"Next, taking care of you, getting you to where
you need to be." Ian answered back
unforgivingly.

"Well, I can go nowhere until after Monday, so I'm kind of stuck for a couple of days. You on the other hand, we can get you out of here quick."

"If you're here till Monday, that means I'm staying here to Monday as well. I will plan to leave on Monday night."

Both men paused,

"And you?"

"We will arrange for my departure on Tuesday, in the morning. Let's get all loose ends finished by Monday, including that new Chief of police, I do not like the idea that he could have the information as well."

"James, are you sure, he was fishing, like I said. Yet, maybe it is not worth it?"

"Do we have the people to do it?"

"Yes, Jimmie should be available, I will send him up with Martin." Ian stated it matter of fact like.

"Do we trust them?" James inquired.

"Jimmie, without a doubt, Martin, not so sure? I tell you what, Jimmie will take care of it he truly hates Tim Martin like you would not believe, even after Tim saved his life."

"Tell you what, one more call from the Chief up there and he signs his own death warrant, if he does not call us again then he lives, we take our chances."

Thirty Eight

"What do you mean it's not human blood?"

Deputy Sheriff Max Kinkler is a conscientious police officer. He has just one black mark against his record. It seems that of all the County's officer involved TAs, that is, Traffic Accidents, he was involved in most of them. He hadn't meant to earn the nickname of Wrecker, but it became appropriate. In his eighteen year career, Max had been involved in twelve TA's. Nine of them were single car crashes. After the usual internal investigations, Max had been cleared of fault each time. Only the department's insurance carrier had trouble finding the humor in this. A single car accident, usually the one driving is at fault?

But accident number thirteen proved to be different. Dispatch received the signal that the airbag in Car 43 had deployed. Men started converging at the dispatcher's desk to be first to hear yet another outrageous explanation.

The first thing they heard was Max saying "Oh, shit. I just hit the median to avoid hitting a pedestrian running at me from across the street. More soon...out."

"Max, are you okay? What's happening?" the dispatcher asked, trying not to laugh.

The woman continued running toward the patrol car while calling "Sir, sheriff. Follow me! Something terrible has happened!"

Max was struggling to climb out of the cruiser because of the airbag, and at the same time trying to calm this woman. "Ma'am, what are you doing? I almost hit you! If I hadn't swerved you would be the something terrible."

"Please, please, come with me! There is blood everywhere! Mr. Tom, he is not at home as he should be! His car is there, he should be home!" She said excitedly with a slight Hispanic accent. Then she began to repeat it. Max wanted to calm her but recognized her fear was hindering her communication skills.

"Ma'am, calm down and show me." Max worked to keep up as the woman took off like a bat out of hell down the block. "Tell me where we're heading," Max panted from behind while trying to thumb his shoulder radio to report.

"I'm running after the woman I swerved to avoid.
She said 'there is blood everywhere' so I'm
checking. Will get back to you from the scene,"
he huffed. Max knew they already had the GPS
location of the car, so assistance was being
dispatched.

Max could barely keep up. He was amazed
that her short legs could propel her so quickly.
She turned and ran through open outer gates of a
mansion. Although he had never been here
before, he had the distinct impression he
recognized this place.

Max took an extra stride so he could slow her
down by placing his hand on her shoulder. They
stopped just outside the huge double door
entryway into home. Both doors were standing
wide open.

Max took in a huge gulp of air and started to
question this woman. "Ma'am, do you live here?"
"No, no, please find out where..." Her voice
trailed off as she anxiously stared through the
doors.

Max tried to get her attention again.
"How do you know this place? Is anyone else in
there? Who lives here?" Max had to be quick
with the questions, her attention was obviously
elsewhere. She was tugging at his uniform trying
to urge him to enter the house.

"Sir, please find my boss, Mr. Griffin. Please, so much blood, something is wrong!"

Max was stunned when he heard the name. That's why he recognized this house. Magazines and newspapers had run photos of these grounds many times.

"You mean the former Senator Griffin lives here?" Max asked.

"Si, officer!"

Max walked her up to the porch, "You stay here! Understand? Stay right here!"

"Yes, I stay here." She started crying and continued to weep as she watched him enter the house. She did not move other than to slump down a little.

Max thumbed his radio and said, "Dispatch, we have a possible intruder at 1407 Wharton, the gates and front doors of the home are open. I'm entering the home now..."

"Max, give that address again."

"You heard me right the first time, the Griffin home."

"Back-up is on the way to your car's location, I'll steer them to you and start other notifications."

Max knew that meant it would soon be a circus around here, regardless of what was found.

Max drew his weapon and cautiously entered the house through the vast foyer. Max noted nothing unusual. He didn't notice the clear puddle he walked through. He turned right into a library. On the hardwood floor he saw an enormous pool of blood. He couldn't see a body anywhere in the room

Max methodically made sure that no one else was in the house and retraced his steps to the entryway. As he walked out two units were coming through the gate.

He asked that one team check the exterior and the other team secure the woman and start on her statement.

He turned around at a noise and could tell that the circus had begun.

"Wow, they made good time" Max muttered under his breath. The two officers interviewing the Senator's maid looked up and silently nodded in agreement.

"Captain, Deputy Kinkler, I was first on scene," Max introduced himself as his superior hurried up the drive.

"Deputy, tell me what we have here?" The Captain ordered succinctly.

Max quickly went over the details of the crash and following the hysterical woman to this house. Max led his captain into the library to show him the blood pool.

Within thirty minutes the street beyond the gates was overflowing with off duty detectives who wanted in on this, as well as agents from the FBI and the Secret Service. Everyone seemed to be jockeying for jurisdiction. Max wanted to leave to check on his unit and get it off the street, but being first on the scene had its responsibilities, so he stayed.

Once it was agreed that the Sheriff's Department would take the lead with the FBI and Secret Service assisting any way possible, they re-entered the bloody room. The blood pool was the only unusual thing in the room. Otherwise it was clean and orderly, not even a piece of paper out of place.

The CSU took samples of the blood. The senior CSI would perform the test itself,
"This was not human blood."
"What do you mean it is not human blood?" The Sheriff stated slightly louder than he should have. The attention now switched, all heads turned in his direction after the statement.

"Test it again, please." The Sheriff held his hand up, motioning for everyone to continue their duties. The FBI and Secret Service on station, avoided his signal all together, they would migrate next to the CSI that was performing the test, for the second time.

After a few minutes it would be announced again, "Not human blood, more than likely it is pigs blood."

After this one detail was relayed, the CSI team would go back and complete their duties at hand. They photographed and dusted the entire room for prints, as well as the front and back doors. The puddle that Max and others had walked through was finally noticed and a sample was taken as well. At first, the composition of the puddle was unknown, but as the smell suggested, it was soon identified as urine. Who had left it was unknown.

The secret Service Agent that was present, immediately was on the phone, he knew the history of the former Senator. He would get to the Senators son, before anyone, this would not stop the travel.

Since the sheriff was in charge, he had to make the necessary notifications. He hated this, especially over the phone. Even though he was unsure of what to report, he nevertheless requested that the Senator's son, a Senator himself, make the trip north. Tom Jr. was soon on his way.

While they waited for the son to arrive, they again searched the house and grounds and found nothing else. If the maid, Maria, hadn't returned on Saturday, the blood pool would not have been discovered until Monday.

Thirty Nine

"Dirty."

Nick Had not really left the previous evening. They had gone out to dinner, dry meat loaf always hits the spot. Their only choice was to get out of the office and go to the diner across the street, in Schrader you were limited to you options. It was, at first to be a group thing, one by one they would fall off. In the end it was just Nick and Kristi, the others had opted for a pizza delivery, in hindsight, they should of as well.

It was nice to just get out of the office for a little bit, the three beers that he had was pleasant as well. They would agree to not talk about the case, they did talk about other things, where she went to school, the LAPD mostly basic run of the mill stuff. For that time, just over an hour and a half, it was nice to take his mind off of what really bogged it down.

The next morning was slightly different, he knew that sometime today he would go see the mayor,

"That will be fun." He thought.

After dinner and a little more work, it dawned on him that Kristi would have a long drive back, and this late, so he suggested that he could take the couch of the motel that he was staying in and that she could have the bed.

"Oh, what a gentleman. I was going to get a room of my own, actually in the same hotel."

That was what happened, rooms were available so she ended up with a room two doors down. He would not have to sleep on the couch, that couch was uncomfortable to sit on, sleeping on it would be another venture into pain that he wanted to avoid.

They would both return at the same time, Nick giving Kristi a ride, which was fine with both of them. He immediately started in the conference room, she started on coffee.

"We're going to be going over everything we know and everything we're working on and that we are on the same page." Please ask questions whenever you notice something we may have missed or if you get lost."

Nick started with the "cold" case. That Charlton case and why he questioned if it was a murder suicide at all, had come full circle, he know had what many might consider the smoking gun, it was as clear as the nose on your face.

"So let's start in a timeline fashion, beginning to present, David and Julie Charlton had escaped the rat race so to speak, a week after her former husband died of a heart attack, they did not go to the funeral.

Instead they went to their cabin, located just a few miles away.

Her former husband, Marcus Reynolds had died outside of Boston, not too far from his company that he co-owned with James Bennett Macmillan. There is no reason why a cop from down there and a cop of investigators would put these two cases together, somehow Sam had. We will more than likely never know why?"

Nick paused, as he spoke he wrote on the board. Not much of the detail, just certain names.

"It is entirely plausible that a man could kill his wife, by many means, in many different ways. As the report, the file and even the pictures state, David Charlton stabbed his wife numerous times and then because of this, walked a few feet over and then collapsed and died of a heart attack."

"The Chief at the time considered this case closed and, besides adding some things to the file after they were returned, whether he had read them or not, nothing more was done."

"Everyone following so far?"

"So let's evaluate this," Nick showed the group two original photos from the scene, one was a David Charlton where he collapsed and died, this picture clearly showed both of his hands, there was no blood on them, at all. The second pictures showed both bodies, the bloody corpse of Julie with her husband lying some five or six feet away.

"How did he clean his hands, on what?" Nick asked? Kristi immediately jumped for the pictures, scanning both, back and forth.

"If you're going to stab someone that many times, you're going to get blood somewhere, especially on your own hands."

"Do you want to know what the final point is?" Nick asked, maybe it wasn't the final point.

"Julie Charlton, as per the coroner's report, was some 12 weeks pregnant."

The room gasped, Caroline was the first to make the connection.

"And if there was a baby clause, that 12 week old kid became a billionaire a little over a week before its own death, depending on when someone is alive etc...?"

"The husband kills the wife and baby, bye-bye baby clause." Kristi stated this, even though she knew, it still touched an element in her.

"Or so everyone thinks?" Nick easily retorted.

Next he covered Sam Clark's death which at first was thought to be from natural causes. He moved on to the vacationing Robert Morris, who was the Company's attorney and also James MacMillian's personal attorney, and his mistress Pamela McKnight who had mysteriously gone on vacation as well.

They all looked as if their heads were swimming with information overload. Where should they start asking questions? Since no one spoke up, Nick continued his recitation.

He talked about the band aid, the finger prints and now that they had the toxicology report, they could conclude that something was injected into Sam that killed him. Nick did not go into detail about the cocktail itself.

"So what kind of hard evidence do we have?" Zach asked this, out of all the people in the room it was Zach.

"Good question Zach, wish I had a better answer, not much evidence really."

Nick stood up again. "I think we should try to solve these deaths by first coming up with a plausible hypothesis while using mostly circumstantial evidence. My hypothesis starts in 2001 when Marcus Reynolds died in Boston from a heart attack. His will stated that if his ex-wife, Julie Charlton, had children or was pregnant, then her offspring would inherit his 50% of Reynolds/MacMillian.

If Julie had no children then Marcus's 50% would go to his partner, James MacMillian.

Julie died a week later apparently childless, but the autopsy report showed that she was indeed pregnant.

This fact was apparently kept quiet or just went through the worm hole. The case was closed here, so why bother, and now James MacMillian is the sole owner of the Company."

Sometimes overload is not noticed until it was too late. Nick, could see the swimming minds in front of him, he had other questions which he would ask on his own and then disseminate the information. Hopefully on Monday he would have more, there was only so much anyone could do with what seemed to be so little.

Nick was tired, he wanted many things. He would ponder what everyone else wanted, it was Saturday, "try and enjoy it?" He waved them all off. "Back to regular duties etcetera, this will all be here on Monday, sadly enough."

Nick retreated to the confines of his office, Kristi followed.

"Well, I thought that a night or at least the rest of the weekend would do everyone good, nothing is going to change over that time period don't you agree?"

Kristi just shook her head up and down, she agreed, she just wanted to hang out longer. The meat loaf sucked last night, the conversation was fantastic.

Out of the blue, he asked. "Would you like to go to dinner tonight, and no, not back to the diner?"

"Would love to." Her response came quick and sweet to his ears.

"I need to make a call, it is time to fish and see what was really going on."

Nick had an idea, why would they kill the chief, unless he had some outstanding proof that scared them, scared them enough to kill? He wanted the answer to this question, more so than anything else? They had called all the numbers, for the most part, some had rung through, no pick up no answering machine.

This time he called a number that was identical, yet just off one number, from the number of the President of Reynolds-MacMillian.

He got them both a cup of coffee then sat down. He pushed the nightly reports aside to help keep his mind clear. He glanced at his watch. Not too early, never too late, for this.

He dialed the number at hand, the one that he expected to go back to the secretary at Reynolds-MacMillian.

It rang three times before being answered. "This is James, what do you have for me Karl?" James MacMillian answered his own phone, he was not expecting the Chief that was for sure, at least not with this call.

"Don't hang up." Nick stated firmly and waited for a response.

"Okay, I won't hang up," a voice said.

"This is Nick Sheridan from the Schrader Maine police Department, is this James MacMillian?"

James pushed the alert under his desk. The 'System' silently linked into the call. Security had told him to stay on the line as long as possible. The 'System' had proven that short phone calls were the hardest to pinpoint with absolute accuracy.

"Yes this is James MacMIllian."

"I would like to discuss with you some of the same things you discussed with my former Partner and friend, I want the same that he wanted." Nick would avoid at all costs of saying anything specific, he did not want to give up his leverage so soon, and after all, this was still just a calculated bluff. Of course he wasn't even fully aware of his leverage.

"Let's talk about other things first. I know what happened to your former partner, and about the baby clause in his will which means I know why his ex-wife, who was pregnant, was killed."

"No, no, no, she was killed by her husband, don't try to put that on me. That was a terrible tragedy, I had nothing what so ever to do with that. Was not even in the states that happened when I was traveling." James struggled not to sound agitated. He knew he had to keep his caller on the line.

"Oh really? Are we talking about the same child who would have inherited Marcus Reynolds share of your Company instead of you?" Nick paused for effect. When there was none he went on. "Nothing to say? Maybe you want to talk about a dead Chief of Police that got too close and maybe asked for certain things, I want the same. It seems he gathered the sordid details with the help of your former attorney. I would ask the attorney about it, but he is on vacation?"

Nick paused, he really wanted a response, but again there was only silence. He thought he heard a slight groan when he mentioned Robert Morris but he couldn't be sure. Maybe it was just a chair scraping or something. "Still nothing to say? Let's move on then. Have you noticed a pattern? It seems that if you are a friend of James MacMillian your life expectancy is pretty short. At least presently."

"Same amount?" Now Nick was silent.

Nick quickly waved Kristi over, he held the phone out so that both may hear. Their heads at least a portion were touching each other.

"And, what assurances do I have?" James asked.

"Maybe I should ask that very question, with what happened to my former partner and friend."

"Let us just agree, since I'm in a trusting mood right now, I will get you what you want, as asked before. The drop will be in the same place..." James paused. Nick wondered what was the same place was?

"In the cabin?" James added.

"Yes, same place. When?"

"It will take me some time, how about Wednesday evening?"

"Fine by me." Nick answered after pausing himself slightly.

"You said, previously to my Lawyer that you had lost some files or they were stolen from you?"

"That is true."

"So how did you discover all of this?" James asked wondering aloud."

"Well, not all the files were taken, he has recordings as well." Purely a bluff, yet it sounded really good. Nick thought he was being recorded, so turnabout is fair play, sometimes.

"And you will destroy everything?" James asked.

"Yes, it will all go away."

"If this is an open investigation who is to say it will not be reopened by a co-worker or something to that affect?" James now inquired, in Nick's eyes this was a good question.

There was silence on the phone for a couple of seconds that seemed longer for both.

"Because there will be a fire, it will all go away. And then I will go away, in the middle of the night to a far off beach, without another word said."

"Wednesday night it is, are we done here?" James asked.

"Yes, were done."

The phone went dead, Nick hung it up and then he swiveled in his chair to look at Christi.

"How long had you suspected?" Kristi asked.

"Not that long, it could only be a few things. If Sam was really investigating, more than just he would know. Keeping something this close, well it leads me to believe that he was..." Nick stopped.

"Dirty?" Kristi almost finished his sentence without pause or hesitation.

Forty

"Point and pull the trigger."

Conoscalo was used to living frugally. Sure he had assets stashed around the country so that he had easy access to whatever he might need no matter where he was. But his home was very sparsely furnished. There were no personal items here. The authorities would never find a lead from anything kept here. He had not been back to that home for some time, he missed that, he wanted to rest.

Something told him that he was safe, that there was no need to worry about things, even he had left the door open to the room, just like normal people. He'd brought most of the medical supplies she would need from the 'hospital', they still sat in the two duffle bags that had been placed in the closet.

Again he had been told that she was severely malnourished. Through the IV drip they, the staff were doing what they could as quickly as they could, it was all a matter of time. The young woman began to stir. She groggily threw the covers back and staggered to her feet.

Conoscalo watched with concern, he raced to the other side and would arrive to catch her as she collapsed.

He tried to help her back to bed when she mumbled, "bathroom." He picked her up, and grabbed the IV stand and pushed it while he carried her. He was sure that staff could help with this, for her it seemed urgent he gently lowered her to the toilet. He turned his back, but he kept a close eye on her in the mirror. When she was finished he helped her wash up then led her back to bed. This time she walked, while leaning on him, he pushed the stand with one hand trying to hold a hand behind her in case she fell again.

She lay back with a sigh. He noted color coming back to her cheeks and was relieved that the drugs, whatever kind they were seemed to be wearing off.

Her eyes opened and actually began to focus when she quietly asked, "Was that you?"

Not knowing exactly what she meant, Conoscalo answered, "Yes, it was me." He liked hearing the sound of her voice.

"At Jackson's place? The warehouse?" She wanted to make sure he understood the question.

"Yes, there." Conoscalo answered openly even though in the back of his mind he was beginning to worry how much to share with her.

He knew that when she was better, she would have to go, hopefully not made to disappear, just go.

Of course, he had fantasies, but he had no idea what would really have to happen as she regained strength and realized where she was and who and what he was.   Would she cause trouble? How would he take care of that? Could he do it if it became necessary?

Maybe it wouldn't be needed. He knew that the godfather would have sent a cleanup crew into the warehouse to remove the bodies. Even if she went to the authorities to report the rape, she would have a hard time getting them to believe her about the circumstances.

Her voice brought him out of his reverie. "You're my angel, you know?" she whispered while smiling up at him.

"No, I'm no angel, I just did what anyone would in the same situation," Conoscalo replied quietly, smiling back at her.

"What's your name?" She asked.

"My name?" Conoscalo was surprised that he hadn't anticipated the question, he should have been better prepared.

He chuckled lightly, then smiled.

"I'm called Conoscalo." He didn't make eye contact with her.

"Cono...scalo?" She repeated hesitantly.

"Yes, Conoscalo." Her question had pleased him. It had been a long time since anyone had asked his name. It felt right to tell her what he considered his true name.

"Faith, would you tell me what you were doing in that place?"

He could see the indecision in her eyes, she seemed to want to answer, but then she stopped. "It's okay, I'm not judging you. I just want to know. Please tell me. I already know it wasn't for drugs." Conoscalo reached out for her left hand and slowly turned her palm up so they could see the inside of her elbow. No track marks scarred her bruised skin.

"Was it for the money?" Conoscalo asked softly.

"No, I was involved..." Faith silently wept and the tears started flowing, but she continued, "...I was involved with the wrong guy. And to settle a drug debt he sold me to Jackson. I was in no position to disagree. I had nowhere else to go." Conoscalo held up his hand, signaling her to stop her explanation.

"I don't want to hear any more, I don't need to know. Until the time comes when you want me to know more, just be comforted in knowing that none of those men will ever bother you again. Faith smiled up at her angel.

"I will go and arrange a wheel chair and a walker, please use them if you need to. I have to go in an hour or so..." Conoscalo paused, unsure of what to say.

"In the drawer next to the bed," He pointed to the drawer that stood next to the bathroom that she had just used.

"There is a weapon, have you ever fired a weapon?" Conoscalo asked.

"No," was her simple response. Conoscalo moved to the drawer and removed the weapon, and an envelope. He check that the weapon was loaded, it was a 22 caliber with a suppressor attached. One was in the chamber.

"If for some reason, someone comes here, which I highly doubt, yet just in case. For that piece of mind, point and pull the trigger, can you do that?" Conoscalo paused.

"If, again, for some reason you want to leave or have to, there is five thousand dollars in this envelope, take it with you for a fresh start." Conoscalo showed her the contents, he had already placed the weapon on her night stand, later she would move it to the drawer of that same night stand.

She looked at him for what seemed like a long minute, "What if I don't want to go, anywhere?"

Conoscalo smiled, "Then I will see you tomorrow."

Forty One

"I'm sure my old man will pop up sooner or later."

It had been a quick trip from D.C. to Boston. Even though Tom Jr. almost always flew commercial, this time he took his Secret Service's advice and flew up on a private Gulf Stream, to ensure his safe arrival and lessen the attention from the media. Of course the media found him anyway and were armed with more speculation than the authorities were willing to share.

So far the investigation had turned up a missing Senator, a blood pool of pig's blood no less, a puddle of urine, and a very scared maid. In the hours since the discovery of the blood pool, nothing new had been found. They knew the house alarm had not been tripped and they hadn't found any witnesses. Tom Jr. arrived expecting that more information had been uncovered while he was in the air, but all he heard was that they were doing everything they could.

"Senator Griffin, please follow me." His Secret Service detail got out of the SUV ahead of Tom Jr. who headed straight for the largest group of officers.

All they reported was that his father was missing and when they showed him the library Tom Jr. realized their concern to begin with. In the two hour trip up, they had discovered little else.

A man approached. "I'm Sheriff Morton, it is a pleasure to meet you Senator even under these circumstances. Let's sit down and I'll brief you on what we have so far."

After listening to the Sheriff's recital, Tom Jr. said "That's it, you have nothing more?" The Senator realized they were trying to placate him by saying they were doing all they could.

"Right sir, nothing more," the Sheriff replied as he dropped his eyes to his hands.

"And so where do we go from here?" The Senator asked.

"We have dusted for prints, we took samples of the blood for the lab, yet we are pretty assured that it is not human blood. We will conduct interviews with the rest of his staff."

"You could have told me all this over the phone." Tom Jr. wasn't sure whether to be angry for being pulled away from D.C. or to be thankful, at least for now, that his father may still be alive.

"Is there anything you need me to do now or should I just go out and face the media?"

"Senator, just between you and me, I would have preferred a phone call, too. But asking you here now was decided by people way above my pay grade."

The Senator nodded, "I see."

"Sheriff, this is my personal number, call when you have something." Tom pulled a single business card from his inner pocket and handed it to the Sheriff.

"Yes sir."

"I mean anything, no matter how small it might seem."

Tom Jr. walked away and reached into his pocket to get his cell phone. He quickly typed in a code and then dialed a number.

"Hello, can we finish this thing up this weekend? With everything going on at the moment it might be the best time, even while I'm in town." The Senator waited for the response.

"That is no problem, consider it done!" The voice on the line confirmed.

"Wait one..." The senator held out his index finger, slightly shaking it toward the oncoming men who were walking in his direction. With the same hand he covered the receiver. "Gentlemen, let me finish this call, then we can talk."

Sometimes the media acted like vultures. Pouncing on any fresh meat they found but this group was actually the FBI and Secret Service contingent, sometimes hard to tell the difference. They backed off deferentially as the Senator put the phone back up to his ear.

"Yes, that would be great." He paused, then quietly finished his thought,   "Yes, sir."

"In public, would be the best. As we had originally discussed?"

"Yes sir."

Tom placed the cell phone back into his pocket and looked directly at the men patiently waiting. "Yes gentlemen, how may I help you?" Being ever the politician, he extended his hand to shake theirs as if he was campaigning.

"Just wanted to discuss the matter with you. We will follow all leads, etcetera, we will work with the local Sheriff's office to ensure a sound investigation. Although it should be brought up, about past happenings and all..." The secret service agent speaking had paused. It is always a touchy subject, when trying to tell or remind one senator of his generally fucked up father, a former Senator and some of the things he pulled in the past.

Disappearances and similar incidents spotted the record of the Senator, although the common person or even the media would have fully grasped what the past had brought.

"No matter how things look, I'm sure my old man will pop up sooner or later with an extraordinary story that will explain all this. Yes, we all know about those past antics and all. I would suggest that you do not place too many man hours on this, he is off with a flavor of the month or something."

"Just for the record, the last time you spoke?"

"Yesterday, around noon or so. I would have to check the records, around noon."

"Yes sir, we understand." Both men walked away, they too, as had many others in that room had wasted a good portion of a nice day.

Without further discussion he merely turned and headed toward the SUV with his security detail. The fanfare and shouts were about to start as they drove toward the gates where the media had been impatiently waiting, cameras and microphones at the ready. Because the car windows were rolled up, they wouldn't get a statement from the usually talkative Senator.

Forty Two

"It had been a while since she had back to backs
as she called it."

Maggie had never received her orders
directly, and this job was no exception.   She
knew what he wanted and the timeframe in which
it needed to be accomplished. Yesterday even
Maggie had been within ten feet of the target, but
because the target was with people who knew
her, Maggie had to back off.

On this Saturday evening Maggie followed her
mark going out again. She would receive the call
to go forward with action, even though she might
have jumped the plan the day before without the
forward notice. She liked to get close prior to the
act, just to get the particulars if it was to be a
forward action plan.

For Maggie, it was something to be in close
proximity of her next victim, as if she would lean
over and inform them, in a slight whisper
"Tomorrow, I will kill you." It did not happen like
that, nor could it ever really. She did like to get
close. Although Maggie couldn't understand why
some people loved to shop, she had learned to
blend in with them and not be noticed.

Maggie wore uncomfortable zip up vinyl boots, a plaid skirt, white blouse, and an expensive but worn jacket. She carried an oversize white canvas shoulder bag with heavy duty straps to allow for the weighty contents she always had near.

This was different from the previous evening. It had been a while since she had back to backs, as she called it.

Maggie's hair had been dyed the previous week which had faded only a little, not that anyone noticed or cared. Her sunglasses were the darkest kind but fashionable and resembled the ones worn by the woman who was now only ten paces ahead.

Maggie appeared to be fumbling around in her bag but she was actually assembling the device she planned to use. The device was about six inches in length. It had a three inch screwdriver-like handle which contained a CO_2 cartridge to power it, similar to a pellet gun. The other three inches was a small, hollow ice pick like extension which protruded from the handle.

Maggie followed her target out a second store. The target now held two shopping bags with store logos emblazoned on each side, proclaiming to all where she had been today.

Maggie walked faster to match her stride. Five paces and their gaits matched. As the target raised her right arm to hail a taxi, Maggie took a step forward and another to the side making it look like she was trying to avoid a collision. Maggie placed her left hand behind the woman's right shoulder for balance. The pssst sound wasn't heard by any passersby as the device penetrated cloth and punctured skin. The small metal poison projectile killed her almost immediately by passing through her lung and driving straight into her heart where the Ketamine and Potassium Chloride were released. Ketamine is a tranquilizer used on large animals and the Potassium Chloride is the drug of choice for death row inmates that have run out of time, fast acting and supposedly painless.

Maggie quickly pulled the device away from the woman and returned it to her bag as she caught her falling body and carried her toward a store front bench. Olivia Morehead didn't cry out in pain or even move under her own power while Maggie was putting her on the bench.

In fact, she never felt anything again. This was her final resting place. Maggie propped her up while discreetly taking her purse and shopping bags making sure to delay the identification of the victim. Olivia slumped but it took another fifteen minutes before anyone noticed that a woman had fallen from the bench. Finally someone called 911.

Maggie was long gone.

Later that evening the fire department responded to the largest fire they'd seen in some time. It gutted an entire building. Faulty wiring would be the cause, the offices below hers was a total loss, little could be salvaged from most of the offices but absolutely nothing was left of the office of Olivia Morehead, Therapist.

Forty Three

"The balls, asked for the same amount as the
other guy."

This meeting between the two was just a
quick phone call, no one's name would be said,
and more importantly no key words were uttered.
The everyday verbiage was used.
"It's a go?"
"Do it,"
"The balls, asked for the same amount as the
other guy."
"Did not see that coming."
"Nor did I....."
"Make sure we keep that back door open, on the
system." James asked that to make sure it was
not being dismantled as well.
"Working on it now, with the protocols."
"Keep them for yourself, you never know when it
could come in handy, you know what I mean."
"I do, and thank you for that."
The 'System,' labeled such by the team of
scientists, technicians and all around nerds who
had perfected it through years of covert research
within Reynolds-MacMillian.

When activated the 'System' could locate within ten feet the source of any phone call in the world, whether it was a land line or cellular signal. The Research and Development funding for this project was well concealed. Everyone knew its use would be considered an invasion of privacy.

Then the President signed an executive order which made the use of the 'System' practically legal, and necessary. Being able to pinpoint the location of callers making terrorism plans anywhere in the world could protect property and might save hundreds of thousands of lives. The 'System' would go on to be combined with the ever expanding satellite systems and GPS. This gave the controllers of the 'System' an advantage.

This was how the original contract proposal had been presented to the government. As the 'System' was perfected, the ideologies of those that manned the controls changed. James MacMillian, along with several of his friends, began to discuss how useful it might be if used privately. Once the technology caught up with the idea, the 'System' was put under the jurisdiction of the U.S. government. The funding to maintain and then enhance it was paid through untraceable sources.

When the NSA originally looked into the idea, and its promising prospects in the war against terrorism, they wanted it for their exclusive use.

Congress had other ideas. The Democrats wanted to set up yet another Department which would answer only to the Clandestine Services Unit. Of course the Republicans rejected this idea easily by having the majority vote in Congress at the time.

The President decided to set up an Agency under the Department of Defense, thus A-11 became a reality. The man responsible for the idea would be brought on board, regardless of the baggage he carried.

As the NSA worked with the originator of the system to protect and perfect it, Reynolds-MacMillian was doing the same, without officials orders or for that fact any idea from any outside source. The team the James MacMillian had designated to covertly enhance and then start-up the system was even placed into other buildings, with the Reynolds name attached. For the rest of the team, they would be systematically folded into the NSA program. For the ordinary American and even those with especially high clearances, the 'System' would be nothing more than science fiction. Only a handful of people knew what had been created, and what it could do.

Reynolds-MacMillian had essentially cloned the program, bad thing about clones, sometime they get replicated. Others were using the system as well, it seemed as if it was the best new toy out there, and every little boy had to have it.

Because the project was no longer with Reynolds-MacMillian, neither was the money that came with the contracts, James had to find other ways of making money. Once the system was up and running, even though they had not completely perfected like the A-11 and one other group, it still was affective. And then the money started to roll in.

Forty Four

"The second, third, fourth, fifth and sixth would
be in the groin."

Atlantic City seemed never to change, new
casinos and hotels would go up and old ones
would come down. It was one way to reinvent or
maybe in this case cover over the actual Atlantic
City. Conoscalo had never really been a fan of the
City itself, he did like that fact that things were
accessible, with his line of work it was nice to
have a lax feeling of law enforcement, it was a
little different on the boardwalk near the casinos,
too many cameras, too many watching eyes.
Away from the casinos and some of the more
popular touristy attractions, life was easy his life
anyway.

It would be a consensus that most that all
U.S. Senators active or retired would have some
kind of continuing or ongoing Secret Service
Protection. Conoscalo thought the same, until he
had opened the manila envelope, he would have
bet the farm that this was an unattainable goal.

He would have no time to investigate, this time unlike many others in the past, he could not sit and watch. His usual routine would be to see the target and to figure the best place for the hit. Because of time constraints, this time he would have to rely on his 'Father'.

The manila envelope had precise times, locations and possibilities. The writer as Conoscalo noticed seemed to have a great amount of inside information. The first hit would be public, Conoscalo would try to make it as quiet and private as possible, for obvious reasons, the second would be more difficult although secluded.

The night came quickly for Conoscalo and just as the envelope of information had stated, target number one was dressed in a plaid worn down jacket with an angler's type of hat, the individual was wearing a wig of a different color, according to the envelope. The Target had just left a back room poker game. He entered the bar through the seldom used back door. The bar was a quiet bar, dimly lit, a place where no one made eye contact, nobody wanted to make eye contact for fear of what could happen or just the fact that they may be to inebriated too do so.

Senator Ben Whitefield was a Republican from Utah. He loved Atlantic City.

He had fallen in love with this city. It was very different from his usual surroundings. In his home state of Utah, he was known far and wide.

Getting into a cash game was even more difficult, and even the short drive to Vegas could be trouble, he was easy to follow.

Going to Atlantic City, in those off weekends to spend time with a fellow Senator, for this conference or for that reason became easy.

He had been known to go to bed early, which was not entirely untrue, depending on what you call early. This worked well for the senator, when he wanted to elude his detail. Having a set pattern, going to bed, would be his go to idea. Leaving his room, as in the past was just as easy, give them a half hour and they were where ever they were, just not around him anymore. His proclivities would ultimately begin his demise.

He took a seat in the bar that he enjoyed, tonight had been a good night for cards and when he left the back room, he left with the money that he had entered with and twenty thousand extra.

Ben enjoyed his beer, it was a domestic, which was not what he preferred but as he said when in Rome, you drink what they drink or at least what they have. When his beer was finished he left the same way he came, that would be his second mistake, his first was that he was out.

He walked down the alley way and when he heard what sounded like footsteps behind him he turned, it was nothing, when he turned back to begin walking again it became something.

Conoscalo looked at his watch, he gently pressed the barrel of the gun against the junior Senator from Utah's temple, Ben Whitefield did not have time to react or even call out, the bullet entered his head and his body dropped to the ground.

Conoscalo acted quickly, he did not want other casualties or eyes to descend upon his actions.

He removed the man's watch, wedding band and his Utah State graduation ring, he removed the money from the inner part of his jacket and his billfold he took his key card also.

When he stepped away from the body he glanced down at his watch, the whole process took a minute and fifteen seconds. Conoscalo walked away from the body he dropped the wedding band, then the class ring, he removed all the money from the billfold and then threw it onto an overhang, he wanted the cops to look prior to finding that relic, for it might make some poor detective's day catching this case.

When he was three blocks over from the first incident he flagged down a cab and headed to the West Side Motel. The second portion of his night would be more difficult, this he knew for sure.

For the past ten years Senator Tyler Hansford was on the straight and narrow, there had been some discussions in the past about his transgressions, for what he liked and as he said "could not live without."

The family, with their money had covered over the past. Very few knew what really had happened, a fortune had literally dropped on those that had been intertwined with his desires, whether they had wanted it or not. Luckily, both for the Senator or the victims, depending on your views and morals, more money was thrown at the families and the "little" issues as one of his lawyers had argued went away.

When Tyler's Father died three years ago, he started back just like old times, within the walls of therapy he had stated that it was a disease, that his current wife regardless of her beauty could not help him with his desires. Tyler liked hitting from both sides of the plate, frankly speaking the younger the better, boy or girl it did not matter. As disgusting as that was to most, he had other hobbies, and therefore the need to leave his properly trimmed New Jersey home, elude his protective detail and sit in with all his pleasures at the little West Side Motel, which was for all intents and purposes on the south side.

After reading the packet of information, Conoscalo had hoped that a child, male or female, would not be there. He tried to conclude that he could let someone walk away.

Conoscalo could persuade them, to never mention the transgression and he could allow this because of the circumstances involved.

He knew that would never happen, for he would have to kill all the occupants of that room. Although, he had let someone go, she was presently at a facility recovering, could he do this twice in a week?

The room that Senator occupied was in the back of the motel, as the truth would have it, he owned this hotel. It was off the books and had not yet been discovered. It would not last like that much longer. Tyler Hansford's room that he was currently enjoying his pleasures in was never rented to another soul for it was "paid" on a permanent basis.

Conoscalo had decided that he would just kick in the door, he had every intention to do just that when he walked up to room 8 at the West Side Motel, he glanced at his watch and at about the same time the door opened. When a young woman started to exit, he was relieved, Conoscalo forced the girl back into the room, locked the door behind them. His weapon with suppressor, the same one that he had just used pointed simply at her forehead. His other hand had one finger up pressed to his lips. It was the international sign of "keep your fucking mouth shut or I will kill you." This time it meant that and there would be no further explanation for it. Sad point about all this was that he would kill her anyway it was just in his best interest to keep in her good graces at this time.

"Sit down on the bed," Conoscalo stated quietly.

The young woman did just that with no sound what so ever, her focus was clearly on the gun still pointed toward her multi colored hair. When he turned down the television, he could clearly hear water running from what he presumed to be the bathroom.

"Is the man in there," Conoscalo asked. Again, the young woman said nothing, this time she just nodded.

"Is he alone," he asked. Again, she nodded yes, the young woman, as he thought was of legal age, not much more. He would guess later that she was maybe twenty-two and definitely, a professional that meant her significant other or just maybe her pimp would come looking if he was not already waiting outside. Conoscalo would deal with that later, if it was necessary.

"Do not move," Conoscalo stated, again pressing his finger to his lips.

He walked to the door of the bathroom and opened it, remarkably the water shut off at the same time, the curtain opened and a man brought his head out from behind the shower curtain, again there was not time. The first bullet entered his forehead, the second, third, fourth, fifth and sixth would be in the groin. That was how it needed to be, that was how the paperwork in the manila envelope had it.

When Conoscalo exited the bathroom, the young woman was visibly shaken, she was not crying, just rocking a little with her head down. Conoscalo removed the man's wallet, ring and watch, for he would do the same as he just had with the other man's personal items.

For a minute, he wanted it to be different, for deep down inside he had a heart. Conoscalo thought what it would take, right now, she was scared, scared to death and would do anything. That feeling for her would go away in time, and then what. Who knew where she had been previously or more importantly with whom, and then when you figure in her prints and DNA. After spending thirty seconds of thought upon the idea he raised the weapon to her forehead and pulled the trigger, she fell back onto the bed.

After all, he had done the right thing. He had done, just like he had in the past, another time and he would remember it differently, how he should have shown some consideration, some idealism to be different. For he had the control, and only he could change what had been or even what should be, later in life, he might look differently at this. Now was not the near future, he had other things to do.

He placed the weapon on the bed, neatly besides the person who lay bleeding. Conoscalo unlocked the door and quietly closed it behind him. When he walked from the room, he walked with his head down, just in case. The ring, watch and wallet became easy to dispose of as he continued to walk.

Conoscalo wanted to exit from the area quickly, he figured that he had no idea when discoveries would be made and when the first would be realized it could become a circus, no actually he knew it would become a circus, and as this played out Conoscalo would be correct.

Forty Five

"Sir, it wasn't a heart attack?"

Senator Griffin decided some time ago to spend this weekend at his Capitol Hill office. Of course there was that, what is now labeled by the Senator himself, the unnecessary flight to his home town because of the "disappearance" of his father? Senator Griffin's father had pulled loosely veiled and more than likely labeled stupid stunts previously. These past events, were more of the same, just as this one resembled.

Finding no real reason to return to his home state just to sooth the local voting populace. He did have an enormous work load and wanted to get some of the mundane items clear prior to all the holidays. He was not alone in this, some others of both parties had stayed for the same reason.

He had been invited to go to Atlantic City to participate in what was called by the media a good surrounding of both parties to hash out what really needed to be done in the Senate.

The Senator had labeled this as a boondoggle and nothing more. Two of his friends, both senators had decided to go to some local meetings in the Atlantic City area.

They were both coming back and had planned for a nice dinner together on Sunday evening.

It had been a while since he and his friends had gotten together as a group, most would find out by mid-day Sunday that they still might have that dinner, just a few of them would not be there.

Tom Griffin was actually in a meeting when the Secret Service, the actual lead agent for his security detail, came in, pulled him off to the side and informed him that Senator Ben Whitefield had died.

"Dead, what do you mean dead? I know he was in Atlantic City. They had meetings scheduled for today. Poor Bastard, I told him if he did not take care of himself that heart was going to go."

"Sir, it wasn't a heart attack," the agent said.

"Then what," he replied.

"The Senator was found in a back alley, not the best part of town. He had been mugged,"

"Mugged, what about his security detail," Senator Griffin replied acting had never been one of his strong points. He hoped that through the years he had gotten better. His acting would have to be good, he too had sometimes lead his detail in one direction when he was headed into another. It was a taboo subject for many reasons, regardless of what might have transpired.
"He somehow eluded or ditched the team, they had no idea he was even gone until seven this morning."

"The body had been found in that alley around two thirty in the morning, no wallet, no I.D. and he was wearing a wig," the agent had grown more solemn in his recollection of the events, as they had been passed to him.
"Does his family know I should call Mary? We were friends, I just feel that I should do something," The Senator had taken a seat, everyone else that had been in the meeting was waiting in the hallway. He removed his cell phone from his jacket pocket and called his other friend. Some would even say his best friend.
When the call went to voicemail, he assumed that Tyler was dealing with the same stuff and he would just call him back.

"Sir, this issue cannot be discussed with anyone at this time," the agent said this with much authority.

"I was Calling Senator Hansford, no answer. Probably dealing with the same stuff," the Senator returned to his seat, he wanted to be busy with something he was just not sure what that something was. The secret service agent had not and would not leave his side, Tom figured that would be the case, so much so that he figured someone would more than likely be sleeping with him. He chuckled to himself and wandered if the agent would be cute, it was not the proper time to laugh, and if Ben were here, he would be saying the same stuff.

It had only been a few minutes, he figured that he was in some kind of lockdown until the threat or all the ideas of a threat had been ran through, when three more secret Service agents came into the room. He did not recognize the other men, he thought that he knew everyone, with all his other duties he did see many faces.

"Senator, this is Agent McCall he is the lead agent in our Investigative Division," Agent McCall shook the Senator's hand after he stood up.

"Sir, we would like to ask you some question. We would like to get them out of the way the sooner the better."

"Sure, whatever is needed to help," the Senator responded with ease for he too wanted to get past this.

"When was the last time you spoke to Senator Whitefield?"

"Yesterday morning, he called me and I had to call him back a few minutes later, I missed the first call,"

"Did he say anything about his intentions in Atlantic City, where he was going with whom?"

"No, just which they were going to have dinner, early and he hoped to get some gambling in,"

"Dinner with whom,"

"He just said they, I figured he meant Tyler,"

Tom's mind was racing, not that he was worried. He did not want to miss anything, as it would work out, he did not have much information to provide.

"Senator Hansford,"

"Yes, Senator Hansford."

The agent during the questions had taken a seat across from the Senator, the two agents that had walked in with him. They took seats on each side. Those agents furiously wrote down all utterances, the Senator figured that somewhere a tape recorder was recording everything, just in case.

"Speaking of Senator Hansford, when was the last time you spoke with him?"

"Sometime yesterday afternoon, my secretary would have the exact time. I also tried to call last night, got his voicemail and then I just tried this morning, say ten minutes ago, voicemail," the Senator wondered what this was about, so he asked the obvious question or at least it was obvious to him.

"Do you think that Tyler, Senator Hansford had something to do with Ben's death," the Senator asked.

"No, we do not think that Senator Hansford was involved in the death, problem is we cannot seem to locate Senator Hansford," the agent looked as if he had lost or as the Secret Service was famous for saying, misplaced the Senator.

"What do you mean? They both eluded the Secret Service Protection details. Heads are going to roll aren't they Agent McCall," the Senator stood up. "So what exactly happened to Senator Whitefield?"

The agent started and left no detail out, he told the sitting Senator everything the Secret Service or what he at least knew. Sadly enough, when Agent McCall thought that he finished and was indeed about to leave the small conference room that they had been debriefing or possible interrogating the young Senator in, the call came through.

"They found Senator Hansford, holy shit," the phone almost dropped from his hands, again the agent had a ghastly white color on his face.

"What's wrong?"

This time the agent sat down, "They found Tyler Hansford, shot to death, once in the head, several times in the groin. In a rundown hotel on the lower south side of town, they also found a dead woman with him."

"Who was the woman?"

"They will call back in a few minutes, obviously extremely early with this situation."

"Sir, Senator Griffin, we need to get you back to your office. Please follow us, and Sir, this information is not entirely public," the lead agent of his Security detail would ensure that nothing happened to his charge.

He was hurried through the corridors deep under the rotunda and then finally to his office, he was a little amazed at all the people that had converged around the T.V. that were set up throughout the offices, it almost reminded him of the last election.

"Senator, what is going on? The Capital and surrounding buildings are on lockdown, and we have no cell coverage. I can't make a call and have yet to receive one," the Chief of Staff said this in almost a disbelief state of mind.

"Agent McCall just received a cell call, not twenty minutes ago," Tom Griffin reached for his phone and dialed his speed-dialed number twelve, his Chief of Staff. When he pressed the buttons on the phone, he did this as if to show that he could make a call.

His lead agent walked up and whispered in his ear, "It won't go through. The city is pretty much in lock down, nothing can get through. It's bad, just ride this out, we will try to get you any information that you need."

The Senator changed directions, "I'm sure it's just a glitch, let's try and get some things done, I will need a response for these heinous actions, Mike who is around today. Let's see if we can graph a response and statement. We also need to get something to the Whitefield and Hansford families." All the while, he removed the cell phone from his hand, turned it off and placed it back into his inner pocket.

Sometimes the calming voice of their leader could change their actions and inner thoughts, for some they started to do work that they would have been doing all along. Others started to become reactive to what had happened. The time to be proactive had passed, it was time to see the different light, and maybe they would still be around to see it.

Forty Six

"They won't bother you anymore?"

The trip back was not eventful. He had left
Atlantic City by train, as had many others he had
waited for a repair and then a new train, he left at
almost eight in the morning some two hours late
to the other early Sunday morning travelers, for
Conoscalo he had nothing but time. He was in a
hurry of sorts, first off it was good to get out of
town, prior to all the excitement that would start
soon enough.

Conoscalo had other reasons to get back, he
had left her in good hands, yet still he felt
something by not being there for her in this time
of her recovery. His attachment had become
uncanny, especially for someone who was not a
regular at getting attached to anything. Let alone
something who breaths.

This situation had connected to his soul, he
truly believed that, somehow that switch came
on. The killing of the young woman touched him
even more, more so than any other recent death
by his hand.

He wished he could have saved her somehow, if he had been there three minutes later, she would have been gone.

He could have told her that he was going to knock her out and that if she ever said a word, he would find out. And, by the way that would not be good for her, he could have. This time as with many of the past he took his easiest way with the situation and ended it all there.

He could think that he was saving her, by some means, killing her did remove her from what could be a messed up life with little expectations for a future. It did not matter what he thought or rationalized at present, she was dead. He did not need to worry about that loose end, ever again. He closed his eyes again, trying to sleep or act as many others on the train had, by dozing in the early morning hours.

No sooner would he close those eyes and he would see, clear as day, the eyes of the strawberry blonde that he now called by her name, Faith. He remembered those eyes, not when he first picked her up, her eyes were closed then. They were open in the vehicle as he moved her. There was a clear line of sight, from him to the rear view mirror to those eyes. They seemed not to blink, nor shed a tear,

"I'm sure she has shed many tears. This girl was sold?"

"For what?" Conoscalo said this to himself, accentuating "for what?"

He wanted to go after the individual who sold her, actually he wanted her to make a list he would do the rest. That was not practical, what was practical was asking if he could take down one Ian Thompson, he could ask that. With what he presently knew, Ian was key, he knew of the team that was at Jacksons, he needed to take care of the one called Jimmie, who obviously has more than one life after what happened at that house.

He needed to make that happen, he needed to be able to tell her that these people will not harm her ever again. This would not be a word play "They won't bother you anymore," he needed for it to be true, and absolute.

Even though he wanted to go see her, he would not. He would make the contact to ask, that message would be relayed and soon he would hear if he could with permission, or if he just would regardless of their position.

Forty Seven

"Godfather, may I have a minute. Godfather just a little time?"

Through the years things change. Everything changes. Some subtly, some with a name change or a way of doing business, the mob, mafia, or whatever slang term that you wanted to use to describe the Family, well they changed also. A few within the confines of the family did not want to change, maybe it was the Sicilian blood, and maybe it was just stupidity. They thought that the FBI and any and all other agencies that had descended upon them would go away with time. The FBI and others would get a little here and there, never really that much, with all things considered. Too many within, that was a good assumption, it was the sixties after all and in time that would change.

A few, and in the beginning it was not every faction, thought that being legit was the way to go, to totally shield how they had made the money, just to make sure that it had been properly and thoroughly washed.

Through the years they did just that, they would start with small business, with regular people working within the confines of that business.

There would be no kneecapping at these places, no strong-arming, and when the mafia boys came around to collect the usual monies they would be paid, no questions asked. As time went on, a few stores became a dozen, a dozen became a hundred and then a select few had become legit. As you know the Mafia was still active, there was a godfather or what at least the modern day media would suggest as the godfather, and for every family leader there were also family leaders that were not public, if they walked past us today, you would not or could not even recognize who they were.

That was the whole idea of it, a legitimized mafia, a certain Godfather had that dream, he never seen it fully into fruition. He had picked the new leader, the one that would take it to the next level, his successor.

When they met, it was not like a gathering of overweight men, placing a ring or watch on a platter, for that was the old days and for the movies.

It was a high tech initiative with no faces shown and voices that were altered. For their system, this new Mafia to work, the secrecy of its members would be unprecedented. They had no catchy names, and since the leaders, the people that made the decisions had never met, they had no secret handshake or group rings.

The Godfather was not new at this. He had been controlling the seven men for some time.

They seven men had never seen him, they knew nothing except that he controlled them, the money was very nice for all, and as long as the money was nice, the questions were few. Unlike his predecessor who knew these people, who had interacted with them for years, he was not. In life, things are not always, as they seem. The piece of mind given by the previous Godfather enlisted the men to follow the new person. The handpicked one, as he called himself.
For the future, for the family to work, the secrecy would be its guardian.

When it first started, it was a makeshift society at best. There was not a meeting schedule or anything that you could place on your refrigerator to remind of where you needed to be. You, however, would receive a call, from the usual throwaway phone.

The call would never be to the primary to the person that needed to attend. A Captain or even a lieutenant would receive the call, and it would go from there. There were many rules, when contact could be made, and by whom, for a secret society or at least one that constantly reminded itself to be a secret society, it had some holes.

With the new Godfather, things changed, he instituted the correct way to contact the individuals and gave the individuals a way to contact him.

He provided the equipment for a price and only with that equipment could you make contact, he started a society within. As for the Godfather only eight people knew who he was, it was hard to believe even for him, and deep down inside he knew his secret would be out. It would be historic on many occasions. Over the course of the next few weeks, as it would work out, others would know his identity as well. Some of these individuals would still breathe and move about like they had previously, other would just no longer breath.

One day it would all be for not, of the eight people who knew of his identity, three of those individuals were dead, not by his own hand or by his order. Besides himself he had four individuals that worked directly for him, very loyal employees, these employees were much like that of the old mafia, they knew what would happen if they talked, to anyone. The fear of that was not the reason for their loyalty, their loyalty was sheer greed and the possibilities to do things that some only fantasize about.

To say that this new Godfather enjoyed this, enjoyed the power would be an understatement. He relished the fact that he has a hired killer to use for anything, he relished the fact that no one was the wiser as to what he did.

He had discussed with his loyal second in charge, earlier in the day that a meeting of the Family would be the best considering everything that had been going on.

For his number two, as he had referred to the man after seeing and even drawing some comparisons to a popular movie that had come out, that was all that needed to be said. By the early afternoon, the meeting was set they would meet at eight in the evening.

He could never use his own home it would easily draw too much attention, his day job was demanding, factor in that of the neighbors and it made it just impossible. When correspondence or meetings like this became necessary, it was an easy transfer. Years before, many years before some thought during the times of prohibition a secret passage was made, for almost 70 years it laid dormant. When discovered it easily fit into the new man's agenda, after all with a secret society a secret passageway was cool.

He transferred over, this night was easier than previous times, and when he sat down the meeting began. They did not need introductions, with a simple, "Gentlemen," the meeting started. A few of the men proclaimed, "Sir," while a few others said "Godfather," rather exuberantly.

"Due to the recent events in Atlantic City, I thought that a meet would be necessary."

"Maybe for my own piece of mind, I know that many of you still dabble in the old ways, after all it is easy money to augment. In addition, as the rules go, this is your choice. I would just like to ask the question, did anyone okay this, for any reason," He stopped short.

These men had been around the block they knew what the consequences could be. He wanted to enforce or even remind his 'Family' that this, those actions would not help the 'Family', at least he could see no justification for it.

"Any comments, ideas," he asked.

Silence was a funny thing. It meant either someone's guilt or the fact that someone wanted to try to answer the question, they were just not sure of how they could, without repercussions. "Godfather, this is my area, I've lived my whole life here. It is my home. I did not order any of this, and with what has come out in the public today the same person did this to both Senators, same weapon. This has all the markings of a hit, yes I know, I did not and would not order this without prior consultation," one of the 'Family' members at least sounded to be in anguish with his statements.

"Yes, I do believe that to be true, that this order did not come from, or for that fact that anyone involved is a part of the 'Family'."

"We still may need to control what is publicly stated, sometimes even we need to be a little proactive as to what the facts may be," The Godfather said this and was silent, there were no other sounds that were made, until he added "That's why, gentlemen, I need your assistance, your guidance as to what we should do next. This will come toward the 'Family' in some way and we need to direct it elsewhere."

The Godfather could not hear what the other men were saying all he heard was silence. He figured that a few would be more than surprised that a man who had lead with a heavy hand for so long was now inquiring as to their help.

"Godfather, do we really need to do anything?" A member from the west coast asked.

Another one of the seven reiterated the same words, and if they did something and it was wrong, it could affect them worse.

"That's true gentlemen, what if it is wrong, and it comes back, maybe not to us, but to other hard working members of our extended family?" He asked and with that once again there was silence.

"What I will suggest is that we, through legitimate legal channels, through our media friends have them do our dirty work and pose questions like who would benefit."

"They could attack the Senate records of each and meet on common ground, something that they were both a part of." The Godfather said it, the bait was there, now how long he thought, how long would it take for one of the members to pick it up.

Silence ensued again.

"They both were a part of a vote. They both switched their votes at the last minute, so it was reported. Although that could hurt our overall goals," a man said.

The conversation ensued, so much so that on several occasions he had to ask them all to slow down and that everyone would have a chance to speak their minds. All members of the 'Family' gathering had spoken out but one, "Godfather, may I have a minute, Godfather just a little time."

"Let's let our Midwest member speak out," the Godfather said and when he did, silence ensued once again.

"Godfather, thank you, I've seen this argument from many sides. Yes, it is true we need something to shield us.

It is a practical idea to have questions asked about that vote, why did they switch at the last minute.

After all, we all know how hard it is to break into the Defense Contracting business. We have tried for a few years now to purchase the right company.

This could hurt us, this new government way of doing business, with all the oversight," the man stopped short of finishing.

"You are correct, it could hurt us, it could, however, draw down the price of the company and, therefore, make it better, much better," another man said.

The Godfather said nothing, he did not need to. The conversation and the men conducting it had done all the work, or at least they thought they had. Moreover, when they finished conversing, one of the men asked what he thought,

"There is intelligence beyond all, so if I am to understand, we want our direction to go toward what that vote consisted of, that they changed for a reason to be against their own party, the republicans, and to assist the other party and that someone had these two individuals killed because of it."

All men agreed that should be the action, they left it in the trusting hands of their Godfather. He closed the meeting with salutations to all, or as he said, "Continued health and wealth to all."

As he was ready to return to his daily mundane life, his last offering to his 'number two' would be to contact their favorite person at the Times, it needed to be a reliable source, he did not care what was written.

As long as the contents were clear that the direction of any further investigation should point toward all Defense Contractors' companies, possibly one in particular.

Forty Eight

"In these fantasies, both followed in their Father's footsteps."

Robbie was surprised the day he received the acceptance letter. His step-father was delighted, his Mother not so much. The original agreement with Robbie's father had warned her, but nothing could actually prepare her for this day. She had never been allowed to discuss any part of this agreement with her new husband, or for that fact anyone. That had been the price for her freedom.

The Acceptance by Harvard was far more than Robbie had dared hope. Of course he had applied there, but without expecting even an acknowledgement.

His friends and school mates applied to as many colleges as they had postage. Most kids either wanted to be with their high school chums or their high school love. Robbie fell into another category, few friends, no love and no earthly idea of what he really wanted to do, with help he had finally concluded that his future should be in the business category.

Harvard certainly fell into that category. Did this surprise acceptance make him curious about the how's of it all, never gave it a second thought. Robbie Robertson was Harvard bound.

Robbie's luck continue. The admissions people deemed it a coincidence, after all someone had to be assigned that room. His east coast roommate was not as surprised as to his new surroundings. Robbie (his biological father called him Robert) liked the extra size of the room and the other perks that had come with it.

Robbie's "real" father had not played an active role in his only child's life until his sixteenth birthday. Then, per the agreement, he was able to join his only son on outings, telling him of the hardships of living and traveling overseas. These stories, as with others, were told to explain his lack of attention during Robbie's youth. This was not true, but it sounded better than the truth. Robbie's father had always sent gifts, cards and made the obligatory phone calls.

Robbie knew he existed, but wondered why he had never been available to participate in his life. His "real" father hated the idea that his son would be known by another name, but according to the agreement, he had to allow his son to be adopted, leaving his given name of Robert Victor Manelli behind. The adoption accomplished the one thing his father valued more than his son's name, it added a special layer of protection.

As Robbie started his first year at Harvard, he felt the same as other students, a little lost and lonely.

Maybe that was why he and his new roommate hit it off so quickly. His roommate, Thomas Griffin Jr. was a celebrity, of sorts. He was the son of a sitting U.S. Senator and former U.S. Ambassador. It seemed that Thomas Griffin Sr. was mentioned every time the Democrats looked for another cabinet member, or when trying to win or keep the White House. This type of media coverage served to raise the profile of Tom Jr. His Mothers mysterious murder some year's before, helped feed that media frenzy as well.

Robbie's father had kept his business very private from his son until this point in his life. Now it had become time, for the truth. At Harvard the discussion started in Robbie's freshman year and continued well into his sophomore year. It was hard for Robbie to understand exactly how it worked. His Father held the position, aptly called Godfather.

This Godfather was different from those in the not to recent past. He was not the flashy type, never had been, as the don of all the crime families or syndicates, he had looked at other more earnest ways to make money for all the families that he controlled.

This Don, or Godfather as he was called, had through the past years taken his business and those that he controlled and brought them more into the legal way of doing things.

This is not to say that he did not use the old ways, when necessary, after all he had a large and extended family to protect and control. This Godfather, at least when he ventured outside of his rather large compound, always traveled with body guards and advisers, just in case.

If circumstances had been different, their friendship would have become one for the ages. Robbie and Tom Jr. shared nearly everything. Before the end of their third year, they did everything together, almost inseparable. By then Robbie had finally comprehended what and just who his father really was. He also knew what his father wanted for his future. Robbie shared this information with Tom Jr., although he had been warned against it. After all, many with the future of Robbie's would consider it a blessing to have a friend, such as Tom Jr. with Tom's father's connections. As children do, they would openly discuss what either of their futures could hold, in these fantasies, both followed in their father's footsteps.

Forty Nine

"As an American, he wanted to do more."

Nick's Sunday was like many others, at least after the noon hour when all of the news broke. He had stayed close to a television, just getting the updates. It did not seem to be enough. Thinking he should do more was always a part of his chemistry. As an American, he wanted to do more. This would be reiterated throughout all news cycles, with two Senators dead, everyone at first wanted to do more, then the real news came out.

Questions had started about why he was in that alley, where was that security detail. The Secret Service had gotten a head of it, seemingly to suggest that many were now on administrative leave with the head of the Secret Service stating emphatically that heads would roll. Sunday evening would present a large opening in the Secret Service, some twenty individuals would by that time have already resigned their positions within the Secret Service.

The information that followed, especially as to why a Senator, an extremely wealthy Senator would own such a dive hotel, and why was he there. Of course with any portfolio you pick up the 'undesirable' as a part of the bigger picture.

This would compound the several accounts as to why another Senator would conceal himself to gamble in the backroom of an establishment, in disguise.

In the end, or at least for that Sunday, it had been brought forth that both men and the young woman had been shot by the same weapon.

Nick was mesmerized, as were many individuals for many different reasons. He had originally gone to the office to start placing all the pertinent and some that might be deemed not pertinent information into the packet for the Mayor. He had attempted to talk with the Mayor a few days before, being stopped by the Mayor "to bring all your information, once the investigation is complete."

That statement complicated things for Nick, he wanted to give an update, not a lengthy information brief. At least with the packet of information the Mayor could review it on his own and then ask questions, at least that was the hope. By the time Nick started focusing more on the television and less on his gathering of information, the packet was up to three hundred pages. Every time he would add information to the packet, he would write on the point paper as to how this new information connected to the previous and future material, it would become convoluted and even more so complicated.

While his Sunday was ended with the television on and still stating the same old thing every fifteen minutes. His Monday would begin in similar fashion.

It had never been important to Nick to turn the television on as soon as his feet hit the floor, he would be more apt to listen to the radio. Getting the traffic information when he lived in LA could save time traveling to work, understanding the weather also helped during the dry time of the year with the fires that would pop up over a spark of this or that. Now that he was in Schrader, he did not need the traffic report, and if there was anything like a fire, he would be notified, so now he turned to the television.

Kristi was the only company after about four in the afternoon, while they had been together for several hours, and then returned to separate rooms at the hotel they had conversed. Both being immersed in what was on television, and with her proofing what she felt comfortable with concerning the report. There conversations where not all about work, even during dinner, pizza again, they had discussed other things.

He had decided to go out to Sam's cabin starting Monday night. He had two days to set up what would happen on Wednesday.

He was off the opinion to silently cordon off the entire area, somebody drives in and they take them from that point. It would be an overpowering, he hoped, take down. If they came with nothing, then he could always address that. If they had weapons, well that would make it easier. This is why he needed the Mayor behind the overall plan, to lessen the mistakes that would certainly happen.

There were a lot of ifs in his idea. To say the least they had been lucky. Something in Sam's body had originally rejected the insertion of the Ketamine-Potassium-Chloride solution, which had been verified, without that and the band aid it may have never been noticed. Even Kristi had suggested without it, it had been ruled a heart attack and nothing more.

Missing files would come up, yet the importance of those files and the happenstance of a department that maybe did not have the best system would have been blamed on down the line. The other lucky portion was that Sam had taken the file of the Charlton's and asked for outside help with it. Kristi finding or being given that file was lucky, and the file might have come back in a timely manner, but when.

The Charlton murder or whatever you would like to call it was misleading at best. He could have killed his wife, coincidence being that the previous husband of Julie Charlton had died a week prior. Marcus Reynolds death, and the subsequent baby clause, compounded by the fact that Julie Charlton was pregnant at the time of her death brings the idea of coincidence to a new level.

Being unable to talk with Robert Morris, at least for another week or so, as Nick had been told, pushed the idea of what was said and by whom on down the line. Not getting the full story from Ian Thompson, the chief counsel for Reynolds-MacMillian and then James MacMillian accepting the fact that the same amount with the same drop area, the cabin, would be acceptable told an entirely different story.

"Was Sam going to take the money, would he?" This was the question that Nick kept asking himself, over and over again. Could his friend, mentor do this? What was the end game for Sam? Nick had not left any part out of the report, he wanted the Mayor to ask, and be properly answered... problem was?

"You want me to read this? Nick, I would not understand the medical stuff, you said the coroner reports are in here?"

"Everything, or at least copies of everything is attached and within the file."

"Yes, I see that everything is in here." Sarcasm was not what Nick wanted, he would have rather had the Mayor place it to one side and just suggest he would get to it.

"Mr. Mayor, Zachary, this is more of a reference. I can sit here and explain it, I even brought the Coroner, Mrs. Jensen to assist on the medical within. I would really like you to understand all that has gone on. We ultimately could wait until..." Nick paused.

"Until what?" The Mayors response was quick.

"Until Wednesday night and see where that all goes?"

"Is that in here?" The Mayor asked.

"No sir, I have that plan. It is in the safe, I have the only hand written copy."

"Why is that?"

"Just think that maybe we have been compromised, in some way."

"With an employee?"

"No, unequivocally not with the employees, any of them. Just a feeling I have."

"Okay Chief, you have informed me. Let me know if there are any changes, and call me Wednesday, regardless of the time, okay?"

Nick had penciled in the afternoon for the Mayor, by the time he walked back to the office, he had not been gone a full half hour. He was disappointed, yet relieved in the fact that the Mayor wanted to know, yet did not. Nick assured himself that one day, this might affect the relationship, especially when things go sideways.

Caroline had reviewed, just as Kristi had. Nick wanted the others to take some time away. Wednesday would be a busy day for all, so he gave Patti the opportunity to use Zach, Ernie and Caroline on the little office things, her list that needed doing. That was their task, for Monday and Tuesday they would perform the little things.

Nick had packed up from the motel, he and Kristi had checked out at about the same time. Since the Cabin was owned by the city and then leased to Sam at a lower rate. Nick asked for the same, and was given the same rate for his lease, whether he would stay in the cabin long term was another story.

His day would end, as it had begun, watching the television. They still had no real leads, depending on what channel you watched. They, the authorities, government and all others had not arrested a soul. Both bodies now laid in the capitol rotunda, for viewing. Another story had seemingly broke on the national stage as well, another Senator, this one retired had vanished.

Fifty

"Sorry for all the lies I'm guilty for."

Once again they were both seated in the dark paneled room, they had with some kind of mystified content watched the younger Senator Tom Griffin Junior, amid his own sorrowful angst eulogize both recently deceased Senators, his former friends, members one and all of the little known group of friends that some referred to as the group of fourteen. Whose numbers, if the group's name was true, had tragically fallen to twelve?

When James turned off the television, the conversation shifted, "and our affairs," he asked Ian.

"Tomorrow evening and everything within our control will be handled," he said as if he was reporting on yet another stock option or legal tactic.

"And your guys, the one will take care of the other, and then?" James asked.

"No this time, after completion Jimmie will go on through Canada, and we will meet up later, he is not expendable." He made that statement with all the comfort he could muster, he knew what the boss had wanted, Ian had decided some time ago that he could not have this one, especially after his miracle survival and all.

In Ian's eyes he was untouchable, and Ian had other plans for Jimmie, once things settled down.

"You trust them, to get this one last job done without fucking it up. Best that we get it done prior to our original Wednesday arrangement. " he asked.

"From our information, they have plans set up for Wednesday, catching them or this individual the day before, might just get them off guard enough to get it done. Jimmie will be careful, he has learnt a big lesson, trust me with that."

"And you Ian, are you ready to take your exit," James said this without looking at him.

"You sure," he asked.

"Yes, I too will be leaving, like we discussed, later tomorrow." James made the decision, it was not hard, it was time to go. Selling would be part of the process. At least he got a fair price. If he stayed around, he would however have to answer many questions about past transfers and his profitable businesses. He was ready for that, he had been for some time, and maybe he just did not have the desire to wait it out. He in ways that were unique and profitable had already gleaned his company for more money than he could ever spend, only a few past accountants, and a best friend knew this and he could guarantee that they were not talking.

"And the company, have you sold it?"

"Yes, actually it has been sold, to a company that has a solid background. The Government will have no problem with this sale. It will be announced later in the week. After I have already left the country, just in case."

"What is your background for leaving?"

"Medical, all made up. I will be going through some new Cancer treatments in Switzerland."

"And what about that information about the Senators past?"

"That will come out on Wednesday as well, they will be digging up his front yard soon after, I will guarantee that. Speaking of the Senator, what really happened to the two guys?"

"We have their phone conversations, everything checks out so to speak. After they took care of the senator, apparently they got into his safe, or he opened it and there was a lot of cash. They decided after disposal to not go back to the safe house. They bought plane tickets, we have an idea of their location, and in the next couple of weeks we will take care of them."

At first it remained a curious mystery, as it turned out plane tickets were purchased, the remaineder was a matter of time, of this Ian was confident.

"On your own with that?" James asked.

"Yes, they betrayed me. I will take care of it."

"So, I believe that is it?" James asked.

James reached over and shook his hand, "Thank you for everything." Ian shook the man's hand, and even twisted a little to check that no one was over his shoulder, with all the house cleaning, he figured he was next. After all, if he were in that position that is what he would do.

Ian removed several files from his office. Those files that he did not shred, he kept and went into his satchel, he looked at his watch, within fifteen minutes he would be at his apartment. He would use a corporate car, that one he would leave at the apartment, for he did not care anymore, he had no reason. His reward was large, larger than he expected, and now in his later years would retire off to some cheap place of the world and live well. He would have some loose ends, yet he figured they were easy enough. For those two who took the cash and ran, they were stupid enough about it to not cover their tracks very well.

He opened his apartment like any other day, removed his outer jacket, turned on the lights and went into his bedroom. He opened the safe and removed other files, special files. He pulled out a duffle bag from under the bed and filled it with several different types of currency and the files themselves.

When he turned back around to face the safe, he noticed it, by that time it was already too late, "Stupid me," he said.

"Oh I don't know about stupid you, well okay maybe," Conoscalo said.

"Let me guess, you're the guy we tried to finish off last week," Ian asked.

"Yes, that would be me. And unlike the person you sent, I'm not a talkative Fuck, I actually have somewhere to be," Conoscalo said this and then went into thought. Get it over with, he said to himself.

"I have a lot of money, more than you'll ever need,"

"And I will take it after I have finished here, and how do you know how much money I need, get up slowly, interlock your fingers behind your head, slowly," Conoscalo spoke slowly himself. Conoscalo slowly and methodically searched the man. He removed a small caliber twenty-two from his inner jacket pocket, he found nothing else. He then started to move the man. He placed the weapon in his own pocket. From that, Ian followed his every command, when they were finished. Conoscalo had Ian sitting on the couch.

"What are we waiting for," Ian asked.

"I have a problem, I need you to write a note and then kill yourself," Conoscalo asked.

"What do you want it to say," Ian asked calmly. Conoscalo almost wanted to comment that if it was this easy he had been going about his business the wrong way all these years.

"Sorry for all the lives I'm guilty for," Conoscalo stated.

"May I get up," Ian asked.

"Where are you going?"

"To the desk," Ian pointed to the small desk across from the couch.

Conoscalo went over and methodically checked the drawers. He set a pen out and moved the pad of paper to the middle of the desk. He then guided Ian over to the desk and sat him down, he instructed Ian not to make any sudden moves, and moved in behind him. Conoscalo squatted behind Ian to one side, while keeping his 9 mm trained on Ian he removed Ian's twenty-two from his pocket and removed the clip. He removed all the bullets except one. He removed the bullet from the chamber and reinstalled the magazine he chambered a single round.

"Who was the one that set me up, where did the orders come from," Conoscalo could clearly see that Ian was a follower. Someone else was in charge.

"Mr. MacMillian, he called the shots,"

"Ian, are you done with the note,"

"Yes,"

"Read it too me," Conoscalo asked.

"It is my sad conclusion, for my life must end. I believe that I have assisted in ending too many lives, directly or indirectly. I' am truly sorry."

Conoscalo was almost speechless.

"So James MacMillian ordered it all?" Conoscalo asked.

"Everything came down from MacMillian, my best team took the action," he answered.

"Your very calm, almost want to commend you,"

"Thanks, you got me, what can I do," Ian stated with what Conoscalo would later consider as true professionalism.

"I said almost commend you, any other teams, I might contemplate over," Conoscalo asked, not expecting the answer he would receive.

"After the Senator was finished, my b team flew the coop, so to speak. I thought I would go after them, they are presently on a beach somewhere." Ian answered as if almost bragging as to what he was going to do to them.

"What Senator," Conoscalo asked because he did not know of any other political leaders dying, beside of the two he had taken care of, and the one still missing Senator.

"Senator Griffin, good job on our parts, one less loose end." Ian stated rather proudly.

"And this other team that is still out there, what dirty orders do you have them marching on next," he asked.

"They get to take care of a little problem in Schrader Maine, looks like you took care of one Chief. You did that, correct, and then as we all know, because we followed you, Robert Morris. That was some handy work as well?" Ian stated.

"Yes, that was my work, all of it?" Conoscalo wryly grinned. "Was I that blatant when I left, the apartment?"

"Yes, cocky might be the best word for your actions, even too big for your britches."

"Yes, I guess cocky might say it all." Conoscalo did not grin this time. He paused, reflecting on something that was already mentioned.

"So now round two, with another Chief of Police."

"In the same place?" Conoscalo asked.

"Yes, tomorrow night."

"Is that so," Conoscalo stopped talking. He actually wanted to know more, he just did not want to get caught off guard and have the table's turn.

"I'm going to place a 22 caliber weapon. You're 22 on your left side, since you are left handed. Do not touch the weapon until I say, okay," Conoscalo continued with "It has one bullet in the chamber, you will not need to chamber the round, and if you think you could turn and hit me, before I shoot you, think again."

Conoscalo slowly walked over to the desk, and placed the weapon on the left side, Conoscalo moved slowly back. This time he moved to a different side, and further back.

"Wait, who are you sending to take care of that second Chief of Police?"

"Your friend from the house."

"The one with the accent, he's mobile?"

"Yes, itching to find you."

"And his partner, the blonde one?"

"He will be up there as well, that is the team that will be sent."

It was time to stop the chit chat, he asked Ian to pick up the 22, Ian did just that, he placed the barrel to his temple and pulled the trigger. Ian slumped to the desk his head with one more hole located in it, fell to the desk, blood poured quickly from the wound and slowly dripped to the floor. Conoscalo was silent. He went back into the bedroom and emptied the remainder of the safe's contents he placed them into the partially filled duffel bag. When he was finished he would have two duffle bags, almost full. He questioned where Ian was planning to go, the bag had several currencies in it, Baht, Yen, Won, American and Australian Dollars.

This time he had parked closer, even saying hi to two women that were in the lobby of the building as he passed through, two duffle bags in tow. Conoscalo removed his gloves and placed them, along with his weapon into the duffle bags, atop the files. Conoscalo glanced at his watch, it was just after six, he had one other job, and they were waiting.

He had been of a dutiful mind.

His preparations would never be known to the common man or woman, though for everything that he had done, he had always prepared.

Through the years Conoscalo had attempted the arduous task of getting to know, or at least know about his next target, he had always had the time to do so. Now it was different, what had happened the other day, where he had lazily entered that home? Where he had, if he would admit it, taken too many things for granted, was he again going to miss step into someone else's shit.

As he had been asked, on a previous phone call that he should not look to the next assignment until he was ready for it. This was something that the Godfather had done previously. He wanted Conoscalo to act on the first job, prior to looking ahead. Even though Conoscalo had not looked ahead, he still feared the worst. In this job he would have no control, the plans and preemptive actions had already been taken. It could be said, that it, the task at hand might even be finished prior to his arrival. He would not be that fortunate.

This time, opening the file on his phone would trigger the GPS. This had been another "new" thing that Conoscalo had hated, and actually still does.

As he opened the file, just after he had read through it, quickly, the GPS for the next location would show on the phone.

Immediately thereafter another message popped up, this one was from a third party. "Target has already left the building. My people are in position, text me at this link upon arrival, Maggie."

"Maggie, who the hell is Maggie?" Conoscalo muttered this as he drove, he would soon find out who Maggie really was.

The drive out into nowhere would take only fifteen minutes, as Conoscalo was texting that link, so that this Maggie knew he was arriving, he would see the explosion. He would finish with the text and send it as the smoke and flames rose from the area, which seemed to be just before him.

Then his phone rang,

"Yes," Conoscalo answered.

"Park your vehicle next to the Lincoln, that you are about to approach. I'm on the crest of land, in front of it."

Even when he had been sitting on the floor, on his knees with his ankles interlocked, his stomach had not turned, as it presently did. He might not be fully prepared, yet he would remove his weapon from the bag and ensure it was fully loaded, and ready to go. He would not wear gloves, this time.

Even though the plume of smoke was still present, as he walked the ten or so feet up the crest, he heard nothing else.

As he topped the crest of the hill he could see a smallish woman figure knelling, both of her hands were raised to her face.

"You won't need that." She stated, without turning around.

Conoscalo paused, slightly glancing from side to side. Checking to ensure that she was not given information from someone nearby, he checked that they were alone.

"Won't need?" He didn't finish his question.

"The weapon you presently hold put it away. We are merely here to assist, clean up and then gather. You are actually here, for backup."

Again Conoscalo looked around, this time with more effort, not hiding the fact that he was looking for something.

"How the hell did you know that, who is helping you?" Conoscalo asked, trying to keep his voice somewhat down.

"Because, under these circumstances. I would as well, although my weapon might have been directed at someone, or thing, just in case." She stated, still with both hands on binoculars, raised to her face.

"Okay?" Conoscalo had been taken aback slightly, her truthful sound and honesty rang through her statement.

"So, the explosion?" Conoscalo asked.

"My team is taking care of it. By the way, I'm Maggie."

"Conoscalo, nice to meet you. You have a team?" Conoscalo asked.

"You don't?" Maggie countered with.

"No, no team, just..." Maggie would cut him off, "So you're the one that I occasionally clean up after?"

"Yeah, I guess so, how many people on your team?" He asked.

"We'll have time for that later." She let the binoculars fall, the small rope carried their weight around her neck. A single finger went toward her ear.

"Copy that, target is in the bag." She said out to the air in front of her, while depressing her ear piece.

"They are bringing him to me, we have about four minutes until we have others arriving. We need to get going." She stood, as did Conoscalo next to her.

"By yourself, really, you're not all that big?" Maggie stated. This being stated by someone who is all of just five feet, one hundred pounds, soaking wet.

"Excuse me?" Conoscalo now gave her the once over.

"Just saying, not trying to be offensive, I suppose we have proven a myth wrong."

"Which one is that?" Conoscalo asked.

"Size doesn't matter, in our case anyway."

Conoscalo didn't have the chance to respond, he had thought to himself. I'm six foot, not small? A white panel van would pull up to them as they reached the bottom of the little hill.

No sooner had the van stopped as the side door opened and two men jumped from the vehicle. Both men, reached back into the van and removed a gentleman in a suit, his head was covered by a black bag, something that resembled a dark black pillow case.

"Put him in my trunk." Maggie whipped the keys to one of the men, who caught them in mid-flight, like he was expecting them all along.

"And the others?" She asked.

"All dead." Stated the same man who had caught the keys.

"Why did I need to be here?" Conoscalo asked, he had been told that he was backup, which was difficult to believe if he was five minutes later they would have been gone altogether.

"You were my back up, just in case something went wrong. Don't you usually have a backup plan, Mr. Lone Wolf?" Maggie asked.

"Usually, I guess?" Conoscalo questioned his own answer, didn't he?

"Well were done here. Lovely meeting you, big fan of your work, until next time." Maggie was ten feet away, by the time she had finished her sentence.

"Yeah, nice meeting you and your team." Conoscalo stated this in a lower tone, since he had not really met the team.

"Hey, who was in the van? Who was the guy?" Conoscalo asked.

"You just took care of his Security guy, didn't you? Well we got the boss." Her keys had been passed back, in a similar way as she had thrown them to the man that had come from the van. Before Conoscalo had fully digested what had just transpired, both vehicles, first the van, then the Lincoln town car had backed up and then left the scene. Conoscalo would quickly do the same he had a couple more things to do.

Fifty One

"Finish it."

One Friday evening, all their hopes and fantasies would change. They, willing to blow off some steam, toward the end of the school year were invited to a party down in the warehouse district. Tom had driven that evening. The normal security that had been attached to the senator's son, had been removed the year before, mostly on Tom Jr. insistence, ultimately Tom Sr. agreed. Tom Sr. wanted for his only living child to have the college years that in his eyes, everyone should, and the freedom to enjoy that time in life.

Not really getting the full directions prior to leaving campus, made Tom Jr. unsure of where they were going. As he had in the past, especially in his home town of Boston, he would simply just pull over and ask someone for directions. Later Tom Jr. would tell two similar, yet different stories of what happened.
"And then, what happened Mr. Griffin?" the detective asked.

"After he fired, four or maybe five times toward the passenger side, he changed his aim toward..." Tom paused.

"Go on. This is vital, it will help us find the person who killed your friend and almost...." The other detective nudged his partner to remind him to just let the story flow.

"He aimed at me and then I just don't remember."

"Just take a deep breath, and try..." the second detective directed.

"Yeah, it happened rather fast, I'm not sure if I heard him fire at me or if it was the sound of my car hitting him. That's what I can't remember." Tom tried to rise from his seat, the first detective pushed him back into his seat, in a not so flattering way. Tom quickly turned and brushed the man's hand to the side, yet still falling back into a seated position.

It really did happen like that. Tom knew that five shots had been fired into his friend. Tom then saw the gun turn into his direction, he could see the shooter, looking in his direction, then down to the gun.

As the man moved toward the front of the vehicle, walking from the passenger side toward the driver's side, that was when Tom popped the car into gear and accelerated. He could see that same man fly into the air and then bounce off of his hood, falling out of sight, in front of the vehicle. As Tom Junior's attention immediately turned to his dying friend, the man that had just been hit stood back upright and then started to limp as he tried to run away from the vehicle and the scene itself.

"Oh God Robbie, stay with me. Listen to me, stay with me Robbie." Tom Jr. felt for a pulse, nothing.

He felt for a pulse again, still nothing. He could tell Robbie was not breathing. This did not diminish his hopes for Robbie. Like a jet, he exited the vehicle and ran to the passenger side, he opened the door and removed his friend, lying him gentle on the side walk beside the car. In the process of removing his friend he kicked the man's gun. When the vehicle made contact it must have jarred the gun from his hands.

This is where the official story changed. Tom would never mention kicking the gun, or seeing it outside of the man's hand. Tom would never mention at least to the police what happened afterward as well, at least not the correct version.

He quickly looked at the gun, lying near his feet.

He then turned and could notice the man trying to run, limping badly in the process, trying to get away, and not having much luck with his injuries.

In that split second of thought, Tom would decide to leave his friend, grabbing the gun, mustering all the speed he had to pursue. His pursuit would not take long, turning once into another alley and he would find the shooter, still limping, still trying to flee.

As Tom Jr. caught up to the man, he would with the force of his younger body, and the force of his lengthy stride, would push the man to the ground. Leaving nothing to chance he pointed that gun straight at the man's head, even nudging it against his temple.

"I'm going to kill you just like you did to my friend. In fact I'm going to blow your ever-loving' head off!"

Tom Jr. hesitated. He pulled the gun slightly off of the man's temple.

He yelled, saying nothing in particular, just a low keyed primal scream of frustration.

Gaining confidence to accomplish what he just stated, he pushed the gun back into the shooters temple, nearly pulling the trigger, when over his shoulder, coming from behind him he could here footsteps. Running sounds, weighing heavily on the pavement as they moved getting closer every second.

"DON'T!"

"STOP!" This yell did not come from the shooter, this statement came from one of the running men.

This startled Tom, they didn't say police, stop. He thought.

He stepped back from the man, now a good two or three feet from his temple, from where the gun just rested.

"Why not, he killed my friend." Tom shouted this, crying these words out to no one in particular, to the voice that had just asked him not to.

"Because you shouldn't have to do this, we are the ones that failed tonight, we should have been nearer. We are the ones that have been entrusted to protect his only child." The bigger man of the two stated this. Both men had stopped running by this time, both men could have easily removed the weapon from Tom Juniors grip if they had chosen to do so. They had not, they wanted Tom to do this on his own accord.

Tom Jr. knew who they had just referred to, Robbie was also an only child, this they had discussed as well. These two men represented the security that should have always been around Robbie, never in plain sight, just nearby, just in case for something terrible like this should ever occur.

Robbie had actually joked about it. After he fully understood his situation, he stated several times. "Not sure what would be worse, if someone were to attack me, my pain or the pain of those that were to protect me and keep me safe."

No one was laughing now, no one worried about what was to be, now.

"Tom, listen. We need you to set the gun down. We are limited on time here. We need you to return to Robbie, even though you may not help him. We need you to return to him and await the authorities. We will take care of this."

"But, I need to do this. I want to kill that son of a bitch." Tom quickly pointed back to the man that wriggled in pain of his own.

"Go Tom, go back and tell the police you chased the man and found nothing." The man that had originally stated to stop said this, he placed his hand on Tom's shoulder and with his other hand, gingerly removed the gun from his tight grip.

Tom Jr. would return to the scene. He would see paramedics and police, others had assembled as well. Curious bystanders and witnesses would identify Tom as the man that had chased the shooter.

"Look Mr. Griffin, just a couple more questions, please?" This came from the detective that had not pushed Tom back into his chair. That detective had retreated to the corner of the room, he had not and would not make eye contact with Tom for the remainder of the interview.

"Okay, what?" Tom snapped back, still glaring at the other detective in the opposite corner.

"So why did you leave the scene?" the detective asked.

"My friend was dead, or close to it. I thought that...."

"Go on Tom, you thought that?"

"I thought that I should chase the man that shot him. He was limping, I saw the direction he went..." Tom's voice trailed off.

"Trying to be a hero, were you?"

"I don't know, maybe. He just killed my friend. I just took off after him." Tom stated.

The questioning of Tom Jr. ended soon after. The police had pursued in the direction that Tom and other eye witnesses had given them. By the next morning they had nothing, that man, the shooter had seemingly vanished.

Four days later, at the funeral of Robbie Robertson, Tom would grace the podium and speak about his best friend. As he looked down into the crowd of well-wishers, classmates and others, he would recall the good times that they shared and of the future friendship that he would miss. It would be stated on that date, during the most difficult of times he had shown a grace for his future, the future he had always wanted.

He had brushed off the 'new security' that his father had wanted for him now, "Just in case." As the local papers had reported, it was what everyone currently discussed.

"That Senator's son, yea the one the lost his Mother, he was attacked, someone tried to kill him, killed his friend instead."

This was what everyone repeatedly stated, even the nightly newscasters for the first few evenings after the incident, stated this. No one gave another thought to the actual victim. Robbie came from Denver, his mother was a homemaker, his step father a dentist. If anyone dug any deeper into that it never showed up in the papers or on that nightly newscast.

Tom Jr. had asked, and it had been granted that he could walk, just by himself, in order to reflect and clear his head. This had been granted only for the confines of the walled in and semi secluded cemetery and no further. His new security detail would be just outside the gates.

During his walk, as he thought of what the future would hold for him, for what it should have held for his friend, he would be approached. He had seen the three stretch limousines circle around the large road that encompassed the cemetery, where his friend's funeral had just been held.

The first one passed moving slowly to his right, the second one moved slower, as it rolled by, a window lowered. A man asked in a quiet yet calm manner asked,

"Did you really mean what you said the other night? About killing that son of a bitch. Or was it just the adrenaline speaking, now that you have had time to reflect on the statement itself."

Tom Jr. turned toward the window itself, he did not hesitate once the man had stopped speaking, "I made the statement, would have done it then, given the opportunity would do the same now." This caught the man in the vehicle off guard, he was not prepared for a response such as this. "Then join me, we need to take a ride."

Tom would enter that vehicle without hesitation. Even though they would not be properly introduced. Tom knew who sat across from him, it was Robbie's father.

It was not a long drive, nothing was said between the two in the back or with the two that sat up front. They walked into a warehouse, there were two tables of men playing cards. When these men noticed the older man walking with the younger one, they all jumped up and hurriedly placed their suit jackets back on, he noticed that every man had a shoulder strap for a weapon, it would be easily concealed by their jackets. All these men in the room, respected the man that walked beside him, they all addressed that man as Godfather.

They would leave the main room and two doors would open, inside were other men standing near what looked like the same man from the other night. The man was sitting in a chair, his legs, arms and torso were duct taped to the chair, with a rag was stuffed into his mouth. "Do you recognize this man," the Godfather asked.

He waited to answer, he glared at the man who killed his friend.

"Yes, he is the man from the other night," He answered.

"That is correct, do you still wish to do what you said." The Godfather asked.

"In a heartbeat," was his cold dry answer.

The Godfather nodded to another man that man brought over a 9 mm with silencer, he handed it to the young man.

"Do you have any gloves," The young man asked. Again the Godfather nodded and one of the men removed their own gloves and handed them to the young man, he gentle put on the pair of leather gloves, "Can the man talk?" he asked. Again, the Godfather nodded and yet another man removed the rag from the individual's mouth.

"Why did you kill my friend?" He asked of the man who sat in front of him.

"Go fuck yourself," Said the man who knew that his end was near.

"Well, I'm not going to go that far, maybe with someone else later tonight," Again the young man answered without hesitation in his voice. The other men in the room including the Godfather, laughed at this.

"Is there a bullet in the chamber," he asked.

"Chambered and ready to go, safety is off," answered the man that provided the weapon.

"Whatever, I want," he asked while looking at the Godfather, as if almost to seek his approval. The weapon, pointed directly on the individual seated before him, it never moved or wavered.

"It's your show, do whatever pleases you," the Godfather said, while he enjoyed every moment.

"I will ask one more time, why did you kill my friend," he asked?

The man hesitated, "Go fuck yourself," As spit flew from his mouth when he spoke, he responded louder than the first time.

The young man didn't hesitate, as the Godfather remembered some twelve years later on his deathbed, "You surprised me kid, you totally blew me away with what you did."

The young man didn't look for the approval, the weapon never wavered he did however lower it from the middle of the torso to the left knee cap. That is where he pulled the trigger. The men that stood behind the seated man would complement the Godfather on his choice. Even as the bullet discharged from the weapon, he didn't blink or quiver because of the recoil. It would be stated by others later "That shot was perfect center of the knee cap."

The man screamed it was a sound that the young man didn't hear, even though he stood directly in front of it. For his attention lied with other thoughts, it would be years before he would recall those sounds and many years beyond that before the remembrances of what occurred would leave his sleeping thoughts.

When the man seemed to calm down somewhat, he was asked again "Why did you shoot and kill my friend," he asked.

This time the individual's response was different, "Fuck you."

This time there was no hesitation, the young man, methodically moved the weapon toward the other knee, again, the man screamed as before. And as before he heard nothing, for he was in some kind of zone. And yes another perfect shot.

"One more time," He would ask, "Why did you shoot and kill my friend."

Again, the answer was different, amidst the individuals wailing and crying, he answered, "If I tell you, then what."

The young man bent over a little, to look the man in his eyes, "Then all of this will be over."

The other men including the Godfather were pleasantly surprised they were almost astonished.

"The Massena's, Loreto Massena gave me the order, he wanted to hurt the Godfather, he wanted to take away his future," the individual said.

The young man turned and looked directly at the Godfather. He just shrugged his shoulders as if to ask what next.

The Godfather walked closer to the young man, he placed his hand on his shoulder and leaned in to his ear, it was a whisper, one that wouldn't be heard by the other men in the room. There would be no need to keep it quiet with the group in the room, for they were the loyal of the loyal, true to what the Godfather would do, when ordering something like this. Even in his profession, there had to be deniability.

"Finish it," he whispered. The Godfather turned the young man back toward the seated man. He raised the weapon back up, not to the knee cap or even the torso. This time he directed toward the head, and pulled the trigger. The man in the chair slumped, He grabbed the weapon with his other hand and handed it back to the man that gave it to him he then removed the gloves and again gave them back to the man who had provided them. He turned to the Godfather and asked, "What now."

The other men in the room started to clap, as the Godfather led the young man from the room they were still clapping. The other men that were located in the outer room started to do the same, it never dawned on him as to why or even how they would know, just that they did, it would become quite a badge, a merit badge of sorts.

They would meet again, many years down the road. Just as they had previously they would meet prior to another funeral.

Fifty Two

"I won't let you go just yet, but I'm confident that
you will give me everything."

When she removed the handkerchief from
his mouth, he was fully awake and very agitated,
as anyone would be that had been abducted from
the comforts of their home, thrown in a van, then
into a trunk and now?

"Do you know who I am?"

"Nope, don't care."

"Right now my people are on their way."

"Good let them come, then you'll have your
people dead here, with you."

"I'll take it from here. Good work, any other
problems." The man in the shadows asked.

"No, just as it was said it would be, sir." The
younger woman answered rather quickly. She
didn't like to be this near to the man. Even with
her skills, he could have people killed with just
the nod of his head. With him, you never knew
who was next, the why didn't matter.

"Maggie, you have permission, not to call me sir."

"Yes s..." Maggie paused, catching herself.

"Yes Godfather." She said. Unlike Conoscalo's time, he had never seen this new boss. The new generation as he called it, would see him. Those that did the dirty work, should see him, sometimes the need to be face to face was necessary. Risky, as his aides would say, still worthwhile and necessary. The number of people that had actually seen him would be few, still it was a growing number. With his job, he either needed them to fear him and be loyal, or just be loyal beyond loyal.

"I know that voice. Where are you?" The man that was bound in the chair asked, as he strained to locate where the voice had come from.

"Maggie, as I said good work. Take some time off, I'll be in touch." This time she did not answer, she left. She now had other instructions to take care of.

He dragged the chair behind him, he did not care about the noise that was being made, and he had no reason to worry about any noise that was to be made in this warehouse.

He had been here before, it had been some time, yet still he had been here.

As the dark figure that pulled the chair, walked closer to the man, the light that had been on the floor before him, now shown into his eyes.

Even though he tried he could see nothing beyond the light, and the legs of the chair. Even when someone was seated into that chair, still, even now he could only see the feet of the person who sat there.

"So do you recognize the voice?" He asked.

"Tom?" Now the man that just spoke, questioned his own words.

"Tom, what the hell is going on? Is that you, you let me up now. Get this tape off."

"Very good."

"Take the light, shine it upwards, its time he knew." The other man in the room moved the light that had shown in his eyes, moving upward toward the ceiling made the entire complex light up somewhat. After this had changed, now that his eyes re-focused, he could see who sat before him.

"You may go now." The Godfather waved the other man off, he left as directed.

"Yes Godfather."

"What did he just call you, Godfather? That's silly, why you're a Senator. What is going on, let me go, you've had your fun or whatever."

"The fun is yet to begin."

"I have people, soon, if not already they will come."

"Like your people, in your vehicle."

James waited, he thought. His mind now race.

"But they'll be found someone will find them. And then they will contact others and they will find me."

Actually that would not be the case. This had already been made clear to the Godfather. The bodies that had been left behind, the burning vehicle, while still in flames, would be found, but then what. What would people, the authorities really think? Hours would pass, and then would he ever be found.

"No, not anytime soon. James your people are not coming, at least not here. See, our system is better that yours. Yes same creator, but we don't have the bugs that your system does. I made sure of that. So they won't be following you to this place. So let's get down to the matter at hand." Tom paused.

"What matter at hand? What do you mean that your system is better, are you talking about..." James MacMillian asked inquisitively, wanting to know about what system he was actually referring to.

"You know that you're a family killer. Someone who preys on others families."

"What do you mean, please Tom? You're a fucking Senator for Christ's sake. What are you doing with all this? Let me go, and I'll give you anything."

"I won't let you go just yet, but I'm confident that you will give me everything."

"Tom, this isn't what you think. It's very complicated."

"Well then take the next few minutes to explain it."

"I... It just is a matter between old friends and all, and it's about survival."

James stopped speaking.

"Guess who is going to survive, this one. So where is my father?" Tom asked, wanting to get some answers from the man prior to expending some shells.

"Tom, I had nothing to do with that. I found out after the fact, Ian Thompson, now he's the man you need to speak with. He's the guilty one here."

"Is that so?"

"Yes, that is correct. You see, once I was told. I let him go, he's gone. And he is the one that needs to be..." James stopped, seemingly he still mumbled, yet said nothing.

"Needs to be, needs to be what?" The Godfather asked.

"He needs to be the one.... to talk about, all of that, and all."

"Well that is no longer a viable option. You see, we can't ask him anything. He's dead."

"Dead, no not Ian, he's still around I'm sure of it."

"No James, he's dead, pretty sure of it."

"No, can't be. I can help find him, I'll find him."

"Cut the crap, just own up to it and you'll be able to leave. To go anywhere you choose, just no longer in the United States. Just come out with it and all will be done, and we both can go on our way."

"Really, you mean, just leave the country. I can go?" James asked.

"Yes, you'll be free to go anywhere. I will assist in getting you there."

"Honestly, anywhere?"

"Yes, just come clean, everything. The disappearance of my Father and about my Mother, Please help this child to discover the truth. And then it will be done, and you may move on. Trust me as I say, I will do nothing in stopping you from leaving."

"Your Mother, Katherine was so vibrant, what a love of life that she had." James stopped, wanting to say more, not really being able to.

James wanted to make sense of it all, although his thought lamp was burning brighter.

"Go on, tell me." The Godfather muttered in a low tone. He had moved closer to the man that was still seated, still taped to the chair.

"Yes, as good as time as any, right, then we may both move on?"

"Yes, then we may both move on." The Godfather said under his breath, and then repeated for himself.

"It was an accident. We had an argument. She wanted to tell your father that she was leaving him and wanted me to leave my wife. But I couldn't, I needed your father for the contracts that made my business flourish and for future business. So we argued. And it was just an accident, she tried to hit me and stepped on her long robe and fell, she hit her head and that was it."

"Accident, you say?" Tom inquired.

"Others were there, they know about it. What really happened, they will back me up. They would have, yet you took care of them, didn't you. It was you?"

"Others you say, what others?" Sometimes it is good to know all the answers, prior to the question at hand, Tom thought.

"Well, my lawyer Robert Morris, he could have, but you know..." Again James was interrupted.

"Yeah, I know. Know all about Robert and Harlan, least you forget about him. You see a little boy saw it all. Took some time for it to come to light, yet it did."

"You saw what happened, and all this time?" James questioned.

"Just recently I discovered what my full knowledge held about it."

"It was an accident, just that." James yelled, into the darkness, past the man that stood near to him, hoping that some kinder soul would discover the sound and actually be able to do something about it.

"No, it was no accident?"

"Yes, an accident. Now I've told you, can I leave now?" James asked

"Why didn't you call someone, the police, a doctor, an ambulance to help her?"

"I checked for a pulse but she was dead. There was nothing I could do and if I was found there people would talk and it would blemish her reputation. I didn't want that for her."

Voices could be heard from beyond the reach of the light. "That son-of-a-bitch, let go of me." Tom didn't bother to turn toward the sounds but James did.

"Who is that, who is over there, come out of the darkness, let me see who you are?" James shouted. Tom ignored him. The voice from the darkness did not come forward as well.

"Oh, I think you might recognize that voice as well." Tom said, watching for realization to show in James' manner.

"Recognize it, I don't know who that is, sounds familiar, but..."

"Well, I will just let the voice have its revenge. I know what is needed for me," Tom Junior said as he left the man's side.

"Let him go."

"Oh, thank you Tom. None of this will ever be repeated, trust me, not a word." James stated in a fast almost unrecognizable way, much different than is regular tone.

"No, not you, time for you to recognize that voice."

It hadn't actually happened as it had been previously reported.

During in his days in the Senate he would have burst from the darkness with the announcement that his death had been overly exaggerated, a la Mark Twain.

This time he did leap from the darkness. The two men that had been controlling him released their grips, upon the command of their boss. With amazing control Tom Sr. strolled toward the man that had ruined his life years ago and recently tried to kill him.

"You ordered me killed, you bastard." Tom Griffin Sr. stated through gritted teeth as he walked into the lighted area.

James was trying to think of a way to refute this statement, but he failed. He was trying to figure out what had gone so completely wrong.

The death of Tom Sr. on Friday night had obviously not gone according to James' instructions. It happened in the following manner:

"You jerk," The senator growled as he pulled a weapon from the pocket of his robe. Tom was reaching for it at the same time McKinley aimed and depressed the trigger of the stun gun. He slammed the weapon into McKinley's forehead. He would lay bleeding and unconscious at the Senator's feet.

The Senator waited until McKinley shook himself awake before saying, "When you use a stun gun, you have to touch skin for it to work. This isn't a Taser that shoots darts at the target. You should start thinking about another line of work."

Here was the reason why this man always drove the van and was never asked to do wet work. This was why he was always delegated to clean-up duty.

Once Tom kicked the stun gun clear, he knelt down and aimed his small caliber weapon at McKinley's forehead.

"Okay dumbass, tell me what was to happen next, or else."

"Or else what?" The kid looked back at the Senator trying to sound brave. He followed the Senator's gaze toward the weapon and became visibly shaken.

Sometimes you get a feeling, maybe that you are being watched. Maybe, it's simple paranoia. For years, he had seen his only child rise to such a level that few see of their own off spring. Where his luck was that of old fashion stuff, his child, his only living one had the good sense to stay clear of the cameras, he never said the wrong thing, on or off camera. For a politician, a son of a politician this was tough, nearly impossible. The kid on the floor said it openly.

"I'm here to kill you."

Well as he said a bit later he was there to subdue, his partner in the van was going to do the dirty work. Now Thomas Griffin Senior had to make a choice. He could get his security team back, they could handle this. With that would be an extreme amount of questions. Questions he would not want to answer directly.

And what if this kid, the one that lay at his feet, wondering what was actually to be the next move for the man he was supposed to detain. What if he knew too much, then what, too many dark corners of this former Senators closet to worry about? So, he did what he thought was best, for the situation, especially for himself.

He called the number that his son had given him, in case there was trouble in the future. It was given to him, after another long lost weekend. Where there was not as much trouble as this current situation might present.

The call went through, a pleasant woman had answered, and then placed the call on hold. She had not asked his name, nor did she give him the time to state it. Fact was, they already knew.

The same voice would come back on, "The orders are for you to shut your door, subdue the individual, and do no harm to him. Somebody will be there in less than five minutes, they will knock two times, pause and then knock two more times. Let them in and then follow all orders as given without exception, do you understand?" "Yes," Again the phone fell silent.

Maggie had made an impression all around, she had become the go to girl, as it was. She would be on his father's doorstep in less than five minutes, she had been in a holding pattern just waiting. She had gone out in the afternoon to 'research' some things, never was she too far away. She took someone from her team, just for the heavy lifting.

He had closed the gate, hadn't he? When he heard the knock, he waited just as the person on the phone had stated. Was it someone else, could it be. Then what would he say if the police did show up, for whatever reason. "Watch out for the urine puddle, by the door, come on in."

Then the second set of knocks came.

He stepped over the puddle, it had been left by the now whimpering kid, who every ten seconds pleaded, "Please don't kill me," in the most annoying voice that Tom had ever heard.

He glanced through the peep hole, it was an older male, with what looked like a three day growth on his face. Just like the young one in his den that was now tied up, who had blood coming from his forehead. This man had it coming from his mouth and nose. He pulled his head back, then went back to the eye hole, this time he could see a young Asian woman, who was a foot shorter than the man who was bleeding, she now shouted,
"Let us in, damnit, I'm here to help."

He unbolted the door,
"Watch out for the puddle." He told the two that had walked through. He still held tightly to the weapon as he had since he first removed it from his robe.

"Where's the other one?" She asked, while holding a zip tie that had been securely fastened around the larger man's neck. She too held a weapon, from the sight of it he could determine it was a 9 mm with a suppressor. Though he had never seen one up close, he had seen many in the movies. As she spoke, she rolled the lolly pop that was in her mouth from side to side as she spoke, even with this in her mouth she did not slur her words.

"He's in the den, this way." He led the two into the den, the other one was seated on the floor in the middle of the room. She pushed the larger man down next to his partner.

"Okay, I need to get some information boys," she calmly stated.

"I want to know how you were to kill him. What you were to do next, and who were you to contact?" She paced in front of both men, the Senator watched from behind. She was short, maybe five two if five feet at all. She had black hair, long and straight.

She wore it in two pony tails, extending from the sides of her scalp. Even with the chill of the night, still she wore short shorts and an extremely tight blouse without a bra. If the circumstances were different, he would have done just about anything to get near her for other purposes, now this little 'girl' scared the bejesus out of him.

"Come on boys, first one to talk gets the reward."

"I was to subdue him and then he was going to kill him. He was supposed..."The younger man, McKinley tried to speak, he was sounded over and interrupted by his partner, whose mouth and nose still bled.

"You dumbass, not one of us is walking out of here. It is the oldest trick."

"Do you want to continue?" The woman asked.

"Yes, I'll tell everything. Then I get to go?"

She said nothing, only nodded.

She then raised her weapon to his bleeding partner, one shot and he fell backward onto McKinley.

McKinley peed himself again and the retired Senator gasped.

"Oh my God, what did you just do? You can't..." The Senator began,

"You were told to stay quiet and follow instructions." She pointed the gun at his head. He immediately shut up and stood stock still.

"Thank you." She said as calmly as ever.

She turned back to the young man and said, "Go on."

The young man did. He told her everything he knew, the place they were to go after the job and the text that he needed to send to confirm it. "What kind of time frame were you given?" She asked.

"Just this evening sometime," he answered, his whimpering had started to subside as he believed this cooperation would keep him alive.

The Senator seemed calm as well. "Anything you want to add?" she asked.

"That's all I know," he replied optimistically.

"Okay, thank you. You will soon be on your way..." Again she was interrupted by the Senator, "We can't just let him go..." She quickly turned to face the Senator,

"I already have permission to kill you, if you do not shut up, completely shut up I will do so. Do you understand?"

"Yes," The senator backed away slightly, this was not what he expected.

"Okay, like I was saying..." She turned and glared at the Senator, "Prior to being interrupted. I need you to make a call, where is your phone?"

"In my back pocket." The young man stated.

Maggie reached behind the kid and removed it from his back pocket.

"It's wet, oh this is piss." She immediately dropped it onto the floor.

"Cut him loose." The other man that had come with her did just that, the kids face lit up.

"Do you have a credit card?" She asked.

"Yes, in my wallet."

Maggie would inform him that she was going to make flight arrangements for both. He had questioned this, since his partners brains were not where they once were. How could he travel? She simply stated, that it would better for him if his people thought they both had left. After presenting him with the notion that he would get fifty thousand to just leave and never speak about the situation ever again made him forget about the two tickets. A hotel reservation was also made, with the credit card as well.

"And that's it?" He asked

"Yes, that is all, stand by and we will get you out of here."

She reached into the back pocket of her tight shorts for her phone, flipped it open and spoke. "Going to need a cleanup crew, at my location."

McKinley heard the faint reply, "How many?" Her answer echoed in McKinley's ears. "Two," She said as she turned to fire her weapon, killing the kid instantly.

Tom Sr. gasped and started to speak. "What...how can I explain two. One maybe possible but two is..." She made no sound, only turned and put her finger to her lips. He instantly realized she meant keep your fucking mouth shut or I will kill you. He obliged, and said nothing more.

As he stood over both bodies to ponder what had been done and what was needed, she broke the silence, "I was told that you have a stash of your own blood?"
"No, used to. Not anymore." He answered with a questioning look.

She nodded to the other guy who left the room without question, he would bring back two bottles of what resembled blood.

The home itself would be cleaned. The two bodies would be properly disposed of. Once the home was clean, the blood would be spilt, trying to lead the police in one direction, until it was tested. As per her instructions, as she had been told the former Senator would be cuffed, and blindfolded, where he would be taken needed to stay private.

Now Tom Griffin Senior walked toward his old friend. So many questions rolling through his head, so little time, he thought.

"You tried to kill me, you bastard. And now I hear, you killed her, why. You and her you say, you were my friend, and still you did this, did you?" Tom Senior wanted to know, yet he didn't. Closure was always a good thing, when he was dealing with others, now it seemed to be not of the greatest ideas, within all of the ideas that he now questioned.

Tom Junior, the Godfather had seen his father's act before. The political grandstanding that had occurred with regularity during the earlier years, now as he spoke to his old friend, learning what he just had, escaping by chance just a few days before had taken a toll on the man. In pain, he dropped to the floor. Now on his knees he wept. Both hands covered his face.

The Godfather nodded to the other two men, who stood nearby. They would walk over and gently retrieve his father, bringing him to his feet, and walking him back a few feet.

"So, if this was an accident. Why were your other friends there?" Tom asked.

The look on James face was of horror, the expression he had was of a blank kind.

All the therapy that had occurred and culminated with the one session of deep hypnosis had paid off. So much so that he had to deal with the therapist. She had gone back on her word, to not record any session, she had paid the price. With that loose end already completed, now it was time to address the man in the mirror. "I was at a party once, several years ago...Listen to me."

He snapped his fingers, bringing the attention of the man that was taped to the chair back to him, away from the still weeping man that had now been repositioned further away.

James's attention shifted, he now looked at the Godfather directly.

"Like I was saying, at this party some years ago, something was said that for some reason always stayed with me, my every thought, even somehow getting into my dreams. I thought it was just me, nothing more. As my heavy tendencies started to weigh in on me, I decided to see a therapist to discover more about these dreams. These constant reminders of seeing a distant man, in a mirror, all the while as I could see my mother lying in a pool of blood." He paused.

As he began to speak, once again, he removed himself from his chair. For the remainder he would pace, one side to the other, while staying in front of James as he paced.

"Do you know what was said, at that party, do you remember?" He asked James.

James did not immediately answer,

"I don't remember, what was said. A lot of things have been said."

"Like I said, it stayed with me. Your friend, Harlan Schmidt inquired as to where Robert Morris was. Because, as he stated, either he is up your ass so far that he can't be seen, or is nearby in the bathroom, cleaning the shit off of him. And you responded in saying, "and typically Harlan, you're kissing that ass." Neither one of you are ever too far away from me at any time. The people around you laughed, some even did it exuberantly."

"And this stayed with you?" James asked, sarcastically.

"Yes it did, for reasons I don't know or at least didn't, until recently. You see in that mirror, I saw it all. Not in a dream like status. I was there, watching from the stairs.

I saw a man arguing with my mother, that same man hit her, several times. And then you left, you never approached her once you hit her for the last time. You see, after you left I walked to her, in shock, not knowing what I should do. No sooner that you left that the door opened again, so I hid." The Godfather paused, switching directions as he paced,

"And as, for many years I could see no one's face, then like I said. Through that mirror, as I hid, behind the wall, that mirror was my line of sight to the living room. I saw the three of you, clear as day, Harlan Schmidt, Robert Morris and you, James MacMillian walking back into the room. Not a care in the world, no worries at all. And then it happened she was still alive."

"She was not, she was dead already." James shouted, trying to get his point across, to no avail.

"Then why did Harlan Schmidt, straddle her, place his hands around her neck and choke her until she stopped breathing. Was he trying to kill her again? And if she was dead, why did he have two cheerleaders, yourself and Robert Morris telling him to continue, just to ensure that it was so, that she was dead."

"You three, it was not just one man in that mirror that I could not see it was the three of you at different times. That is what was so confusing?"

"For years, I just thought it was a flash of the face, a grey area of a person, yet as my fog lifted it was you that I saw, then Harlan and Robert, together and separately. Overall, James it was you. You were that man in the mirror that for so many years I could not see."

James did not speak.

"And then you tried to kill my father, if not for some incompetence of your people. Then I figure my Mother just might have her soul mate back."

"Soul mate, your mother was a whore, nothing more. If she hadn't married well, she would have been out on her back making a living." He was stopped, not by his own accord. He was stopped by the overwhelming blow that his face just absorbed. The Godfather had made contact, James MacMillian would no longer have the desire to talk, not just yet.

"Father, this is your opportunity." He held the weapon out, another 9 mm with a suppressor.

"To do what?" His father questioned.

"To finish it. However you please."

His father had been standing on his own accord, more riveted to the conversation that had just been held, more so than his personal pain. Even though his son spoke of his deceased mother, his father who had listened so intently would confirm if asked the darker side.

This was where James thought he would get the last laugh, "Do with me what you will, tomorrow you are going to have to start answering some other questions about your past."

"Questions, about what?" Tom Junior asked inquisitively.

James began to smile, the blood from his now busted lip would flow down his chin it had already coated his once bright white teeth.

"About something the authorities will find in your front yard, that information will come out tomorrow, no way to stop it."

James figured there was no way to stop it, he would be correct, even the leader of the crime families would not be able to stop that. His smile turned to a low chuckle.

"So you think you have the upper hand?" The godfather retorted.

James said nothing, he just nodded.

"So you must be referring to that prostitute situation. Where you had my father believe that he had killed the young girl?" The smile on the face of James Bennett MacMillian had disappeared, that chuckle had completely stopped.

"When actually your people killed her. And then you or at least under your orders had her buried by the front courtyard, near the fountain?"

"How do you know this?" James asked, now with a disbelief look on his face.

"James, I know just about everything. I do know that I'm five steps ahead of you at all times. So let me tell you what they will find there, a previous pet of ours.

A dog that we used to have, that died right after he had moved into that house..."

"I will verify this, after all a Senator in good standing will be difficult to refute. They will still dig, my father will insist to put this all behind us. He will give some political type of speech that he always seems to do, of course this will be after he returns from his "long" weekend." Tom Junior placed his fingers in the air for the imaginary quotes as he said long.

James said nothing, a beat man knows when it is over. This bell has just rung for one James MacMillian.

"You see, with the power that I have. I will inform the authorities that my father was out on a boat fishing. The pig's blood will be explained as a joke, a sorry one at that. In fact he did not even know about the deaths of the other Senators until earlier today."

The godfather now held the weapon out toward his own father, who walked toward the weapon and removed it from the grip of his child. Holding tightly, he walked up to his former friend and business associate. He raised the weapon toward the man's head, he squeezed the trigger. James's head flew backward and then toward his chest, where it would rest, the blood flowing from the hole that had just been made in the middle of his forehead. He turned around and handed the weapon back to his son, the Godfather.

"Can I go home now?" is all he asked.

Fifty Three

"It's you, my angel."

Conoscalo looked at his watch. He had more than enough time to go see Faith, if from a distance, and then business. His business was located in a smaller town in Maine, it would work out okay, he was sure of it. His time was limited enough that he would not be able to return here. Before he knew it, he was in front of Methodist Memorial Hospital, unlike many other times he strolled in through the front doors, no disguise, no knives and certainly no weapon. He was not worried. There would be no reason, after all who knew him.

When he arrived at room four hundred seventy-eight he noticed that something that he had not previously, for her room was in the nice part of the Hospital, the expensive part. He walked to the door and opened it, it was literally the decisive moment, was this was another set up in any manner it would be now.

Much to his surprise when he opened the door, there was no one in the room, except for one young woman lying on the bed.

He approached her, from a distance he could tell that she was sleeping, or at least in a state of near sleep.

He checked the medical chart at the end of the bed, the name said Faith Morgan, he approached the side of the bed, the side that she was facing, and it was most definitely the woman that he had found bloodied and half-dead. The same young life that he had visited before. So easily you could forget what some one looks like, minus the eyes, that strawberry colored hair. That was all he really remembered. He was glad to see the rest, now to see it all. To envision, all that was before him.

He pulled a chair closer and sat down, Conoscalo felt the need to explain, he was not sure of what he needed to explain, just that he wanted to. He had only been in the chair for a few minutes, when she opened her eyes, and again, looked directly at him. Her face lit up, in a positive way, "It's you, my angel," she said.
He took a finger to his mouth, "Shhh, yes it's me."
"Thank you for everything," she added with an exuberant tone.
"It was my pleasure, how are you feeling,"
"Sore, I'm really sore, they are giving me some pain killers. I think it is morphine."

The other drugs that had been in her system had finally cleared out, now the staff could go back and start working with some of the other issues. This brought Faith back to a stage of grogginess and the altogether feeling of blah, disorientated somewhat. Almost a feeling of Déjà vu, without really comprehending the concept of it all together.

"Have the doctors suggested when you might be released," he asked.

"They have said soon, I asked to stay longer, I," her words stopped, Conoscalo could see that her eyes were tearing up.

"I need you to stay here. I will be back before you know it. Just be prepared to leave soon, try to get your strength back and be prepared to leave. Do not mention this to anyone, not anyone. I will not call, I will just show up," he started to get up from the chair.

"I will explain, we will have plenty of time to discuss it," he answered.

Conoscalo reached over to kiss her forehead. He hesitated and started to stand back up.

"It's all right you can" she said with a pleasant tone.

He bent over and this time kissed her forehead, twice. He started for the door and left. Faith would sleep tonight. She would be very comfortable and would even dream a little.

Fifty Four

"You had me at gun point, the whole time.
You left this crap and you were gone,"

His Monday, at least after the Mayor was quiet. His time in the cabin was spent with some simple cleaning and then some rearranging of the furniture. Tuesday started late and was more for the procedural at work, he had finalized the plan for Wednesday, the times to be on station and everything else. He had decided that they would watch from three directions, the sheriff's department had provided other individuals, even the Sheriff signed off on it.

The Sheriff, after being briefed, had agreed that if you did not catch them in the act of the payment, if that was to happen, then your circumstantial evidence at hand was all the weaker. If they did not show up at all, then you had nothing, except for a murdered Chief of Police and a lot of talk, nothing more.

On that Tuesday evening he would arrive later than normal, for his dinner time. The last hour at the office was spent on the phone to Kristi, he forgot about most everything else for that hour, for Nick it was nice to talk with a woman who was not overbearing or too forward. He enjoyed the pace of their budding relation's or even friendship.

After dinner, Nick had a beer and started to read, the quality time that he had recently was not of a great absorbing caliber he was probably going to fall asleep in that chair, and even though he had slept in chairs and on couches recently he did not have a problem with that fact.

Ian's people were loyal if anything, their orders were simple, they would follow those instructions and then head for Canada. The money that they were owed had been paid, it was already in the account. For both individuals it would be a vacation until Ian needed their services again. Or at least that was the thought, Jimmie had other plans to carry out, yet those plans were for later.

Little did they know that Ian would never call for them, if they were still able to answer a call? They had already looked at the cabin from a distance, there was snow in certain areas. For the two men it would be best to go around those areas where they could, less to cover after the fact.

Ian's two individuals that he had handpicked were good, they had done things like this before and above all others, they were extremely loyal. Ian had used them together on many occasions. They never had let any boss down.

They spotted a lone Patrol Officer not too far from his car.

He was outside the vehicle smoking a cigarette looking at the cabin using binoculars. The men approached one from the left one from the right.

Earl Kenney did not stand a chance they caught him totally off guard a cigarette in one-hand binoculars in the other. He was dead before the binoculars hit the ground. They grabbed his radio and started for the cabin. They had discussed the door they would enter. They had discussed the whole job. There would be no changing of the particulars unless the situation warranted it. They would have no reason to change the how, they did not care about the why they just had another job to do.

It was after eleven when they both approached the house, from this point out they would have no reason to speak until after. Except for two lights in the front room all other lights would be off, it was their business to notice the ordinary, they had not. He entered through the kitchen door, ten seconds with the lock and it was open. He proceeded through the kitchen, into the living room. His weapon was drawn and extended from his arm straight out. He slowly entered the bedroom.

He could see from the shadows that there was someone in the bed. He walked closer to the bed, he had scanned the room and no one else was there. When he was at the side of the bed he lowered the weapon and placed it against the sleeping target, his finger was on the trigger pulling the trigger closer to his body, when he felt the barrel of another weapon push against his temple.

"No sudden moves," Nick told the man before him.

"Take the weapon, and gently toss it to the bed,"

The man did just what Nick asked of him, without question or hesitation.

"Bring your hands, around to your back and interlock your fingers,"

"We are going to slowly back out of this room, I will then guide you to where you need to sit do you understand?" Nick asked. He was speaking slowly in order to not show just how nervous he was.

"Yes I understand," the man said without emotion.

They slowly moved toward the door of the bedroom, Nick was walking backwards, the weapon was straight out pointing to the back of the individuals head, he was walking in unison with Nick step for step. Nick had just entered the living area when he felt the barrel of a weapon pressing against the back of his skull.

"Okay, small town cop, you thought of one, what about a second one, and if you think your Patrol Officer that was your lookout, he won't be joining us." The second man stated this with a thick accent, sounding as if he had not a care in the world. In fact, the only care that he had was getting this over with and leaving the country.

The words were cold to Nick. He did not change his position at all. He became more concerned, not for his own safety but that of his Patrol Officer, and which one.

Nick responded with the only response that popped into his head "I have a gun pointed at your partner." Nick was not able to finish the response.

"Yea, yea my partner is a professional, he got caught. He knew the risks going in, and yes, he would do the same. You shoot my partner and you die, simple as that, now remove your finger from the trigger well," the man, said in a clear and oh so calm manner.

Nick knew that it would all be over soon, they had him. It was Nick's own mistake he could have had help, he chose to be a cowboy and go it alone. He had always thought about this scenario, looks like one patrol officer picked up on it.

Looks like he would pay the price, he removed his finger and held the butt of the gun with his thumb and a forefinger, the rest of his body did not move. The man in front moved quickly to grab the weapon from Nick. They ordered Nick to go to the couch and sit, much in the same spot that Nick had wanted to place the individual himself.

"What a turn of events here, just when you thought it was all over," the second man said gloatingly.

"What Patrol Officer," Nick asked

"Do not know, older guy it looked like," the second man said.

"May I ask who hired you if you know," Nick asked, if anything it would put his mind at ease or at least he would know if he was right.

Both men looked at Nick and at each other. They decided that it could not hurt anything to tell him. They had other business to take care of. He second man that had come in seemed to be the lead person. He more or less ordered the other man to go out and gather their bag, it was what they needed to finish he said. After the man had left, he ordered Nick to lean his head toward his lap and interlock his fingers over the top of his head. Once he had completed this, the second man started to talk.

"Why would you want to know, why do you care. You were expecting something, typically, we do not make mistakes and yet you caught my partner totally off guard. It is obvious that you were not expecting a crowd."

"I was not expecting a crowd, was actually expecting something tomorrow. I did not have a lookout. That was done on his own," Nick reflected after he made that statement, it was either Earl or Ernie he was not sure which one. If Nick was upset, it was because they had not listened, and they had not come as a team. It was probably a good thing, since these individuals are professionals it would just mean another dead individual, one that worked for him or used to anyway.

"Not expecting a crowd, that is for sure. We were hired by Ian Thompson, do you know who he is."

Nick was one that would not shock easily. However, he became surprised for the actions that happened next. His hands were interlocked and on top of his head, it was a good place to have someone. It would be difficult to move in that position and he could see nothing except his legs and his elbows on each side.

Of course he knew of Ian Thompson.

Conoscalo had been watching for some time, he saw the first man enter through the kitchen door, and he saw another go in the front a few minutes later. He knew the layout and could now see both men standing in front of the couch. He would imagine that the target was on the couch. He did not know how to approach. He was deciding the best and fastest action when the positions changed, the man that had originally entered through the kitchen came out the same way, the man walked away from the house to the nearest set of trees and grabbed a duffle bag, he would then head back to the house as quickly as he had walked into the other direction.

This was when Conoscalo took action. The same time that the man had moved from the cabin, Conoscalo moved toward it. The man's feet were not on the first step when the butt of the gun hit his head. He dropped quietly into the snow, the duffle bag at his side. He removed the individual's weapon, he loosened the shoelace of the man and used that to tie his hands behind his back, it was not the best it would do for now. Conoscalo was fully ready for anything. He dropped the individual's weapon and reached for his 9 mm that he had placed in his pocket.

When Conoscalo entered the house, he had his weapon pointed at the man in front of the couch, he approached him as quietly as possible, the second man standing did not turn around for he fully expected his partner, and after all, they were professionals.

Conoscalo placed the barrel of the 9 mm to the back of the second operative's head, he pushed slightly, "Be careful of your next move it may just be your last."

"Tim," asked the man without moving any part of his body or the weapon he was holding toward Nick.

"Not Tim, Tim has had an accident, he will be joining us soon, and your name is Jimmie," Conoscalo stated.

"Shit," Jimmie stated. He knew who held the gun, he did not have to see him.

Nick heard all of this, he however did not move. Jimmie acted quickly, he would let go of the butt of the gun. His finger would stay in the well of the trigger.

"You're the Chief of Police, right," asked Conoscalo.

"Yes," Nick's answer was polite, yet curious as to who he was and how did he know?

"I need you to get up slowly and pat Jimmie down," Conoscalo speech was intentionally slower than usual.

Nick did just that, he lifted his head and saw a shadow of a man standing behind the individual before him. When Nick was fully standing, he asked "What about the weapon." The weapon was still dangling from Jimmie's finger.

"Grab the barrel of the weapon and then hand it back to me," Conoscalo said.

Nick just did that, he grabbed the weapon by the barrel and handed it back, he then proceeded to pat Jimmie down. When Nick found something in the man's pockets or on his body, he told the new man, he knew the names of the two individuals and he was thinking that Tim was dead. Jimmie was directly in front of him and he was not looking too sure of himself. When he had finished, he motioned to the new man that he was done.

"Okay, good job Chief, do you have handcuffs," Conoscalo asked he was no longer talking slowly. His speech was in a normal pattern and pace.

"Yes, in the other room," Nick did not want to break the trust and be shot before he had a chance to do anything or at least try. He was not sure who this other man was and all he could conclude is that he really baited someone that they would send two groups to get the job done. Nick was not sure who would die next, for he could not figure out the man in front of him.

Nick left the room and grabbed the cuffs, when he entered the living room he was carrying the handcuffs with one finger extended and the cuffs dangling from that finger.

"Why don't you cuff him?"

"Okay," was Nick's only statement?

Jimmie was now sitting on the couch, both hands were laid out on his upper leg portion. His hands were palm up on both knees. He cuffed one hand and then lead the cuffs under his right leg and cuffed the other, this would make it difficult to escape let alone move.

Nick stood back up, "What now," he asked.

"Do you have another pair of cuffs," the man holding the weapon asked.

Nick did not want to be cuffed, if anything was going to happen just do it, he was almost ready to blurt this out when,

"They are not for you, the other guy outside needs some better restraints, just in case," the man said.

"He's not dead," Nick asked.

"No, I need him brought into the house and placed next to my old friend Jimmie." the man answered.

Using the same steps as before, Nick got the other cuffs and went outside, Conoscalo watched from the window, trying to keep an eye on the man on the couch, and the Police Chief that just went outside.

Nick cuffed the man outside, he struggled slightly after being cuffed. Nick led him back into the cabin, the man said nothing, nor did Nick. He led the newly cuffed man, Conoscalo pointed to the couch. Nick placed the man in that spot, next to Jimmie.

Nick returned to stand next to Conoscalo.

Nothing was said, the two men on the couch Tim Martin and Jimmie Rodgers were not even looking at the man or Nick. Nick tried to avoid eye contact with the person that stood next to him, after you are taught that under certain situations. After a few minutes of silence Nick blurted it out, "What now?"

"I think we need to discuss what he did the other night in a certain warehouse in Boston, Look at me," Conoscalo said this, and both men on the couch looked directly at him, Conoscalo said this in such a manner that Nick too looked right at him. So much for avoiding eye contact.

"That was you, you and your partner," he asked. The man looked more at the weapon, than the person "Yes that was us," he answered.

"So after you shot Jackson it was Jackson, right" "Yes it was Jackson," Martin answered.

"You then discovered a young woman in the warehouse. You chased her down, a young woman down and then tell our friend what happened," Conoscalo demanded.

"It was a job, nothing more, was it you friend," the man on the couch retorted back to the man holding the weapon.

"So part of your job was to rape someone, with whatever you used. Part of the plan," Conoscalo asked.

"You're a pro. I can tell that, you know how it works. Sometimes you do what you have to do," the man said again defiantly.

"You're right I'm a pro, I know how it works, and I would never do that. If they saw something or it needed to be taken care of, that's why you carry a gun, asshole," Conoscalo wanted the point to resonate in the man's mind.

"What is this about?" Nick asked.

"This man and his mate, not Jimmie, he was dealing with a knife wound if I remember correctly?" Conoscalo brushed his own neck with his fingers, slightly flipping his wrist. Jimmie watched, and even to a common man you could see the fire burning in his eyes.

"So this guy," Conoscalo pointed to the character named Tim Martin, "And another individual, who has already been taken care of killed someone." Conoscalo shrugged his shoulders, he had no problem with the killing portion. "Then they found this young girl, he chased her down and violated her in every orifice, he left her for dead," Conoscalo stated, while pointing the weapon a little closer to the individuals head.

"Was she a friend of yours," Nick asked trying to come to some conclusion as to why he cared about this now.

"Never met her before, she is doing okay now, after some much needed medical attention," he added.

"You're not a representative of any Police or federal organizations are you?" Nick asked.

"No, what you may call a bad guy. Did not need to come here either, just wanted to take care of something for a new friend," the man said.

"Thank you, I think. Why," Nick asked.

"You're welcome, and yes you're safe, at least for now, we will discuss that in a minute. Why come here and do this, take the chance and all, let's just say I found my Faith again," Conoscalo said this and then refocused all his energy to the man on the couch.

"As for this jackass, is this couch yours, any attachment to it," Conoscalo asked.

"Not my couch, no attachment," Nick answered with a puzzled look.

"Anything you want to say," he asked.

"Nothing," Martin answered, he knew what was next.

The first shot went directly to the man's forehead, as his body slumped to the back of the couch, then next two bullets went to his heart. Nick jumped. He did not say anything he especially did not look at the man, who had just fired the weapon, it worried Nick of what could be next.

"Sorry that was personal, usually I never talk that much, or for that long. I just needed to make sure," Conoscalo, stated.

"No problem," after all what was Nick to say, that he objected.

Conoscalo lowered the weapon.

Both Nick and Conoscalo now looked at the other man who sat on the couch.

"Jimmie, thought I had you before. Is the neck healing? And you were wearing a vest that night, correct?" Jimmie did not answer, either question.

"You know that one of us has to finish this."

"So get it over with then." Jimmie spoke without the unease of what others might, with a crackling voice or with tears, his face was resolute.

This time he fired only once. Now two bodies slumped in some form on that couch.

"Time to talk," Conoscalo asked simply.

"Fine by me,"

"You do not need to know my name. I would like to know yours"

"Nick Sheridan, Chief of Police Schrader Maine, thank you, again for...." He wanted to ask more, he just was not sure where to start.

For the next few minutes, he explained, he did not go back to his origins. He said nothing of the Father figure or his past that was not important to what he needed to explain. He explained that he had killed Robert Morris, and his primal squeeze or whatever you wanted to call a mistress these days.

Nick had some other questions, like it was jeopardy, you never know until you push that button if you are correct or not.

Nick asked, "Could you tell me anything about the Charlton's, David and Julie, died about 13 years ago up in this area?"

He talked about the Charlton's. He actually apologized, "I did not know she was pregnant until afterwards when I saw the cards and noticed the champagne on the table."

"Would you tell me who hired you?" Nick asked.

"Well, in this case I do not know, and if I did I would not tell you."

"I knew it was not the husband." Nick retorted this like getting the last question on Jeopardy correct and doubling his money. His exhilaration was overwhelming, like he would get to keep the money.

"What gave it away, had to be something?" Conoscalo asked.

"No blood on his hands, nothing nearby that he could wipe them on. Little blood on his shirt. It just did not fit."

"It is always the little things." Conoscalo added.

"I would like to ask, what you removed from the cabin, the first time. This was you, correct?"

"Yes it was. Some files, a couple of notebooks," This rolled off the tongue of Conoscalo. It was like he almost anticipated more questions about the cabin and the first time he was here.

Nick became quiet, he wanted to ask about his friend, and he wanted to know about Sam.

"And about Sam, the reason you have been to this cabin before," Nick asked.

"It was a quick job, not sure the reason. I did not talk to your friend, just injected him and left." Conoscalo reported this like he was reading from a book, a book that he had no emotional attachment for. Forgetting that the man that stood in front of him, had an enormous amount of fury, Nick wanted to do something, Nick thought, for he could try to bring this man to justice, which was what burned inside him.

He knew his limitations, and his abilities. As much as he wanted to conclude otherwise it would be for not. And so Nick, in his infinite wisdom, with his hand's pretty much tied, not being able to do anything else, he would almost shout, simple raising his voice,

"He was my friend and he deserved better."

Conoscalo understood, what if it was one of his friends, pending he had any. His heart shifted, what if it was Faith, like he had done just a few minutes ago, and she was not even dead. His friend was, and yet he tried nothing, why. Because he was practical, at least that is how Conoscalo wanted to think about it. He knew there was nothing to do. He would have to take some extra precautions when he left. Changing the subject seemed to be the best.

"Any other questions," Conoscalo asked sounding a little impatient.

"What else did you remove from the Charlton's scene," Nick was talking to the man that stood in front of him like they were old school buddies catching up. It would not haunt him that he was speaking to a killer like this, for he had many times before. To say the least that all previous times he had the upper hand during the question and answer sessions.

"I removed a expecting a baby card, the bottle of champagne, a balloon," Conoscalo was trying to recall all that he had done.

"That's it," Nick asked impatiently.

"I also removed an at home pregnancy test and the box it came in," Conoscalo said.

"Let me just say. I have many files, some from this cabin like I said. Some from other places. Have them all, figure it out, do your police work." Conoscalo stopped short, he did not want to be there any longer, and he just wanted to go.

"You came here to avenge what happened to the young woman, what now," Nick asked.

"I want to leave, I'm retired you will not find me unless I want you too," Conoscalo was suggesting.

"Just leave, how I can after what you have told me, just allow you to walk off and never be seen again." Nick said it in a sarcastic manner. He did not want a confrontation with this individual. Nick continued with "What would I tell the authorities, don't worry about it, I let that other assassin leave, that is what you are a hired gun," "Yes, I'm a hired gun, was a hired gun. Now retired, you could tell the FBI and others whatever you want, I'm holding a gun that could easily be pointed in your direction," Conoscalo said thinking that they could come up with a story that was decent in structure.

"You do have me by gun point," Nick offered, here he was helping the man who killed. This brought a distress of some sorts over Nick. No one should walk away. His friend and many others sacrificed their lives for what. Think practically. Think practically Nick said, to himself. Conoscalo's, reply was "I have you by gun point." This eased the feeling somewhat, Nick had the key in front of him. It was nice to hear that he had it mostly right. He wanted to ask the man what was next.

"You had me at gun point, the whole time. You left this crap and you were gone," Nick, stated this, with a sensible tone. He wanted to talk himself into the fact of letting this person go. After all, he did have a gun.

"You better leave," Nick, suggested.

"Before you try something," Conoscalo answered.

"Yes, before I try something."

Conoscalo wanted to shake his hand, he decided against it, and headed for the door. Conoscalo went out through the front door.

Nick looked at his watch it was one forty in the morning. He immediately made some calls. Soon the Sheriff and his team would be there. He went into the kitchen and started the coffee. He looked out the kitchen and saw the duffle bag just off the porch, almost where he had been when he retrieved that Tim, who now lay slumped on the couch, with a couple of holes in him. When he returned to the kitchen, he sat down at the table and proceeded to open up the duffle bag, his day was just starting, again.

Fifty Five

"Have a good retirement my friend, I'm glad you found your faith."

Conoscalo started to drive south as soon as he left the cabin. He was feeling good about himself. That feeling had been vacant from his soul for some time, he almost broke into a smile, and it had been sometime since he had that feeling as well. By the time he reached Methodist Memorial, it was early in the morning. He walked through the lobby, with not a word said. He stopped by the gift shop and bought some flowers.

When he arrived at the door to her room he took a deep breath, and opened the door, the flowers dropped to his side, his heart sank. The stripped bed was vacant as was the room he could see nothing in the room, nothing at all. Still holding the door open, he looked back to ensure it was the room he wanted, 478, sadly enough it was the room.

He heard a sound in the bathroom, his heart started to beat faster, when he turned there she was. She slowly and gingerly walked up to him and gave him a very gentle hug.

She kissed his cheek, and then moved to kiss his lips.

"What's a matter, you did not think that I had left, did you," she asked inquisitively. She moved by herself, slowly yet still she held on to nothing. Conoscalo could see that she was sore, that there was still much pain, her pain would continue. As with other things, it would all take time.

"Well actually I did," he said honestly.

She kissed him again, "Hope that is okay," she asked just to make sure that he approved of the kiss.

"A little unexpected, but nice," he added.

"I still need to check out," She was fully dressed, Conoscalo wondered if she had been fully dressed yesterday in anticipation.

She walked over to the closet and opened the doors. On the floor of the closet was a black overnight bag, a plastic bag hung from one of the hooks. The medical supplies had been given back to be destroyed or used, she did not care when she gave it to the staff.

"That was delivered, by a friend of yours or so he said," she pointed to the overnight bag.

"Did you open it," Conoscalo asked.

"The man who brought it, said not to, so I did not," she added.

Conoscalo walked over to the bag, he removed it from the closet and placed it on the bed. He hesitantly unzipped the bag and noticed the note sitting on top. Faith noticed the contents under the note,

Conoscalo opened the note, he read every word aloud,

"Thanks for everything,

Call me when you are settled,

If you want to.

Have a good retirement my friend, I am glad you found your Faith," He looked over to Faith, they both smiled, he continued to read the note. *"Take care of her.*

You're Friend,

G."

He folded the note, and placed it into the bag. He too looked a little deeper, just to see. He zipped the bag up and they headed for the door, he carried the overnight bag and her plastic bag, she held tightly to his arm.

He would gradually dismantle his cell phone, one piece in the trash here, another over there. By the time she had checked out, his phone and possibly his past was in the trash cans in that hospital, there was no other real or common way to follow him, this time he watched.

Fifty Six

"I wonder if renters insurance covered that."

Nick had some cleaning to do, he would have to buy another couch.
"I wonder if renters insurance covered that."
He had been in with the Sheriff and his two investigators for some time. Shortly after they arrived on scene, he would begin to explain.
"And this guy said, he was not here for you. To take care of something personal with these two other men?" The investigators would state many times, that they had never seen anything like this before, not even close, Nick would agree.
Nick would also have to address his lone wolf, the one that 'they' had taken care of. It was Ernie, for all the good of it, this part turned out the worst. Arrangements and notifications would be made, it was the soberest of times for this little group to have to deal with two losses, and the fact in the back of his mind, told him it could have been worse, for everyone.

Nick knew there would be other interviews, this was a lot to grab at any given time let alone at once. The files had helped, once the FBI was called in, federal warrants would soon follow. The search for James Bennett MacMillian would go on. Ian Thompson would be found rather easily, other pieces would follow.

Nick would relish the fact that he would survive this, that the individual had not just killed him. He would wonder repeatedly as to the real reason why, or was he just lucky this time. This would be the topic of discussion between Nick and Kristi for many days to come. She would be the one that he could talk to, the one he could show his true feelings and the emotions that come with it.

The Senator that was missing, had been on a fishing trip and was fine. They, all authorities over several states still searched for the killer of the two Senators that had died in Atlantic City. That killer would never be found.

The End